The Ghost in Roomette Four ———————

Praise for the Mysteries of Janet Dawson

"*Water Signs* has many delights.... Following a Jeri Howard PI investigation is so enjoyable that the reader won't care [whodunit].... The beautiful descriptions of the Oakland-area estuary and the visits with the irascible floating homeless make this mystery smart and highly enjoyable."

—Betty Webb, *Mystery Scene*

"Terrific Jeri Howard page-turning adventure. Great plot twists and true-to-life characters, and Dawson brings the neglected Oakland waterfront into full view."

—Jerry Kennealy

"Solid... Dawson downplays danger to life and limb amid lengthy narrative passages devoted to the sad state of change in this beautiful city and its environs."

—*Publishers Weekly*

"*Death Deals a Hand* is a very authentic trip, rides and reads smoothly.... A lovely step back in time."

—*Mysterious Women*

"Well worth a read... The book is a top-rate accomplishment. My interest in the plot never wavered."

—*BookLoons*

MYSTERY FICTION BY JANET DAWSON

THE JERI HOWARD MYSTERY SERIES
Kindred Crimes
Till the Old Men Die
Take a Number
Don't Turn Your Back on the Ocean
Nobody's Child
A Credible Threat
Witness to Evil
Where the Bodies Are Buried
A Killing at the Track
Bit Player
Cold Trail
Water Signs

SHORT STORIES
Scam and Eggs

SUSPENSE FICTION
What You Wish For

CALIFORNIA ZEPHYR SERIES
Death Rides the Zephyr
Death Deals a Hand
The Ghost in Roomette Four

— The Ghost in — Roomette Four

A California Zephyr Mystery

JANET DAWSON

2018
PERSEVERANCE PRESS / JOHN DANIEL AND COMPANY
PALO ALTO / MCKINLEYVILLE, CALIFORNIA

Copyright © 2018 by Janet Dawson
All rights reserved
Printed in the United States of America

A Perseverance Press Book
Published by John Daniel & Company
A division of Daniel & Daniel, Publishers, Inc.
Post Office Box 2790
McKinleyville, California 95519
www.danielpublishing.com/perseverance

Distributed by SCB Distributors (800) 729-6423

Book design by Eric Larson, Studio E Books, Santa Barbara, www.studio-e-books.com

Cover art © Roger Morris, IKAM Creative, Inc. All rights reserved.

10 9 8 7 6 5 4 3 2 1

LIBRARY OF CONGRESS CATALOGING-IN-PUBLICATION DATA
Names: Dawson, Janet, author.
Title: The ghost in roomette four : a California zephyr mystery / by Janet Dawson.
Description: McKinleyville, California : John Daniel & Company, [2018]
Identifiers: LCCN 2017055342 | ISBN 9781564745989 (softcover)
Subjects: LCSH: California Zephyr (Express train)—Fiction. | Railroad travel—Fiction. |
    Ghosts—Fiction. | Murder—Investigation—Fiction. | GSAFD: Mystery fiction.
Classification: LCC PS3554.A949 G48 2018 | DDC 813/.54—dc23
LC record available at https://lccn.loc.gov/2017055342

To my mother,
Thelma Dawson,
who loves to read,
and my brother, Roger Dawson,
who plays a mean blues guitar

ACKNOWLEDGMENTS

Many thanks to fellow mystery writer D.P. Lyle, who is also a medical doctor. He provided much-needed information on the medical conditions discussed in this novel. Thanks also to Dawn Church for information on how to conduct a séance. Also to Roger Morris, my fellow Pullman pal, who has provided the outstanding cover art for all three California Zephyr mysteries and to Doug Spinn, owner of the Pacific Sands, who first told the story about a haunted roomette.

The Ghost in Roomette Four ————————

Chapter One

I AM NOT seeing this, Jill McLeod told herself. But she was.

Light shimmered at eye level, about ten feet in front of her. The apparition seemed to have no source. None, anyway, that Jill could discern. What's more, she could see through it.

Jill took a step toward the light. It brightened, then dimmed. She took another step. The light flickered and moved into roomette four.

She shook herself. A few more steps, then she stopped at the open doorway of the roomette and peered inside.

Empty.

Of course it was empty. There was no one traveling in this space. When the *California Zephyr* reached Salt Lake City, at 5:20 A.M., the passenger holding a reservation for this roomette would board the train.

But she had seen the luminous flicker. Surely it was just a trick of the light. But what light? How? There was nothing but darkness outside the roomette's window, save the occasional twin headlights of a vehicle at a crossing or a pinprick from a distant ranch. Here in the passageway the electric lights were dim. What Jill had seen was different from those ordinary lights. Different, and hard to explain. What could have caused it?

It was nearly midnight. The train's last station stop had been in Elko, Nevada, at 11:17 P.M. Now the train sped east, heading for the Great Salt Desert that spanned western Utah. The passengers traveling in this Pullman car, the Silver Gorge, had gone to bed.

Jill would have been in bed, too. However, before she could

remove her uniform and put on her pajamas, she and the first-aid kit she carried had been summoned by a porter to one of the Pullman cars. Jill was a Zephyrette, the only female member of the train's onboard crew. Her job was to see to the passengers' needs. That included everything from answering questions to broadcasting announcements on the train's public address system, making dinner reservations, mailing postcards and sending telegrams— and treating a little boy who had scraped some skin off his elbow when he jumped off the bunk in the sixteen-section sleeper near the back of the train. She had doctored the child with Merthiolate from her kit and put a bandage on his arm.

She was returning to her own quarters when she entered the Silver Gorge and saw—whatever it was she was seeing. Or had seen. It was gone now. She set the kit on the floor and entered the roomette, seeing her own reflection in the window.

"I must have imagined it," she whispered.

But she wasn't imagining the chill inside the roomette. It was faint at first, a few degrees lower than the temperature in the corridor. As she stood there, the cold grew more penetrating. It seemed to go through her, to her bones. She moved toward the door. Then she heard four short taps.

Frightened, Jill hurried out of the roomette into the corridor, nearly tripping over the first-aid kit. She picked up the kit and retreated a few steps, stopping at the door that opened onto the soiled linen locker. Her heart pounded. She took a deep breath, willing herself to calm down.

She struggled to find a rational explanation for what she had seen and heard. And felt.

I did see it, she thought. I really did. And I heard those taps. That cold feeling. But... No, no, I must have imagined it. I'm tired, that's all. It's just because I'm tired.

She breathed in and out. The rapid beating of her heart slowed. Now all she heard was the rhythmic *clickety-clack* of the train's wheels on the rails below her. A rumbling, wheezy snore erupted from behind the closed door of the nearest roomette. The passenger inside was sawing logs, as Jill's father would say.

The Silver Gorge was, in railroad parlance, a ten-six sleeper.

That meant the car had ten roomettes, five on either side of the center passageway where Jill stood, and six double bedrooms facing another passageway at the front of the car. The roomettes were designed to accommodate one person, while the double bedrooms had two beds, one upper and the lower a bench seat that converted into a bed. At the soiled linen locker, in the middle of the car, the passageway jogged right, then left again.

Jill pushed away from the locker and turned to her left, entering the corridor that fronted on the bedrooms, with doors to her left and windows to her right. She heard a loud, whistling snore coming from bedroom E, then the two-long, one-short, one-long whistle, a warning as the train approached a crossing.

Jill went through the vestibule to the next car, the Silver Crane. The Pullman porter, Darius Doolin, sat in his tiny compartment. He stood up when he saw her. Threads of silver streaked his close-cropped black hair and wrinkles wreathed his coffee-with-cream face. He'd loosened the collar on his white shirt, preparing to settle down and get whatever sleep he could before the train arrived in Salt Lake City.

"I thought you'd long since turned in for the night, Miss McLeod."

Mr. Doolin's quiet voice was flavored with a Southern drawl. He'd once told Jill he was originally from Oklahoma, though he'd lived in Oakland for years. He was a veteran of more than twenty years as a porter, most of it on the Western Pacific Railroad, one of the three railroads that jointly operated the *California Zephyr*. That morning, the sleek streamliner, pulled by three Western Pacific locomotives, had departed from the huge shed called the Oakland Mole on San Francisco Bay. The WP took the train over the Sierra Nevada Mountains and across the Great Basin to Salt Lake City. There the locomotives and train crew would swap out for the Denver & Rio Grande Western crew and engines for the journey over the Rocky Mountains to Colorado's capital city. The Chicago, Burlington & Quincy Railroad brought the train across the Great Plains into Chicago's Union Station.

Jill, a Zephyrette, was considered an employee of the Western Pacific. The Zephyrettes were a small group of female railroad employees who traveled aboard the *California Zephyr*, which was called the *CZ* or the Silver Lady, because the sleek stainless steel cars all had "Silver" in their names. There were two trains per day, one eastbound, one headed west, each with one Zephyrette as part of the crew. The trip took two and a half days, and the Zephyrette had a layover of two nights in Chicago or San Francisco before boarding the *California Zephyr* for the return trip.

"Good evening, Mr. Doolin." Train crew members were expected to keep things on a "mister and miss" basis, even though they had traveled together frequently, as was the case with Jill and Darius Doolin. She gestured at the first-aid kit she carried in her left hand. "I was called to the sixteen-section sleeper. A little boy hurt himself when he jumped off a berth."

"A lot of children on the train this trip," Mr. Doolin said. "And many of them running wild, as they sometimes do."

Jill kept her voice quiet as well, not wanting to disturb any passengers. "Yes, there are lots of kids traveling. That's to be expected since it's summer. I've had such a hectic day. There were a couple of boys playing cops and robbers in one of the chair cars, and later a little girl who took a tumble on the stairs in the dome-observation car. I'm tired. That must be—"

Mr. Doolin looked at her. "Is everything all right, Miss McLeod? You look a bit peaky."

"I'm tired," Jill said again. "That's why I saw—"

"Saw what?" Mr. Doolin asked. When she didn't answer, he smiled. "Oh, you saw the ghost. On the Silver Gorge."

Jill stared at him. "You've seen it, too?"

He nodded. "Twice."

"I don't believe in ghosts," Jill said. "There has to be a logical explanation for what I saw."

"Miss McLeod," he said, "you know whose ghost that is. You're the one who found the body. Two months ago, it was. In roomette four on the Silver Gorge. For some reason, that man's spirit ain't resting easy."

Jill looked at him in consternation. "Resting easy? That man died of natural causes. Something to do with his heart. At least that's what I was told."

Mr. Doolin looked skeptical. "That may be. But he's haunting that roomette. Trying to send a message, I expect. Now, you look tired to the bone, Miss McLeod. You need to get to bed. That ghost will keep until tomorrow." He smiled again and returned to his seat.

"I don't believe in ghosts," Jill muttered as she walked through the Silver Crane, through the vestibule and into the darkened dining car, the Silver Banquet, where white tablecloths gave the deserted car a spectral look. The next car was the Silver Roundup, the dome-lounge car. The front section held a coffee shop and a lounge, both long since closed for the night. The back of the car had a dormitory section with bunks stacked five high, for the waiters and cooks who worked in the diner. There were also two compartments, one for the dining car steward and one for the Zephyrette.

Jill's compartment was small, with a bench seat, a toilet and a sink. Once inside, she locked the door and set the first-aid kit in its usual place on a nearby shelf. She removed her uniform, a tailored teal-blue suit that was worn with a white blouse. The left breast pocket had a monogram reading ZEPHYRETTE, and so did the garrison cap she wore on her short brown hair. The blouse had a *CZ* monogram, standing for *California Zephyr*. She hung up her uniform, ready to get back into it if necessary. If she was called upon to assist a passenger in the middle of the night, and she hoped she wouldn't be, she'd have to get dressed again.

She put on a comfortable, well-worn pair of blue cotton pajamas. Then she pulled the sink down from the wall, washed her face and brushed her teeth. When she pushed the sink back up to the wall, the water drained out. Then she lowered the back of the bench seat, transforming it into her bed. She got between the covers and propped herself up with a pillow. Jill usually worked on her trip report before turning in for the night. The report, required to be filed at the end of each run, was an account of each day's activities, the usual and the unusual, and Jill kept a pencil and a small notebook in her uniform pocket to make notes throughout the day. She jotted down problems, such as smoothing the ruffled feathers of that demanding passenger traveling in one of the sleeper cars, and dealing with those rambunctious children in the coach cars. She noted the number of dinner reservations she'd made this first day out and mentioned giving out soda mints to three passengers suffering from motion sickness.

Jill set aside her notes and leaned back against the pillow. Normally she would read before going to sleep. Agatha Christie was her favorite author and she loved the Miss Marple books. She'd already read the latest, so she had brought a couple of old favorites to tide her over until the next Christie release. She looked at one of them, *A Murder Is Announced*, and decided she was too tired to read. She took off her watch and twisted the tiny knob on the right side of the face. The train crossed from the Pacific to the Mountain Time Zone when it went over the border between Nevada and Utah. Jill's last announcement, made around nine o'clock this evening, was to remind passengers to reset their watches. Now she did the same.

She turned out the light, listening to the *clickety-clack* of the rails. It usually lulled her to slumber. But tonight, sleep didn't come right away. She kept thinking about what she'd seen.

I don't believe in ghosts, she told herself again. But what could explain the light she'd seen? What could explain that strange cold feeling inside roomette four, and the tapping sounds she'd heard?

She thought of a scene in Dickens's *A Christmas Carol*, when Marley's ghost pays a Christmas Eve visit to his former business partner. Ebenezer Scrooge didn't believe in ghosts, either. Marley's ghost had asked, "What evidence would you have of my reality, beyond that of your own senses?"

And Scrooge had replied, "You may be an undigested bit of beef, a blot of mustard, a crumb of cheese, a fragment of underdone potato. There's more of gravy than of grave about you, whatever you are!"

Jill sighed. Well, I didn't have any of those things for dinner, so I can't blame this on my digestion.

She rolled onto her side, plumped the pillow. Instead of drifting off to sleep, she thought about a day in May, two months earlier, at the end of a westbound run, when she'd found a dead man in roomette four.

Chapter Two ─────────────

May 1953

THE *CALIFORNIA ZEPHYR* headed through the Oakland waterfront, passing warehouses and piers. Each time the train neared a street, the engineer blew the warning for public grade crossings—two long whistles, followed by one short and another long. The train had already made a brief stop at the Western Pacific station at Third and Broadway, where a number of passengers had departed. Now the *CZ*, at the end of its westbound run from Chicago, entered the vast rail yard, criss-crossed by tracks. Its destination was the Oakland Mole, an enormous train shed on the shoreline of Oakland's Middle Harbor.

Zephyrette Jill McLeod, tired after the two-and-a-half-day journey, looked forward to getting home to her family in Alameda. But her day wasn't over yet. Once the train arrived at the Mole, she would assist departing passengers, those heading for East Bay destinations and those hurrying to catch the ferry that would depart from the Mole, crossing the bay to San Francisco. After that, she had to finish and submit her trip report, due at the end of each run.

Inside the ten-six sleeper, the Silver Gorge, she walked down the central passageway between the roomettes, glancing from side to side. Many of the travelers had already left the train at other stations. At roomette seven, she stopped to help Mrs. Wolfe, an elderly woman who had boarded in Denver, heading to San Francisco to visit family. Mrs. Wolfe had already gathered her book and her knitting, tucking them into her oversized handbag. Now Jill lifted Mrs. Wolfe's suitcase from the overhead rack and handed it to Frank Nathan, the porter, who stood nearby.

"Here's the porter," Jill said. "He'll help you off the train and direct you to the ferry."

"If you'll follow me, ma'am," Mr. Nathan said.

"Thank you, young man." Mrs. Wolfe took a change purse from her handbag, opened it, and handed several coins to the porter. "You've been such a help this trip."

Jill followed Mrs. Wolfe as she and the porter made their way to the vestibule, where two other passengers waited, eager to leave the train at the end of their journey. As she came abreast of roomette four, Jill glanced inside. The passenger, Mr. Randall, was still in his seat, his head tilted toward the window. He had removed his suit jacket and loosened his tie. It looked like he was asleep, eyes closed under the lenses of his horn-rimmed glasses.

Mr. Randall had boarded the train at the *California Zephyr*'s stop in Portola, just after eight that morning. During the journey, she'd seen him eating breakfast and then lunch in the dining car, drinking coffee in the lounge. Mostly, though, she had seen him here in this roomette, his jacket off and his tie loosened, his briefcase open on the floor, a ledger and a notebook on his lap. "Business trip," he told her, looking up from his work.

Later in the afternoon, when she had walked past the roomette, Mr. Randall had his glasses off. Without the spectacles, his face looked exhausted, drawn, as though he was under some sort of strain. He was rubbing his temples. A headache, perhaps. She was about to offer him some aspirin from the first-aid kit in her quarters. Before she could say anything, he took a small bottle from his pocket and removed the cap. He shook a couple of pills into his hand and popped them into his mouth.

Then he put on his glasses and looked up, as though startled to see her. "Didn't see you standing there, Miss McLeod. I'm as blind as a bat without my glasses."

"Are you all right, Mr. Randall?" she asked. "Can I get you anything?"

He shook his head and managed a smile. "No, thanks. Just a little tired. I've had a couple of long days on this trip. I'll be glad to get home." He gestured at the papers. "I've got to finish what I'm doing, though. It's important."

Now he was asleep. Those long days had caught up with him. His neatly folded suit coat was in the open briefcase on the floor.

Jill knocked on the bulkhead. "Mr. Randall, we'll be at the Oakland Mole in a few minutes." He didn't respond. "Mr. Randall?"

She moved closer and called his name again. The train eased around a curve and Mr. Randall slumped to one side. His glasses slipped off his nose and fell to the floor as his head thumped against the window. Alarmed, Jill leaned forward and touched his hand. It was cold. She reached for his wrist and felt for a pulse. There was none. Then her fingers moved to the man's neck, searching again for a pulse. Again she felt nothing.

"We're coming into the Mole, Miss McLeod." She looked up at the porter. He frowned when he saw her face. "What is it?"

"Mr. Randall. He's dead." She stepped back, feeling a pang of sadness. He was so young, and he had seemed like such a pleasant man.

Now Frank Nathan moved into the doorway and leaned over. He, too, felt Mr. Randall's wrist. He shook his head as he straightened, confirming what Jill already know. "He's dead, all right." The porter looked past her as the train slowed, coming into the Mole. "We're here, and I've got to get these passengers off."

"Go ahead," Jill said. "As soon as they're off, I'll find the conductor."

Frank moved quickly to the vestibule, straightening his cap and his jacket. Jill reached for the roomette's door, intending to shut it so the other passengers couldn't see the body. Then she noticed something on the floor, just the other side of the open briefcase. It was the bottle she'd seen earlier, when Mr. Randall took those pills. But now she realized it didn't have the rounded shape or the brown metal cap she associated with a Bayer aspirin bottle. The cylindrical glass bottle had a plastic cap and a label from an Oakland pharmacy. She read the typed words below the patient's name.

Digoxin. Jill's father was a doctor. She knew that Digoxin was digitalis. It was prescribed for people who had heart conditions.

That's all she knew, though. She shook her head. Poor Mr. Randall. He had appeared to be in good health. Except... She remembered how he had looked earlier in the afternoon. He had mentioned how tired he was. And he'd taken two of these pills. Perhaps he wasn't in good health after all.

As she straightened, her hand caught the edge of Mr. Randall's suit coat and pulled it away from the briefcase. She glanced at the contents underneath. Funny, she didn't see the ledger or notebook he'd been working on. The train was slowing for its arrival at the Mole. She pushed the coat back to its place in the briefcase and backed out of the roomette, shutting the door.

When the train stopped, Frank Nathan unlocked the doors and lowered the steps, setting the step box on the ground. He helped Mrs. Wolfe down to the platform and pointed her toward the ferry. Once the other passengers had gotten off the train, Jill stepped down to the platform and looked for the conductor, Mr. Bailey. The big, gray-haired man was standing up by the dining car, talking with the brakeman, Carl Loring. She hurried toward them.

When he saw her, Mr. Bailey raised the watch he held in his hand, the gold links on the chain glittering in the late afternoon sun. "Miss McLeod, back at home in Oakland. An on-time arrival after another uneventful journey."

"Not entirely uneventful," Jill said. "I'm afraid one of the passengers is dead. He's in roomette four on the Silver Gorge."

"Good Lord." The conductor slipped the watch into his vest pocket and turned to the brakeman. "Carl, get a doctor and an ambulance. I'll go with Miss McLeod and see for myself."

The brakeman took off, heading for the Mole, while Jill and the conductor walked to the sleeper car and boarded. The conductor surveyed the scene inside the roomette, shaking his head. The doctor and the ambulance arrived a short time later.

The doctor checked Mr. Randall's body, then he picked up the prescription bottle and examined the label. "Well, a prescription for Digoxin tells me he had a heart condition of some sort."

"That's digitalis, right? For the heart?" The conductor, standing in the passageway, held Mr. Randall's wallet. "His driver's license says he's thirty-one years old. That's awfully young to have a heart attack."

The doctor shrugged. "This wasn't a heart attack. That's different. This man probably had a weak heart, due to some underlying medical condition, even as young as he was. So I would guess this is heart failure."

Jill gestured at the prescription bottle. "I saw him take a couple of pills from this bottle. Earlier in the afternoon. I thought at the time he was taking aspirin, for a headache. But once I saw the bottle—"

"He probably took too much." The doctor shook the bottle and the remaining pills rattled against the glass. "An overdose of Digoxin can be fatal. It happens from time to time. Patients forget how many pills they take, or they take too many in a short time. We'll transport the body to the coroner's office for an autopsy. I'll hand the pills over to the coroner's office as well, just to make sure this is really Digoxin. The medical examiner will determine the cause of death."

"We need to notify his next of kin," Jill said. She turned to the conductor. "Is there a business card in his wallet? Or his briefcase? He got on the train in Portola and he told me he'd been on a business trip, that he was returning home to Oakland."

Mr. Bailey rifled through the wallet. "Yes, here's a business card. Kevin Randall, Financial Department, Vennor Corporation. It's on Broadway here in Oakland. And here's a picture of a woman."

Jill peered at the photograph. It showed a young woman with dark brown hair in an ear-length bob, swept away from her oval face, wearing a pale yellow dress. She was quite pretty and Jill felt a pang for her. Was she Mr. Randall's sister? A girlfriend? Either way, she was going to get some bad news. Jill, who had lost her fiancé in Korea three years ago, knew how awful that news would be.

"If you don't mind," the doctor said, "we need to get this body out of here and into the ambulance."

"Of course." Mr. Bailey gave the wallet, the photo and the business card to Jill. He picked up the briefcase and lifted Mr. Randall's suitcase from the rack, handing it to the porter who was waiting in the corridor. "Miss McLeod and Mr. Nathan, take these things to the office. It's after five but we can certainly call this Vennor Corporation and see if anyone is at Mr. Randall's place of business."

Jill followed Frank Nathan off the car. From the vestibule, the doctor beckoned to the two attendants who waited by the ambulance parked on the platform. Most of the passengers had left the Mole, by car, by bus, or on the ferry that was now heading toward San Francisco, dwarfed by the pilings of the Bay Bridge. The dining car crew, cooks and waiters, was unloading supplies and the baggage man was steering a cart with several boxes on it toward a truck. A couple of Red Caps, one of them seated on a battered wooden chair, shared a bottle of Coca-Cola and talked.

Frank Nathan was already walking into the Mole, carrying Mr. Randall's suitcase and briefcase. Jill followed but she'd only taken a few steps when she heard a woman's voice. "Pardon me, miss."

Jill turned and her stomach lurched. She looked down at the photograph in her right hand, where she held the business card and the wallet. Then she looked up again. The young woman in the picture now stood in front of Jill, the same dark hair and oval face, a slim figure in a wide-skirted dress of green and white piqué, with a small white handbag that matched her shoes. A diamond engagement ring sparkled on her left hand.

"I'm here to meet a passenger. I'm afraid I'm late." The woman smiled. "I don't see him anywhere. Maybe he got tired of waiting for me, and took a cab."

"What's the passenger's name?" Jill asked, dreading the answer.

"Kevin Randall," the woman said.

Jill took a deep breath. "Miss— What is your name?"

"Margaret Vennor."

Jill hesitated, unsure of how to break the news. "Miss Vennor, I'm afraid…" She stopped and took a deep breath. "It appears Mr. Randall was taken ill." There was just no getting around it. Jill signed and began again. "I am very sorry to tell you that Mr. Randall has passed away."

The young woman looked at her as though Jill had suddenly sprouted wings and a tail. Then she turned her head and took in the sight of the ambulance on the platform, its rear doors open to reveal the interior. She swayed. Jill reached for her. The Red Cap who'd been sitting jumped up and lifted the chair. Together he and Jill got Miss Vennor seated on it.

Now Margaret Vennor began to cry, harsh sobs shaking her body as tears ran down her face. Jill held her hand. "Is there someone I can call? Someone who can come and be with you?"

The young woman reached into her handbag for a handkerchief and used it to blot her eyes. She took several deep, ragged breaths and fought to control her tears. "My aunt, Helen Vennor. In Oakland." She rattled off a phone number and Jill wrote it in her notebook.

The doctor and conductor appeared on the vestibule. Jill waved at Mr. Bailey, who stepped down to the platform and quickly joined them. "Sir, this is Miss Vennor. She's here to meet Mr. Randall. I've broken the news to her. She's given me her aunt's phone number."

"I'll stay with her," the conductor said. "Go to the office and make that call."

As Jill moved away, one of the ambulance attendants came into view, holding one end of a stretcher. The conductor took Miss Vennor's hand and moved so as to block the young woman's view of the stretcher and the ambulance. "If you'll come with me, Miss Vennor. We'll go to the office where you'll be more comfortable."

In the office, the conductor pulled out a chair and steered Margaret Vennor toward it. Jill moved to the nearest phone. She glanced at her notebook, then dialed the number. The line rang twice, then a woman answered.

"Mrs. Vennor? My name is Jill McLeod. I'm here at the Oakland Mole with your niece Margaret. I'm afraid I have some bad news."

Chapter Three

JILL WOKE WHEN THE TRAIN reached Salt Lake City at 5:20 A.M. She sat up in bed and turned, raising onto her knees, so she could look out the small window above her pillow. On the platform she saw a tall man in a business suit, holding a suitcase in one hand and a briefcase in the other. He had black horn-rimmed glasses, just like Mr. Randall.

Again she thought back to that day when she'd found his body. Poor Miss Vennor. She'd waited with the young woman until her aunt had arrived. Then Jill had finished her trip report, adding the information about Mr. Randall. After she submitted it, she called home. Her younger sister, Lucy, drove to Oakland in the family car to pick her up. Later, she had inquired at Western Pacific headquarters, and was told that the Alameda County Coroner's Office would do an autopsy. She never heard anything else about the incident. Life moved on and she hadn't thought much about it since, until Mr. Doolin's words last night brought it all back. Now she recalled Miss Vennor's stricken face when Jill told her that her fiancé was dead.

A ghost. Surely not. But Jill wasn't the only one who had seen something strange outside roomette four, according to Mr. Doolin. She would talk with the porter again, to find out what he'd seen—and heard.

The *California Zephyr* would sit here in the Salt Lake City station for twenty minutes before leaving at 5:40 A.M. This was a crew change stop as well as an equipment change. The three Western Pacific locomotives that had pulled the train over the

Sierra Nevada mountain range and across the Great Basin were exchanged for five Denver & Rio Grande Western diesels. The extra engines were needed to pull the *California Zephyr* over the Rocky Mountains. Jill snuggled back under the covers. Sleep overtook her in a few minutes. She woke again when the *CZ* reached Provo at 6:32 A.M. Might as well get up, she thought. As the train pulled out of the station after its brief stop, she got out of bed and pulled the sink down from the wall. A shower would have to wait until she reached Chicago. She made do with a sink bath, put on her uniform, and headed for the dining car.

The diner no longer had a ghostly look. Several other early risers occupied tables, drinking coffee or looking at menus. The dining car steward, Mr. Tallent, stood at the curved counter in the middle of the car, greeting her with a cheery, "Good morning, Miss McLeod. Take any seat you like."

Behind the steward, the kitchen with its shiny stainless steel counters and cabinets vibrated with activity; the white-uniformed cooks moved about, juggling pots, pans, and serving pieces. In addition to the steward, chef and three cooks, the dining car was staffed by six waiters. Jill settled into a window seat at a table for four. In addition to the crisp white cloth, the table bore thick white napkins and was set with heavy silverware and china bearing the violets-and-daisies pattern. Each table held a full water bottle, a bud vase with a fresh carnation, and a heavy silver stand that held the menu and the meal checks, which passengers used to mark their menu choices.

A white-coated waiter appeared with a silver-plated coffeepot. "Good morning, Mr. Lewis," Jill said as he poured her first cup and set the pot on the table.

"Good morning, Miss McLeod." The waiter had traveled with her before and he knew what she was going to have, even as she reached to mark the meal check. "French toast," he said with a smile. "Bacon, crisp, not burned. We've got you covered, Miss McLeod."

Jill poured cream in her coffee and sipped, relishing the first jolt of caffeine. The dining room was filling up and a moment later, an older couple joined her at the table. She had met Mr.

and Mrs. Patterson the day before when they boarded the train in Sacramento. They were traveling in one of the sleeper cars, headed for Omaha, Nebraska and a visit with their son and his family.

"Did you sleep well?" Jill asked as the waiter brought more coffee.

"Oh, yes, we always do on the train," Mrs. Patterson said, stirring sugar into her cup. Mr. Patterson pulled the menu from its stand. "What are you having for breakfast, Miss McLeod?"

"I'm partial to the French toast."

"And I'm partial to corned beef hash and eggs," Mr. Patterson declared, handing the menu to his wife.

Mrs. Patterson perused the offerings. "That's a bit heavy for me. I think the poached eggs on an English muffin sounds good."

They marked their menu checks, which were collected by Mr. Lewis, who had returned with Jill's breakfast. A fourth person joined them at the table, a man who introduced himself as Mr. Dayton, from Elko, Nevada. He was traveling in coach, heading for Grand Junction, Colorado. After he ordered an omelet, the four of them talked. Mrs. Patterson was looking forward to seeing the spectacular scenery as the train went over the Rocky Mountains. Since it was July, it would be light later in the evening, which meant the passengers would be able to get a good look at Gore and Byers canyons, deep in the mountains. Both canyons were carved by the Colorado River, and the train would run alongside the river for over two hundred miles.

Jill looked out the window and saw that the train was nearing Soldier Summit, a pass in Utah's Wasatch Mountains. She excused herself and got up from the table, moving to the train's public address system, located near the dining car steward's counter. She picked up the mike and began her first announcement of the day, telling passengers about some of the sights they'd see on this second day out. That done, she hung up the mike and headed forward through the train, to start the first of many walks through the *CZ*. She walked all the way to the first passenger car.

The consist—the railroad term for the list of cars that made up the train—began with the powerful locomotives that pulled the train. Immediately in back of these was the baggage car, the Silver

Coyote, followed by three chair cars for coach passengers, each with a coach attendant to see to the passengers' needs, and each with a Vista-Dome, an upper-level compartment rising from the car's roof, with seating for coach passengers. Curved glass formed the front, rear and side walls of the Dome, providing unparalleled views of the scenery, for which the *California Zephyr* was famous. "Look up, look down, look all around," was the line used in the *CZ*'s advertising. Under the dome was a depressed floor, lower than the rest of the car, with steps leading down to the men's and women's washrooms.

On this trip, the chair cars were the Silver Dollar, the Silver Rifle, and the Silver Bronco. Next came the Silver Roundup, the buffet-lounge car where Jill's compartment was located, and then the Silver Banquet, the dining car. At the rear of the train were the Pullman cars—the six-five sleeper, the Silver Crane; the ten-six sleeper, the Silver Gorge; and the Silver Larch, the sixteen-section Pullman, where at night seats were converted into upper and lower berths. Then came the transcontinental sleeper, another ten-six car called the Silver Rapids. This car would be detached from the train when it reached Chicago, then attached to a train from the Pennsylvania Railroad, its ultimate destination New York City. The very last car on the train was the dome-observation car, the Silver Horizon, which had four Pullman accommodations, a buffet that served food and drink, and an observation lounge. Above the café was another Vista-Dome.

When Jill reached the front of the Silver Dollar, she paused to say hello to the car attendant, then she answered questions for several coach passengers. She made her way to the second car, the Silver Rifle, where the conductor's office was located at the rear of the car. Jill peered into the office, wanting to introduce herself to the Denver & Rio Grande Western conductor who had boarded the train when the crew was changed out in Salt Lake City. There were two men inside, both drinking coffee. One of the men had a familiar face. Jim Gaskill, a tall, rangy man in his forties, wore the typical conductor's uniform, with a dark jacket worn over a white shirt, as well as a dark tie and vest. A watch on a chain was visible in his left pocket. D&RGW insignia decorated his lapels. His billed cap bore a shiny badge with a snowcapped mountain peak and the words MAIN LINE THROUGH THE ROCKIES, surrounding the RIO GRANDE portion of the railroad's name. Mr. Gaskill would be aboard the *California Zephyr* until the next crew change, in Grand Junction, Colorado.

The second man was younger, with a muscular, wiry build, red hair and a face dusted with freckles. Jill had never seen him before. He looked at her with a friendly smile, a pleasant twinkle in his blue eyes.

"Good to see you again, Miss McLeod," Mr. Gaskill said. "Have you met Don Harding, our brakeman?"

"No, I haven't. Nice to meet you, Mr. Harding." Jill offered her hand and the younger man grasped it.

"It's a pleasure, Miss McLeod," he said. "It's only my second trip on the *Zephyr*. I was in Southern Colorado before, based in Durango."

Mr. Gaskill took another sip of coffee. "The Western Pacific conductor briefed me in Salt Lake City. Sounds like we're having an uneventful run so far. I'd sure like to keep it that way." He glanced at Mr. Harding. "When Miss McLeod and I did an east-bound run last December, we had all sorts of shenanigans going on, including a sneak thief and a murder. Then there was that rockslide."

"I'd like to hear about that," the brakeman said. He flashed his smile again.

If that was a hint, he was being none too subtle about it. Jill was used to attention from the males aboard the train, both crew and passengers. From time to time she had to deal with the wolves, the men who figured the Zephyrette was fair game for their atten-tion. Still, Jill admitted, romantic alliances between crew members were common. One of her fellow Zephyrettes was engaged to a dining car steward, and she herself was dating a man she'd met on that very same December run. A Zephyrette could not be mar-ried, though. Should she decide to take the step into matrimony, she'd have to give up her job, and she didn't want to do that, at least not yet.

Jill excused herself and continued her walk through the train.

She went through the third chair car and entered the Silver Round-up, where the coffee shop was full of passengers having breakfast. She stopped briefly in her own compartment, then continued through to the Silver Crane. Perhaps she could take a moment to talk with Mr. Doolin. She wanted to find out what he knew about the ghost.

But Mr. Doolin was busy, talking with the Pullman conductor, Mr. Grace, a tall, imposing man with dark chocolate skin and tight gray curls under his cap. Crew members like Mr. Gaskill and Mr. Harding, the engineer and fireman up in the locomotives, and the dining car crew, were employed by one of the three railroads that ran the *CZ*. Jill, as a Zephyrette, was considered an employee of the Western Pacific Railroad for payroll purposes. And the porters, who were overwhelmingly black, were employees of the Pullman Company, based either in Oakland or Chicago. During each run of the *CZ*, there was a Pullman conductor overseeing the porters.

She greeted the two men and walked past them. The door to bedroom A opened and Mrs. Lombard, a passenger who was traveling from Oakland to Chicago, stepped out. Jill stopped to admire her outfit, a coat-dress of silky ivory rayon decorated with a coppery print. Her brown leather handbag matched her high-heeled pumps. "Thank you," Mrs. Lombard said. "I got the dress at the City of Paris in San Francisco. Do you shop there?"

"Sometimes," Jill said. "I live in Alameda, so usually I go to Capwell's or Kahn's in Oakland. Did you finish that Raymond Chandler book you were reading last night?"

"I did. How about you, did you dive into Agatha Christie?"

On the previous evening, Jill had encountered Mrs. Lombard in the lounge of the Silver Roundup, having a nightcap while she paged her way through *The Lady in the Lake*. They both had a love for mysteries, with Mrs. Lombard leaning toward the more hard-boiled practitioners of the art.

Jill shook her head. "I was so tired last night I didn't read before going to bed."

"I'm sure being a Zephyrette keeps you quite busy," Mrs. Lombard said. "Since I've finished my Chandler book I'm getting ready to start another one. It's by an author who's new to me, Ross Macdonald. It's called *The Way Some People Die*."

"That's certainly an intriguing title," Jill said. "I'll look for it. Enjoy the book."

Mrs. Lombard waved and headed forward, in the direction of the dining car. Jill walked toward the rear of the train, leaving the Silver Crane for the Silver Gorge. The porter, a young man named Mr. Webster, was making up a bedroom that had been vacated by a passenger who left the train in Provo. The space was reserved by another passenger who would board the train in Grand Junction, Colorado.

"And the passenger traveling in roomette four?" Jill asked. "I understand someone was getting on the train in Salt Lake City."

Mr. Webster nodded. "That's Mrs. Callendar, bound for Iowa." He looked past her. "Here she is now."

Jill looked at the older woman who had appeared in the passageway, walking toward them. The woman was in her fifties, Jill guessed, dressed in a moss green gabardine suit and carrying a square gray leather bag. She had a pleasant face below her expertly coiffed brown hair.

"Good morning, Mrs. Callendar, I'm Jill McLeod, the Zephyrette. Please let me know if there's anything you need."

Mrs. Callendar smiled. "A lot of coffee, that's what I need. And a good breakfast. I had to get up quite early this morning to catch this train."

"You'll have plenty of opportunity to relax between here and your destination," Jill said. "There's lots of coffee and good food in the diner."

"I know. I'm an old hand at train travel."

"Despite the early hour, I hope you were able to get some sleep after we left Salt Lake City, without any disturbances." Jill wondered if Mrs. Callendar had heard or seen anything in the short time she'd occupied the roomette.

"I didn't bother to have the porter make up the bed when I boarded," Mrs. Callendar said, "but I did doze off after we pulled out of the station. I woke up about twenty minutes ago. Now, if you'll excuse me, I really do need coffee." She stepped past Jill and the porter and continued walking forward.

Jill left Mr. Webster and headed back through the train. It was the height of summer, a time when people took vacations, visited relatives and friends or just traveled somewhere they hadn't been before, enjoying the broad tapestry of America from the Vista-Dome. As a result, the train was full. Many of the passengers were children. Most were well behaved but some treated the train as their moving playground, and their parents were content to take a break and let them. In the sixteen-section sleeper, where the daytime seats would be converted to upper and lower berths at night, two little boys were chasing one another down the aisle. Finally the mother of one of them stepped out of the women's rest room at the end of the car and took her offspring by the arm, settling him in his seat with a sharp word and a stern look. Jill stopped to check on the little boy whose skinned elbow she'd treated the night before. He proudly showed off his scab and assured her he was fine.

In the transcontinental sleeper, she talked with the Birnbaums, an elderly couple who were headed back to New York City after visiting their married daughter in San Francisco. Then she stepped through the vestibule into the dome-observation car, the Silver Horizon, which contained three double bedrooms suitable for two passengers each, and a drawing room that could accommodate three passengers. At this end of the car was a tiny compartment for the porter. Jill passed the bedrooms and the drawing room and took two steps down to the depressed level under the Vista-Dome. Here in the car's buffet, or lounge, the porter, Ed Harvey, was behind the curved counter at the small bar, pouring cups of coffee for two passengers, a man and a woman. Jill waved at Mr. Harvey, then she walked up two more steps leading to the main level, where curved stairs led up to the dome. At the rear of the car, comfortable upholstered chairs, lined either side, five on one side and four on the other, where passengers sat with small, round metal tables that had recessed holders for glasses, with ashtrays in the middle.

To the right of the stairs leading to the Vista-Dome was a

writing desk, with stationery and postcards for the passengers. Jill frequently collected letters and cards during her walks through the train, mailing them at the longer station stops. Today, the next such stop would be Grand Junction, Colorado, at 11:46 A.M. There were also newspapers on the desk. Before the train had left the coach yards in Oakland the day before, multiple copies of the *San Francisco Chronicle* and *Examiner* had been delivered to the train and distributed through the cars, including this one. And today, during the stop in Salt Lake City, current editions of the *Deseret News* and the *Salt Lake Tribune* had been added, as would the *Rocky Mountain News* and the *Denver Post* when the train reached Denver this evening.

Jill looked down at the newspapers on the desk. The headlines were full of news about the impending armistice in Korea, promising an end to the conflict. The Korean peninsula had been separated into two countries since the end of World War II. However, war began in June 1950 when North Korean troops crossed the border into South Korea. Later that year, in October, the Chinese army had entered the fray.

Korea. Thinking about the war always caused a pang. She wouldn't be riding the rails had she married her fiancé, Steve Haggerty, the man she'd met while attending college at the University of California in Berkeley. Her degree was in history and she was planning to teach while Steve fulfilled his military obligation, since he'd been in the Reserve Officers Training Corps while studying engineering. Four years of college in exchange for a commitment to serve, so Steve had been commissioned as an officer in the Marine Corps. After training at Camp Pendleton in Southern California, he'd gone to Korea the following year, as the war heated up.

Steve died in December 1950, at a place called Hell Fire Valley at Chosin Reservoir. The battlefield was known as "Frozen Chosin" because of the terrible winter weather that year, with snow, wind and temperatures far below zero.

Jill could still recall every detail of the night Steve's Uncle Pat, a Western Pacific conductor, had showed up at the McLeods' home in Alameda to tell Jill of Steve's death. After months of grieving, she'd wrapped her engagement ring in a lace handkerchief and tucked it into her jewelry box. Then she went looking for a different direction for her life, one that left little time for wondering how things might have been. It was Uncle Pat who had suggested that Jill become a Zephyrette, telling her she'd be good at it.

And she was. She enjoyed her job very much. She'd been riding the trains for over two years now. And there was a new man in her life, Mike Scolari. She'd met Mike last December on an eastbound run of the *California Zephyr*, and they had been dating ever since. Dating, no plans yet, just enjoying each other's company. Mike, a World War II veteran, was using his GI benefits to go to school at UC Berkeley. He wanted to finish his studies and move on to his career before thinking about anything permanent, and Jill concurred. She wasn't ready to give up her life on the rails.

Korea, Jill thought, looking again at the headlines. Now the war that had taken Steve's life, and those of so many others, was coming to an end.

Chapter Four

JILL LEFT THE NEWSPAPER on the table and took the steps up to the Vista-Dome. All twenty-four seats in the upper observation area were taken, with passengers looking at the mountainous terrain of eastern Utah. The *CZ* had gone over Soldier Summit and was heading down Price Canyon, toward the little town of Helper, where the train would stop briefly.

"Why is the town called Helper?" The passenger in the nearby seat was Tommy Reeves, a fourteen-year-old who, with his family, was traveling on the sixteen-section sleeper. He was quite taken by the sights around him and since he'd gotten on the train in Sacramento, he had many questions for Jill.

"There's a steep grade here in the canyon," Jill said. "So as the train went west up the canyon, it would take on additional engines, called helpers, to help with the climb."

Tommy leaned close to the window, looking at the canyon walls, then the buildings of the little town. The *CZ* stopped and started again a moment later, pulling out of Helper.

"How soon will we be in Colorado?" another passenger asked.

Jill consulted her watch. "Another hour or so. We join the Colorado River at Westwater, Utah, and follow the river for two hundred thirty-five miles. The state line is not far from there. Then we go through Ruby Canyon, which is really beautiful. We're due into Grand Junction, Colorado at a quarter to noon."

She stayed in the Vista-Dome until the river came into view, then she went back downstairs, and made her way past the buffet and the sleeping accommodations at the front of the car. She headed back through the sleeper cars, pausing here and there to talk with passengers and answer questions.

In the Silver Gorge, the door to roomette four was half-open, and she saw Mrs. Callendar inside her roomette, a book on her lap. "What are you reading?" Jill asked.

Mrs. Callendar lifted the book so Jill could see the cover. It was one of the earlier Edna Ferber novels, *Cimarron*, about the early history of Oklahoma. "I love historical novels," she said. "How about you?"

"I do," Jill said. "Historical novels and mysteries. Agatha Christie is my favorite author. I really enjoyed Miss Ferber's book *Giant*. Do you like Lydia Stafford's books? Last December she was a passenger on the train."

"Oh, I love her books, especially the one about the California Gold Rush," Mrs. Callendar said. "I hope she's writing a new one."

Jill recalled how Miss Stafford had closeted herself in her bedroom during the journey from Oakland to Chicago, tapping away on her typewriter. "She is, or at least she was working on it the whole trip. She told me the book will be published next year. Just so you know, it's about the building of the transcontinental railroad."

"I can't wait," Mrs. Callendar said.

Just then, the older woman who was traveling in the roomette across from Mrs. Callendar stepped out into the passageway. Mrs. Abner had boarded the train in Winnemucca, Nevada. "Good morning, Miss McLeod. I trust you had a good night's sleep." After Jill assured her that she had, Mrs. Abner peered in at Mrs. Callendar. "Hello, I'm Brenda Abner. I'm headed for Glenwood Springs, Colorado, for a family reunion. We're all going to soak in the hot springs there."

"Sarah Callendar," the other woman said. "Nice to meet you. Hot springs sound lovely. I'm bound for Burlington, Iowa, to visit friends."

"Do you play bridge?" Mrs. Abner asked. "I'm trying to find a fourth for a game back in the observation car. I've got two other people lined up besides myself."

"I do play," Mrs. Callendar said. "Though it's been a while."

Mrs. Abner clapped her hands together. "Wonderful. How about meeting in the observation car at nine-thirty? The others are Mr. Lewelling, he's from San Francisco, and Miss Pomeroy, from Davis, California."

"I'll be there," Mrs. Callendar told her.

Jill left them chatting and walked forward through the sleeper, saying hello to Mr. Webster as the porter came out of a bedroom. She crossed the vestibule into the Silver Crane, where Mr. Doolin was putting sheets into that car's soiled linen locker. "Do you have a minute to talk?" Jill asked.

Mr. Doolin nodded. "I had a feeling you'd be back."

"I'd like to find out more about this ghost." She stopped and shook her head. "It feels odd talking about it, because I don't believe in ghosts."

"Many's the person who's said that," Mr. Doolin said with a chuckle. "Only to change his, or her mind. You saw something last night. Something you can't explain. And it still bothers you, I can tell. 'There are more things in heaven and earth, Horatio…'"

"Now you're quoting Shakespeare at me." She smiled.

"I'm saying that sometimes we are not given to understand, Miss McLeod. We just have to accept."

Jill considered this, then she took a deep breath and expelled it, taking a tiny but still skeptical step toward acceptance. "Yes, I saw something. A flickering light."

"And you could see right through it. I told you, I've seen it twice, and it was just like that."

"There was something else. I went into the roomette and it was cold. Not just cold. Numbing. Then I heard taps. Four distinct taps."

"I haven't heard any noises." Mr. Doolin's expression lit up with interest. "But last time I was working as porter on the Silver Gorge, I had a passenger in roomette four who kept complaining about the cold. He couldn't get warm."

"There's a passenger in roomette four now, though it was empty last night. I certainly hope she doesn't experience any problems this evening."

"Time will tell," he said.

A passenger stepped out of a nearby compartment and beckoned to Jill. "Oh, Miss McLeod, just the person I want to talk to.
Could you come here for a moment?"

"Certainly, Mr. Sheffield. I'll be right there."

As it turned out, Mr. Sheffield had several letters to be mailed.
Jill carried stamps in her uniform pocket, so she took the letters
and promised to post them during the brief station stop in Grand
Junction. The train was nearing the point where it joined the Colorado River, traveling alongside that body of water for more than
two hundred miles. It would be about an hour and a half before
it reached the next stop.

Jill left the Silver Crane, thinking about her talk with Mr.
Doolin. Of all the crazy things she had encountered riding the
rails during the past two years, a ghost—if the flickering light was
indeed such a thing—was not among them. Did the young man's
spirit haunt the roomette where he had traveled during his final
journey? Did Steve's ghost haunt the slopes of Hell Fire Valley in
Korea? Jill wondered about that as she walked through the dining
car, dodging one of the waiters who was setting a table in preparation for the diner's lunch service. Then she discarded the thought.

———

The train wound through twenty-five-mile-long Ruby Canyon,
which took its name from the spectacular red sandstone cliffs on
either side of the river, where spires and arches had been carved
by thousands of years of erosion. At the yellow brick station in
Grand Junction, Jill mailed letters and postcards, said good-bye to
departing passengers and greeted new ones. Then the train headed
east through the fruit-growing town of Palisade. Jill went to the
conductor's office in the second chair car, to check in with the new
Denver & Rio Grande Western conductor who would stay on the
train until it reached Denver. He was a gray-haired man named Ed
Weatherbee, and Jill had traveled with him before.

Jill had lunch in the dining car and was finished by the time
the *California Zephyr* pulled into Glenwood Springs at 1:35 P.M.,
crossing the Frying Pan River and coming to a stop at the station
on the south side of the swift Colorado River. Clouds of steam rose
from the hot springs on the north side of the river. Above this, on

a bluff, was the Hotel Colorado, an imposing brick-and-sandstone building constructed in the 1890s. Among its notable patrons over the years were President Theodore Roosevelt, the movie actor Tom Mix, who'd shot a picture in the canyon, and the Chicago gangster Al Capone. And the hotel was reputed to be haunted. Jill recalled hearing stories of a child in Victorian dress playing in the halls and elevators that moved of their own volition.

Glenwood Canyon was fifteen miles long, carved by the Colorado River, through limestone, sandstone, shale and granite. The caves near the town held many hot springs. The train's Vista-Domes were packed with passengers as this eastbound train went through the canyon, passing the westbound *CZ* at Grizzly Creek. The train had several more spectacular canyons on its route—Dotsero, Byers and Gore.

Jill walked back to the dome-observation car and began making dinner reservations, part of her Zephyrette duties. She carried a binder with colored cards for different seating times. Jill kept track of the reservations in her binder as she handed out cards, covering the sleeper cars first, then moving to the chair cars.

The *California Zephyr* and the Colorado River parted company at the town of Granby. The train headed through Fraser Canyon, President Dwight Eisenhower's favorite fishing spot, and then to the town of Fraser, which was near the ski resort called Winter Park, the slopes bare now in July. The train plunged into Moffat Tunnel, its bore more than nine thousand feet long as it went under the Continental Divide. Then it wound down the eastern slope of the Rockies, with Denver finally visible in the distance as the train came out of the mountains and made its slow descent down the curve called the Big Ten, where the tracks looped in a big S with a tight ten-degree radius of curve. Once the tracks straightened, the *CZ* picked up speed as it went through the town of Arvada and the outskirts of the Mile High City, finally arriving on time in Denver at 7 P.M.

The platform of the big Beaux-Arts station near the Platte River bustled. Passengers got off the train, greeting relatives and friends with hugs and handshakes, handing bags and bundles to waiting Red Caps, then walked toward the building to collect their checked luggage. Other passengers lined the platform, waiting to board. Denver was another crew and equipment change stop, with the Denver & Rio Grande Western locomotives decoupled and replaced by Chicago, Burlington & Quincy engines. The conductor and other onboard personnel were CB&Q employees as well. Jill got off the train and walked along the platform, enjoying the balmy summer evening as she assisted passengers in locating their cars. Soon the conductor gave his familiar call. "Now boarding, the *California Zephyr*. Destination Chicago..."

Jill boarded the train, climbing the steps to the vestibule of the Silver Crane, where Mr. Doolin waited to pull up the steps and close the door. The engineer blew the whistle, and the *California Zephyr* pulled out of the Denver station, moving slowly through the train yards and the neighborhoods north of downtown. Once the *CZ* left the outskirts of the city, it gained speed, heading northeast across the high plains of Colorado.

Jill headed back to the dome-observation car, the Silver Horizon. Two "specials" had boarded the train in Denver. These were special-attention passengers, prominent people who had come to the attention of the railroad when booking their accommodations. They were singled out for extra attention from the onboard crew, especially the Zephyrette. In this case, the specials were an Illinois congressman and his demanding wife. They were traveling in the drawing room on the Silver Horizon, the largest and most expensive accommodation on the train.

The congressman's wife regaled her with tales of their Washington connections and their friendship with President and Mrs. Eisenhower. "You know, Mamie's from Denver," she said. "And Ike loves to fish up at Fraser."

Jill smiled. "Yes, ma'am, I do know that. I grew up in Denver." The Doud home on Lafayette Street in Denver, where the First Lady's family lived, was not far from the home of Jill's grandmother, near Cheesman Park.

She finally took her leave of the congressman and his wife and peeked into the lounge area of the Silver Horizon, where she saw Mrs. Callendar playing bridge again with three other passengers. Then she went up to the Vista-Dome and watched the sun set over the now distant Rockies.

The stairs leading down from the Vista-Dome were edged with

Lucite that glowed with muted light now that it was night. The observation car had a rounded back end, called a fish tail, and all the chairs in the lower-level section were full. Jill made her way back through the car, doing a walk-through of the train. After indulging in apple pie and coffee in the coffee shop, Jill talked with passengers in the Silver Roundup lounge, then went to her compartment just before ten o'clock. She worked on her trip report, read a few chapters of *A Murder Is Announced* and finally turned out the light.

She slept undisturbed until early the next morning. She woke briefly as the train left Omaha, Nebraska at 5 A.M., then again half an hour later as the *CZ* crossed the Missouri River, the sound of wheels on rails different on the bridge than it was on the ground. Jill dozed off again and woke again just after six. She was dressed and in the dining car as the train made its brief stop in Creston, Iowa. Just to be different, she ordered bacon and eggs instead of her usual French toast.

As the food was delivered, she was joined by two passengers who had boarded the first chair car in Denver. Mr. and Mrs. Wells, who appeared to be in their forties, were traveling to Aurora, Illinois, the next-to-last stop before the train arrived in Chicago at 1:30 P.M. "A family reunion," Mrs. Wells added as she took a fork to her omelet. "I'm from Aurora, my husband is from Brighton, Colorado."

"My family farmed there." Mr. Wells deployed the pepper shaker over his scrambled eggs. "We still own the farm, but I have a feed store in town."

"I've been to Brighton," Jill told them. "I was born in Denver, and grew up there."

As they ate breakfast, Jill told them about her early years in the Mile High City, where her father was a doctor. When he volunteered for the Navy, right after Pearl Harbor, the McLeods had sold their house. Jill, her mother and her two siblings had moved in with Jill's maternal grandmother, while Dr. McLeod shipped out for the war in the Pacific. When he returned at the end of the war, they had moved to Alameda, California, where they lived now.

After finishing her breakfast, Jill said good-bye to her companions and began her morning walk through the train. She started in the chair cars, chatting with passengers in each car. Then she strolled through the dining car, which had filled up. After making her way through the coffee shop and the lounge in the Silver Roundup, she stopped briefly in her own compartment. Then she headed into the Silver Crane. Glancing at her watch, she saw that it was a quarter to nine. The train would be in Ottumwa, Iowa, at 8:53 A.M., about ten minutes from now. Already Jill could see the outskirts of the town from the windows on her left. She said hello to Mr. Doolin, then passed through the vestibule to the next car.

In the Silver Gorge, Mrs. Lombard was coming out of bedroom A. Today she wore a polka-dotted dress with a full skirt that swirled around her. "Good morning, Miss McLeod. It looks like another lovely summer day. Is the dining car still open?"

"Yes, it is," Jill assured her. "For another half hour or so."

Mrs. Lombard headed for the front of the car as Jill turned to her right, then left again, walking down the corridor between the roomettes. Mr. Webster, the porter, was at the rear of the car, heading toward her. Then Mrs. Callendar stepped out of roomette four, wearing another stylish suit, this one gray with black trim. As Jill recalled, the passenger was leaving the train in Burlington, Iowa, the stop scheduled for 10:07 A.M. She looked tired and out of sorts.

"Good morning, Mrs. Callendar," Jill said. "I hope you had a good night."

The older woman fiddled with the latch on her handbag and frowned. "As a matter of fact, I didn't. I had the devil of a time getting any sleep at all. The roomette was quite chilly. I had to ring the porter to bring me extra blankets. That seemed to help, but right after I dropped off, I woke up again. Two men were arguing and they went at it for quite a while. It was extremely rude of them to carry on with their conversation at such a late hour."

Jill and Mr. Webster exchanged looks. She knew the porter was thinking the same thing that she was. The passengers traveling in the roomettes on either side of number four, and the roomette across the corridor, were all women. She supposed it was possible that two men had been arguing in the corridor, but Mrs. Callendar said the argument went on for some time. She wondered if anyone else, including the porter, heard the voices.

"I'm sorry your sleep was disturbed," Jill said. "Were you able to make out what the two men were saying?"

Mrs. Callendar shrugged. "Not entirely. I just got the impression it had something to do with numbers. Very odd. Now, if you'll excuse me, I must have coffee and breakfast before the dining car closes."

She stepped past Jill and headed forward, in the direction of the diner. When she had disappeared from view, Jill turned to the porter. "Did you hear anything, Mr. Webster?"

He shook his head. "Nothing like that. And I'm a light sleeper. If there was two men arguing in the corridor, I surely would have heard them. My compartment is at the end of the car, not that far from roomette four." He paused. "I know what you're thinking, Miss McLeod. The ghost."

"You, too?"

The porter smiled. "Yes. Me, too."

"Did you see something?"

He looked over his shoulder before he spoke, reluctant to be overheard. "Once before, when I was working on this car. Late at night, after everyone had gone to bed. I saw a light. It went into roomette four. Which was empty at the time, no one traveling there. Heard some noises, too. Like someone knocking on the bulkhead."

Jill sighed. "I saw a light last night, before Mrs. Callendar got on the train at Salt Lake City. I went inside the roomette. It was chilly, just as she said. And I heard a noise, like tapping. But no voices. Have you ever heard voices coming from the roomette?"

Mr. Webster shook his head. "No, I haven't. Just the light and that knocking sound. But no voices."

"Mrs. Callendar heard two voices," Jill said. "Two voices, two men."

"Two ghosts?" Mr. Webster asked.

Jill shook her head. "I hope not. I should think one would be enough."

Chapter Five

JILL WOKE UP IN HER OWN BED on Wednesday morning, her calico cat, Sophie, curled into a ball next to her. She stroked the cat's head and was rewarded with a purr. Then she stretched her arms above her head.

It was good to be home. She had been gone for six days. It took two and a half days for the eastbound *California Zephyr*, train number 18, to make the journey from Oakland to Chicago. After a two-night layover in the Windy City, Jill had boarded the westbound *CZ*, designated train number 17. Another two and a half days passed and the train had arrived late Tuesday afternoon, at Oakland's Middle Harbor. Passengers who lived in the East Bay got off the train, collected their luggage and headed for private cars, taxis and buses. Those going to San Francisco boarded the ferry that would take them across the bay.

When Jill had finished with her end-of-run duties, she called home and her brother, Drew, came to pick her up. She caught sight of him, waiting near the platform in the family's Ford, and walked over, carrying her suitcase. They drove home, through Oakland streets and the tunnel called the Tube, that ran under the estuary to Alameda. After six days away, Jill welcomed the sight of Alameda, often called the Island City, with its canopy of trees over the streets. The houses that lined the streets were large and small and in-between, some made of stucco, others built of wood, like the McLeod family home on Union Street, just a few blocks from the bay. Alameda was home to many houses built in the Victorian era, and Jill's family lived in one of these. It was a two-story house in the Queen Anne style, painted blue with bright yellow trim. A dogwood tree, which in springtime was covered with masses of white flowers, shaded one side of the front yard. On one side of the house, a Cécile Brünner rose had outgrown a tall trellis and now climbed toward the second-story windows, its green foliage loaded with small, soft pink blooms. The wide front porch wrapped around two sides of the house, with a porch swing and a comfortable glider for outdoor seating. Above the front door was a fan-shaped window made of stained glass, its panes ruby red, blue and gold. Inside, there was a bay window in the living room and a wide staircase leading to the second floor.

Drew carried his sister's suitcase into the house and Jill greeted her parents with hugs. Then she went upstairs. Her cat demanded to be picked up and cuddled, so Jill did this first. Then she stripped off her uniform and took the shower she had longed for during the trip from Chicago. When she came downstairs, dressed in dungarees, a checked cotton blouse and a pair of ballet flats, dinner was nearly ready. Her father had fired up the barbecue grill in the backyard, planning to put on hamburgers as soon as the coals had burned down. Her mother had potato salad and baked beans on the table. Jill's sister, Lucy, had made shortcakes, round sweetened biscuits, which they ate piled with strawberries and whipped cream.

Now Jill looked at the clock on her bedside table. It was nearly eight, and morning sun poured through the white eyelet cotton curtains. A dust mote floated through the air and settled on the leaves of the purple African violet on her nightstand.

She pushed back the covers and got out of bed, putting on her striped seersucker robe. Down the hall, in the upstairs bathroom, she took a hot shower. She washed her short, curly hair and toweled it dry. Then she returned to her bedroom. It was furnished with a single bed, white-painted wrought iron decorated with brass fittings, covered with a rose-colored chenille bedspread. She dressed, wearing the same clothes she'd worn last night. Then she made the bed, dislodging Sophie, who meowed with indignation as she repaired to the nightstand. Jill pulled up the spread and arranged the colorful pillows at the head. "There," she told the cat. Sophie meowed again and flicked her tail. Then she stepped daintily onto the bed, circled and snuggled up in the pillows.

Jill went downstairs and headed for the kitchen. Her sister was at the kitchen table, an empty plate and a cup of coffee, and the morning newspapers in front of her. Lucy wore her blond hair with loose pin curls framing her face. It was the latest style, known as the Italian cut. Jill kept her own light brown hair short in what was called a poodle cut. The style was easy to care for, and went with Jill's fair coloring and blue eyes.

Lucy looked up and grinned. "About time you got up, lazybones. Even your cat has been down for breakfast."

"Did you leave any coffee for me?" Jill crossed the kitchen, to the counter where a stainless steel GE percolator sat on the counter, next to a can of Maxwell House ground coffee. She lifted the pot, which felt as though it had liquid in it. She opened the cupboard above her and pulled out a cup. Once she'd filled the cup with hot coffee, she opened the refrigerator door and took out a small bottle of cream, pulled off the cap, and poured a generous dollop into her coffee. She took a sip. Ah, nothing like that first cup of coffee.

Jill's mother bustled into the kitchen from the back porch, where the washer and dryer were located. Lora McLeod wore a red-and-yellow cotton print wrap dress and carried a wicker laundry basket full of folded towels. "You're up. Do you want me to fix you some breakfast?"

"I'll make some toast. I don't want a big breakfast, since I'm having lunch with Tidsy. You did say I could use the car today. Is that still all right?"

"Certainly," Lora said. "You know where the keys are." She left the kitchen, heading for the stairs, the laundry basket balanced on her hip.

Lucy got up from the table and washed her breakfast dishes in the sink, leaving them to dry in the drainer. "If you're using the car today, could you drop me off at the library? I have some books to return. I'll walk back."

"Sure. Let's leave early. I want to drop off my uniform to be cleaned. And I'll go to the library with you. I have books to take back and there's one I want to look for."

"Okay. I'll be in the dining room working on my invitations." Lucy left the kitchen, singing, *"A kiss on the hand..."* Jill smiled and shook her head. Her sister had taken to singing "Diamonds Are a Girl's Best Friend," ever since her boyfriend Ethan had presented her with an engagement ring in May, right after Lucy graduated from Mills College in Oakland. The song was from the musical *Gentlemen Prefer Blondes.* Jill was looking forward to seeing the recently released movie version featuring Jane Russell and Marilyn Monroe.

Jill took a slice of cooked bacon from the plate at the back of the four-burner stove. Then she opened the breadbox and took out a loaf, sticking two slices into the toaster. She looked out the kitchen window and saw Drew, in khaki shorts and a T-shirt, out in the backyard garden. It was July, which in the Bay Area often meant pale gray fog and the need to dress warmly, prompting the quote often attributed to Mark Twain: "The coldest winter I ever spent was a summer in San Francisco." Today, however, the weather was warm and sunny.

Her toast popped up. She removed the browned slices from the toaster and put them on a plate, reaching for the butter dish. Then she carried her coffee and the plate to the kitchen table, covered with an oilcloth print of cherries and pears. She and her mother had canned apricot jam last summer, and the jar on the table was the result. She scraped jam from the jar onto her toast and took a bite.

The back door opened and Drew came inside. He carried a round metal colander piled with bright red tomatoes and several varieties of squash, from yellow crook-neck to pattypan with their round shapes and scalloped edges, in shades from white to light and dark green. He set the colander on the counter. "Morning, Sis."

"Those tomatoes look good," Jill said.

"Yeah. I ate one out in the backyard, right off the vine."

"I can tell." Jill pointed. "You have a splotch of tomato juice on your T-shirt."

Drew dampened his finger at the sink and rubbed at the red spot near his neck, succeeding in spreading the stain rather than eliminating it. He eyed the plate of bacon on the stove. "Maybe I'll have a bacon and tomato sandwich, right now. How long before you leave town again?"

"I'll have to call and get my schedule. Probably a week, or ten days." Jill took another bite of toast.

The phone rang in the downstairs hallway. The ringing stopped as someone answered it. Then Lucy appeared in the kitchen doorway. "Drew, it's for you."

"Okay." Drew left the kitchen. Jill took another sip of coffee as she reached for the newspaper at the top of the stack. The McLeods had always read newspapers. When they lived in Denver, they took the *Rocky Mountain News* and the *Denver Post*. Now they took the *San Francisco Chronicle, San Francisco Examiner* and the *Oakland Tribune*.

Nibbling her toast, Jill looked at the headlines on the front page of the *Chronicle*. The coming armistice that would end the Korean War was prominent of course, but today a local story took precedence. The American Federation of Labor's Carmen's Union, employees of the privately owned transit network called the Key System, was set to go on strike. That was serious, since the system's network of buses carried passengers all over the East Bay. The streetcars Jill had seen when the McLeods first moved to the area had been converted to buses in 1948, and the rails torn up, a move opposed by many passengers and cities, Jill recalled. The system also ran commuter trains on tracks over the Bay Bridge to San Francisco. When she first started college at the University of California in Berkeley, Jill had lived at home, riding the bus to campus. Later she'd shared an apartment with several other coeds.

Jill knew from earlier articles that in the past five years, fares had gone up, with routes changed or eliminated. Ridership was down. These days, more people had cars, she supposed. She read through the articles, noting that parking restrictions had been lifted in some areas, and people were forming carpools, as they had during the war.

She finished reading the newspaper and got up from the table. Lucy was at the dining room table, with her wedding invitations and lists stacked around her. The wedding was scheduled for late September. Sometimes Jill felt a pang, thinking of other wedding plans. She and Steve had scheduled their wedding for August 1950. Instead, Steve went to Korea.

Now it was Lucy's turn to plan a wedding. She had shopped for a wedding gown, at stores in the East Bay as well as San Francisco. She had finally settled on a dress and chosen the outfits for the bridesmaids and for Jill, the maid of honor. The church and its hall were already booked for the ceremony and the reception that would follow. Lucy and Ethan were going to honeymoon in Hawaii, sailing for the islands on one of the Matson liners.

Her mother brought up the subject later that morning, when Jill was helping her put shelf liners in the linen closet near the second-floor bathroom. Lora McLeod had cut several pieces of oilcloth, covered with bright yellow daisies. She had set one piece on the top shelf and was smoothing it into place. "Does it bother you that your sister is getting married?"

Jill looked at her mother as she handed her another sheet of oilcloth. "Sometimes it does. Most of my college friends are married now, some of them as soon as they graduated. And a couple of Zephyrettes I know are leaving their jobs to get married. So there are weddings happening all around me. It's bringing back memories of all my plans and preparations." She paused, then went on. "I sometimes wonder what my life would have been like if Steve hadn't been killed. Or even if we'd gone ahead with the wedding when I wanted to, before he went to Korea."

Her mother looked stricken. "Then you'd have been a young widow."

"At least I'd have had the experience of being married. Or maybe a baby."

"A young widow with a baby." Lora McLeod sighed. "You'll get married eventually. Maybe you and Mike—"

Jill held up her hand. "I know you and Dad like him, and so do I. But I want to take it slowly. I've only known him since December. And I'm not ready to leave my job. I really enjoy riding the trains and meeting all sorts of people."

"I know you do." Lora smoothed another length of oilcloth on the bottom shelf. "Someday I hope I'll be helping you plan a trip down the aisle."

Jill was eager to change the subject. She was weary of the assumption that getting married and having a family was the only option for a young woman in her twenties. "I have to tell you something funny, that happened on the train," she said. "It was at the start of this last run, after we left Oakland. A man came up to me outside the lounge and told me I was perfect."

She smiled at the memory. The man who had intercepted her had short sandy hair and hazel eyes, large and penetrating behind wire-rimmed glasses. His tall, muscular frame filled out a well-tailored gray suit. He had boarded the train at the Oakland Mole, traveling in a compartment aboard the six-five sleeper.

"Excuse me?" Jill asked.

He leaned toward her and she sidestepped him.

A wolf, she thought. There was usually one on every trip, the male passenger who focused his attentions on the Zephyrette. In many cases they were married men who removed their wedding rings before boarding the train. Others were single. In all cases, the wolves considered themselves irresistible Lotharios. After two years and more riding the rails, Jill was adept at avoiding those attentions, all the while managing to be polite.

"No, I'm serious," the man said. "I'm not making a pass. Please, let me introduce myself. I'm Drake Baldwin, the director. Maybe you've seen one of my movies."

"I don't know," Jill said, somewhat overwhelmed. "What movies have you directed?"

"My most recent movie was *Parker's Cove.*"

"I did see that. So you're the director?" He nodded, looking pleased as she told him she had enjoyed the movie, a romantic suspense picture that came out the year before. "What did you mean when you said I was perfect?"

"I meant—" He took her elbow and steered her out of the corridor as two passengers walked by heading back toward the sleeper cars. "What is your name?"

"I'm Miss McLeod, the Zephyrette."

"I know you're the Zephyrette. That's why you're perfect."

"I'm afraid I don't understand."

"Let me give you my card." He reached for the inner pocket

of his suit coat and drew out a leather card case, removing one card. He handed it to her with a flourish. She looked it over. Drake Baldwin Productions, with an address in Los Angeles. "I have a new project, a film noir, very dark, a thriller."

"Like *The Narrow Margin*," Jill said. Now that was a movie she had really enjoyed. The suspenseful thriller had been released in the spring of 1952, starring Charles McGraw and Marie Windsor, with most of the action taking place on a train.

Baldwin's smile dimmed a bit when she mentioned the other movie, then his face brightened. "Well, similar, in that both films feature the train. Mine will take place on the *California Zephyr*. That's why I'm up here, in the Bay Area. I'm scouting locations. The train, of course. I'm going to shoot in San Francisco, at the Ferry Building. And on the ferry, and at the Oakland Mole. And then the climax, up in Feather River Canyon. I've got a dynamite script and I'm putting together a great cast."

"Well, I wish you the best," Jill said.

"But I need you," Baldwin insisted. "I need a Zephyrette for my *California Zephyr* movie, and I think you're perfect for the role. You have the right look."

Jill smiled. "The uniform helps. This all sounds very interesting, Mr. Baldwin. I really must attend to my duties right now." She moved away.

Baldwin put his hand on her wrist. "Please, give me your phone number, so I can contact you."

Not going to happen, Jill thought. She hadn't completely dismissed the thought that Baldwin was a wolf and this was an elaborate ruse to get her phone number. "If you need to get in touch with me, you can contact the Western Pacific office in San Francisco. Now, if you'll excuse me." She removed his hand from her arm and walked briskly forward, in the direction of the coffee shop.

"I still have his card," Jill said now, as her mother laughed at the story. "So if you get a call from a movie director named Baldwin, he wants to make me a star."

———

At a quarter to eleven, Jill went upstairs to change clothes before heading to the city for her lunch date. Drew was in his bedroom, playing records on his high fidelity system. A driving rhythm and a woman's rough voice reverberated down the hall. Her brother had a longstanding passion for the music known as rhythm and blues. Some people called R&B—along with jazz, blues and gospel—race music because the records were recorded by and marketed to Negroes. However, the term rhythm and blues had become more common in the late 1940s. Drew had a huge collection of records, both the old 78 RPMS and the newer 33⅓ RPMS. Many of the names were unfamiliar to Jill, but she recognized some of them, such as Big Mama Thornton, Bessie Smith and Billie Holiday.

She went into her own bedroom and took off the dungarees and blouse she'd been wearing. She put on a short-sleeved dress of blue-and-green plaid seersucker. A white linen jacket and white low-heeled pumps completed her ensemble. She gathered up her Zephyrette uniform and looked for the library books she needed to return. They were on her desk, and so was her cat, curled up in a sunny spot. She picked up the books and scratched the cat's ears.

As she went back downstairs, she called to Lucy. "Are you ready to go?"

"Give me five minutes," Lucy said.

Jill retrieved the car keys from the bowl on the hall table and went out to the front porch to wait, sitting in the porch swing, with the books on her lap. Agatha Christie was her favorite author, but she had decided to try some other mysteries from the library, including other British authors, such as Dorothy L. Sayers, and Ngaio Marsh, who was from New Zealand. As it happened, all three of the books on her lap were by American authors, *The Bahamas Murder Case* and *Murder is the Pay-Off*, by Leslie Ford and *The Chinese Chop*, by Juanita Sheridan. Jill had enjoyed the books and was planning to look for more by the same authors.

Lucy came out the front door, holding more books, several by Georgette Heyer, who was one of her favorites. There were also westerns by Louis L'Amour and Max Brand, her father's favorite reading material. Lora McLeod was fond of big fat books, family sagas and historical novels, like those by Edna Ferber. So was Jill, when she wasn't reading murder mysteries.

The two sisters walked to the green-and-white Ford Victoria in the driveway, and Jill slipped into the driver's seat. She started the car and backed it out onto Union Street. On the sidewalk in front of the corner house, two little girls in shorts and cotton blouses, their hair in pigtails, had drawn a hopscotch game on the pavement in yellow chalk. Now they tossed stones and hopped through the squares.

At Encinal Avenue, Jill turned right. A few blocks down, she parked at the curb and took the uniform into the dry cleaning shop. Back in the car, she drove downtown. A left turn onto Oak Street took her to the Alameda Free Library, at the corner of Oak and Santa Clara Avenue. Jill parked on the street near Long's Drugstore. She and Lucy walked across the street to the two-story library, which had been built in 1903, with funds provided by Andrew Carnegie. It was a mix of architectural styles, faced with buff brick and with gray sandstone at the basement level. They went up the marble-and-granite steps, where pillars stood on either side of the front door.

After returning the library books, Lucy headed for the stacks to search for more. Jill wanted to read more books by Sheridan and there was another book she was looking for as well. She went to the card catalogs, a phalanx of drawers containing thousands of three-by-five inch cards that catalogued the publications available in the library's collection. The note cards were used to locate the books, which were shelved according to the Dewey Decimal System. Jill pulled out several drawers in turn, rummaging through cards, making a list. Then she headed for the library's fiction section, scanning the shelves. Of the Juanita Sheridan books, she found *The Kahuna Killer* and *The Mamo Murders*. The author's fourth book, called *The Waikiki Widow*, wasn't on the shelves. Someone must have checked it out. No matter. She chose another Leslie Ford book, *The Woman in Black*, then moved to another shelf looking for a book by another author, *The Uninvited*, by Dorothy Macardle.

Here it was. Jill pulled the book from the shelf. The dust jacket was gray-green, showing a dead tree in the foreground and in the background, two tiny figures, a man and a woman, in front of a lonely-looking house. She had read the book before and she'd also seen the movie version, which had been released in 1944, with Ray Milland, Gail Russell, and Ruth Hussey. She was in high school back then, and she and some of her friends had seen the movie at one of the grand movie palaces in downtown Denver. Jill loved the theme song, "Stella by Starlight." Now, with all the talk of ghosts she had heard over the last few days, she wanted to reread this chilling tale of a haunted house on England's Devon coast.

Jill went to the checkout desk, then left the library and returned to the Ford. She headed for the Park Street bridge that led over the estuary separating Alameda from Oakland, and made her way to the Bay Bridge. She stopped in a line of traffic and when her turn came, she paid the toll taker a quarter. Accelerating, she moved forward, driving over the cantilevered portion of the bridge. Ahead was the tunnel that bored through Yerba Buena Island. This was a natural island jutting from the bay. To the right, on the north side of the bridge was the flat expanse known as Treasure Island. It had been built by filling the land on what had once been called Yerba Buena shoals, a rocky shipping hazard. Landfill constructed the island in the mid-Thirties and it was the site of the 1939–1940 World's Fair. After that, plans had been in the works for an airport, but the war intervened. In 1942 the island became a Navy base and there were still Navy facilities located on the island.

The tunnel loomed ahead. Jill drove through it, coming out on the suspension section of the bridge. Below, and to her right, she saw the impressive Beaux-Arts Ferry Building. Now in San Francisco, Jill took an exit and descended onto the city streets, driving through midday traffic until she reached her destination. She angled the Ford into a parking space on New Montgomery Street. As she got out of the car, a streetcar rumbled by on Market Street. A group of sailors walked toward her, wearing their distinctive white uniforms and Dixie-cup hats. San Francisco was a Navy town. There must be ships in port down on the waterfront. As Jill passed the sailors, she heard a chorus of wolf whistles. She kept walking, then turned and entered the Palace Hotel, where she was to meet Tidsy.

Chapter Six

"A GHOST ON THE TRAIN? That's a change from the usual run of passengers." Mrs. Grace Tidsdale waved at the waiter, who hurried to their table. "Another scotch on the rocks, please."

They were having lunch in the opulent Garden Court, at the Palace Hotel on Market Street. The hotel had been built in 1909, rising from the ashes and debris of the 1875 original, which had been destroyed in the 1906 San Francisco earthquake and subsequent fire. The renowned opera singer Enrico Caruso had been staying at the hotel at the time of the quake and famously swore never to return to the City by the Bay. More recently, in 1923, President Warren G. Harding had died in an eighth-floor suite overlooking Market Street.

When she had arrived at the hotel, Jill had detoured down the hall, so she could take a peek into the Pied Piper bar, which was just off the polished marble lobby near the hotel's Market Street entrance. The bar was named after the large painting of the same name by artist Maxfield Parrish, based on the old tale of the Pied Piper of Hamelin. The painting showed the piper playing his seductive pipe, luring children away from the town.

Now she was seated in the opulent dining room. The Garden Court, with its high atrium glass ceiling, marble columns, oriental carpets and tables covered with crisp white cloths, was the height of San Francisco elegance. Woodrow Wilson had hosted a luncheon here in 1919, to drum up support for the Treaty of Versailles and the League of Nations.

On this warm summer day, the dining room was full, with

attentive waiters moving quickly from kitchen to tables. In one corner, a pianist at a baby grand played a song called "Where Is Your Heart." The romantic theme from the movie *Moulin Rouge* was popular right now. During the drive over the Bay Bridge, Jill had been listening to the car radio, and she'd heard the recording by Percy Faith and his orchestra.

Before mentioning her experience with the purported ghost, Jill had told Tidsy about her encounter with the purported Hollywood director. Her friend had responded with peals of laughter. "Director, my foot. It sounds like he was making a pass. An inventive one, at that."

Now Jill gazed around the room of well-dressed women and men in tailored suits. In her seersucker dress and white jacket, she felt like a country mouse who had come to the city. Across the table was Mrs. Tidsdale, who preferred to be called Tidsy, by her friends, anyway. Jill was pleased to be counted among those friends. Tidsy had been a passenger on Jill's train back during an eventful eastbound run in December, and the two women had forged a bond. Now they met for lunch in the city, every month or so. This lunch date had been arranged before Jill left town the week before.

Tidsy was a tart-tongued, brassy blonde in her late forties, a woman of opinions who wasn't afraid to share them. She had a fondness for alcoholic beverages and salty language, liked red dresses and a good game of poker, and smoked like the proverbial chimney. Today her round figure was packed into a form-fitting jersey dress in an eye-popping shade of crimson. The garment's hue matched her long fingernails and the lipstick on her full lips. Her chunky garnet ring glittered as she waved her fork.

Jill pointed out an affable-looking man at a nearby table. "Who is that? He looks familiar. I'm sure I've seen his picture in the newspaper."

"I should say you have." Tidsy chuckled. She waved at the man, and he saluted her with a raised glass. "That's George Christopher. He's president of the San Francisco Board of Supervisors. He ran for mayor in 'fifty-one but got beat. I know him and his wife, Tula. Nice people. George was born in Greece and immigrated with his family when he was just a kid, a few years after the big quake. Word is, George is planning another run in two years. I wouldn't be surprised if he wins. He'll make a good mayor." The waiter brought her scotch and she took a sip. "Now, tell me more about your experience with the supernatural. I do love a good ghost story."

Jill paused, her fork hovering over the broiled salmon on her plate. "I'm still not convinced that what I saw was a ghost. It could have been a trick of the light, or the fact that I was so tired that night."

"Or Scrooge's underdone potato." Tidsy speared one of the roasted potatoes that accompanied her medium-rare roast beef.

Jill laughed. "Funny, I thought the same thing, at the time." Then her expression turned serious. "There was more to it than the light, though. When I went inside the roomette, I felt a chill. And I heard taps. Four distinct taps."

"Curiouser and curiouser." Tidsy sipped her drink. "A trick of the light, yes, that could account for what you saw. But the cold and the taps? Very interesting. So the porter is convinced that the ghost is Mr. Randall, the man whose body you found on the train. How did this Mr. Randall die?"

Jill took a sip of her iced tea. "I'm not sure. I never found out the results of the autopsy. The doctor who examined the body in the roomette said it could have had something to do with his heart. There was a prescription bottle nearby, for Digoxin. That's digitalis, and people with heart conditions use that."

"Digitalis. This man was in his thirties, you say?" Tidsy looked thoughtful. "It happens. When I was growing up, I had a cousin who was born with a heart defect. He used digitalis, too, as I recall, and died fairly young. Now, this happened in May, right?" When Jill confirmed this, Tidsy went on. "I have a friend who lives in Oakland. Her niece was engaged and the fiancé died unexpectedly, in May. The young woman who was meeting the man at the Oakland Mole, what was her name?"

"Margaret Vennor."

"It's the same person. Poor girl." Tidsy spooned more horseradish sauce onto her roast beef. Her face looked a little somber.

She must be remembering last December, when Jill had found a body on the train, while the *California Zephyr* was traveling through a remote Colorado canyon. The murder victim had been Tidsy's friend.

"Then the aunt I called from the Mole was…"

"Helen Vennor, yes." Tidsy reached for her scotch and took a sip. "We've known each other since college. We both grew up here in the city, me in the Mission District and Helen out in the Richmond. But we didn't meet until we went to the university in Berkeley. We roomed together for a couple of years, and then we both got married. My husband was killed in the war and I went off to Washington to work as a government girl. Helen stayed here in the Bay Area. Her husband, Daniel, is a businessman, has a big company over in Oakland. He and his older brother, Alex, were both in the Navy during the war. The brother died. He was killed early in the war, at Midway, I think. Helen and Daniel took in his daughter. I gather the girl's mother left, just took off a year or so before the father died. I think Margaret Vennor is about your age."

Jill nodded. "She appeared to be. I stayed with her until her aunt arrived, and I met Mrs. Vennor briefly. That's the only contact I had with either of them."

"Helen and I don't see each other as often as we should, but we talk on the phone from time to time. In fact, she called just a few weeks ago, to invite me to a party. They have this garden shindig every year. I asked how her niece was doing and she said the girl is having a difficult time getting over her fiancé's death. Not surprising, since it was just a couple of months ago. But you know how that is. Losing someone you love. We both do."

A hint of sadness came to Tidsy's eyes. It was the first time Jill had seen a chink in the older woman's brash self-confidence. "My husband's name was Rick. We knew each other in high school, but we didn't get together until after I graduated from Cal. Got married in November of 'forty-one, a month before Pearl Harbor. He was crazy about flying. Worked at the San Francisco airport before he joined the Army Air Corps. Then he went off to Tokyo with Jimmy Doolittle. Most of those guys made it home, eventually. Rick didn't."

The Doolittle raid on April 18, 1942 had provided a much-needed boost to Americans still reeling from the shocks of Pearl Harbor, the Philippines and Guam. Led by Lieutenant Colonel James Doolittle of the Army Air Corps, sixteen B-25B bombers launched from U.S.S. *Hornet*, an aircraft carrier in the western Pacific. Without fighter escort, the bombers took the war to Tokyo, the first such attack on the Japanese mainland. Fifteen of the bombers made it to China, where they crashed on land or in the sea, while one made it all the way to the Soviet Union. Of the eighty crew members, most eventually returned home, though some ended up as prisoners of war, their fates unknown until the war ended. Tidsy's husband had been among the casualties.

"You lost your fiancé in Korea," Tidsy said now. "All these news reports, about the Armistice and the end of that war, must be bringing up those feelings again."

"Yes, the headlines are definitely bringing back memories. Even though it's been more than two years since Steve died."

Tidsy picked up her glass and took another sip of scotch. "This whole thing is fascinating. I wonder if this ghost—"

"If there is such a thing," Jill interrupted.

"If the ghost is trying to communicate," Tidsy finished. "What about those taps? It's got to be more than the wheels knocking."

"Wheels make a different sound." Jill took the last bite of her salmon, thinking. Then she said, "Taps. I heard four distinct taps. If it was train signals… Trains blow their whistles in different patterns, to convey messages. For example, a train approaching a crossing blows two long, one short and one long. Four short blasts on the whistle means a request for a signal to be given, or repeated. Maybe it's just four taps because it's roomette number four. Or maybe we're both being silly."

Tidsy laughed. "I've been silly before and no doubt will be again. No skin off my nose."

Jill set down her fork as another thought came to her. "Morse Code."

"Morse Code," Tidsy repeated. "I used to know Morse Code, but I'm rusty. I'll have to look up and see what four taps mean."

"I'll look it up, too. Dad has a booklet somewhere. I've seen it in his study."

Tidsy finished her roast beef and reached for her scotch, swirling the amber liquor, the ice cubes clinking in the glass. "We need to have a séance."

Jill stared at her. "You can't be serious."

A wicked smile played on Tidsy's red lips. "Oh, but I am. I've always wanted to go to a séance, and now I have the perfect excuse to host one."

"Parlor games," Jill said. "But this isn't a game. Miss Vennor is a real person who has suffered a terrible loss."

"I understand that." Tidsy rattled the ice cubes again. "But if getting in touch with her dead fiancé will let her move on, it might help. On the other hand, maybe we wouldn't need her at the séance. You would do. You've seen the ghost."

"I saw a flickering light," Jill argued. "I'm not ready to concede that it was a ghost. There could be a perfectly logical explanation for the whole thing."

"Or not." Tidsy smiled. "You should be more open to the possibility."

The waiter appeared at the table, collecting their plates. "Would you ladies care to see the dessert menu?"

"Yes, we would," Tidsy said. After the waiter departed, she looked at Jill. "I have no idea how to hold a séance. I don't suppose there's a how-to manual. I guess we'd need a medium. I wonder if mediums advertise in the *Chronicle*. Or have listings in the Yellow Pages. Further research is most definitely needed."

The waiter returned with dessert menus and refreshed Jill's iced tea. Jill glanced at the menu and decided to try the lemon tart. Tidsy laughed, a wicked smile on her face. "I'll have devil's-food cake. Sounds appropriate. After all, a séance may be the devil's own business."

Chapter Seven

A SÉANCE. WHAT HAVE I UNLEASHED? Jill asked herself. The devil's own business indeed.

She and Tidsy had argued about the séance while they ate their desserts. Jill was against the idea. But the irrepressible Tidsy was determined to move ahead and find a medium. "We could hold the séance at my apartment." She tapped one red fingernail on the rim of her dessert plate as she made plans.

They said good-bye in the lobby of the Palace Hotel. Jill headed out to New Montgomery Street, walking half a block to where she had parked the Ford. She unlocked the car and got in, driving home over the Bay Bridge. In Oakland, she wound through Chinatown and into the tube that went under the estuary to Alameda, coming out on Webster Street on the other side.

She stopped at an intersection, waiting as a couple of boys on bicycles pedaled past. Then she turned and drove a couple of blocks to the McLeod home. She parked the Ford at the curb, behind a familiar red Studebaker that belonged to her sister Lucy's fiancé, Ethan Keller. The driveway was already occupied by her brother Drew's car. The 1949 Mercury coupe was his pride and joy. He'd bought the car two years ago from a sailor at the Alameda Naval Air Station, and he'd fixed it up, painting the exterior midnight blue. Dressed in faded dungarees and a T-shirt that had seen better days, he was using several old rags and a bucket of soapy water to clean the dust from his car. He was tall, like their father, and had Jill's blue eyes and light brown hair, worn with a side part. As she came up the sidewalk, he paused in his washing job, waving at her. "Hey, Sis," he said, reaching for the bottle of Coke he'd left on the pavement.

Lucy and Ethan sat on the porch swing, holding hands, with two glasses and a pitcher of lemonade on a nearby table. Ethan called to her. "Hey, there, Berkeley."

"How are you, Stanford?" Jill said.

Ethan was tall, broad-shouldered and blond with blue eyes, a former fullback who'd played for Stanford University, across the bay in Palo Alto. Jill's alma mater, the University of California at Berkeley, was Stanford's biggest rival. Jill and Ethan were always joshing about the rivalry, particularly in the fall, around the time of the annual Big Game between Cal and Stanford.

Lucy waggled her fingers at her sister. "We're going to see that new movie, *Gentlemen Prefer Blondes*, this coming weekend. Maybe you and Mike can join us, make it a double date. I'm sure he'd like to see Jane Russell and Marilyn Monroe."

"So would I. The movie would be fun. I'll check with Mike."

Jill opened the front door. Instead of going upstairs to her room, she headed down the hall to her father's study at the back of the house.

Morse Code, she thought. She knew it was named for Samuel F. B. Morse, one of the people who invented the telegraph. It was a method of transmitting text, through short and long signals, called dots and dashes. She knew from experience that if the *California Zephyr* was stopped between stations and a message needed to be sent, the brakeman would climb the nearest pole and tap into the line, sending a Morse Code message to the nearest station. Her own knowledge of Morse Code was limited to the signal for S-O-S, three dots for S, three dashes for O, and three more dots for the second S. Her father had a Morse Code booklet, left over from his Navy days. She scanned the shelves, which were full of medical books as well as a collection of the western novels her father loved. Finally she spotted a small beige booklet, the one about Morse Code. She leafed through the pages, looking at the dots and dashes that, in combination as clicks, taps or flashing lights, were used to make letters.

Four dots meant the letter H. She shut the booklet and put it back on the shelf. She thought again of what she'd experienced on the train—the light that moved into the roomette, the sudden cold, the four knocks in rapid succession. If there was a ghost, was it trying to communicate something?

This is crazy, she thought. I can't believe I'm even considering the possibility.

She went up to her room and kicked off her shoes. Sophie had made herself a nest on the bed pillows, curling into a tight ball. Jill leaned over and scratched the cat's ears. Sophie purred and stretched, rolling over so Jill could tickle her belly.

Jill straightened and unbuttoned the dress she'd worn for her lunch date. She hung the dress in the closet and put on soft, comfortable capri pants, adding a short-sleeved cotton blouse. Then she went to her small desk and pulled out a drawer. Inside were the little bound notebooks she used during her Zephyrette journeys, to keep track of what happened on the train so that she could write her trip reports. After she filled the notebooks, she tossed them in this drawer. As for why she kept them, she thought it might be interesting, sometime in the future when she was no longer a Zephyrette, to write an article or a book about her experiences. Now she reached inside the drawer. She dated the notebooks on the front cover, and the most current one was on top. She recalled that she'd been at the end of the previous notebook back in May, when she had discovered Kevin Randall's body in roomette four. She found the notebook she sought and opened it, looking for the phone number Margaret Vennor had given her that day. Then she slipped the notebook into her pocket and put on a pair of sandals.

She used the upstairs phone extension, which was on a table near the door to her parents' bedroom. Jill dialed the number. The phone rang several times, then was answered. Jill thought she recognized the voice at the other end of the line as that of the older woman she'd talked with that day. Jill had stayed with Miss Vennor in the office until her aunt had arrived, then she'd excused herself and gone off to finish her own duties. Now she asked to speak to Margaret Vennor.

"Margaret's not home right now," Mrs. Vennor said. "May I give her a message?"

"My name is Jill McLeod. I'm the Zephyrette who was there that day, when Mr. Randall died."

"Yes, I remember you," Mrs. Vennor said. "You were very kind. I don't think I had the opportunity to thank you, so I'll do that now."

"You're welcome. It was only what I had to do, under the circumstances. I'm so sorry for Miss Vennor's loss. I hope she's well."

"As well as can be expected, considering."

"I would really like to speak with her. I'm in Alameda." Jill gave Mrs. Vennor her telephone number.

Mrs. Vennor repeated the number and added, "I'll let her know, Miss McLeod." Her voice held a note of curiosity, but she didn't ask for further details.

"By the way, Mrs. Vennor, I'm a friend of Grace Tidsdale. I just had lunch with her."

Helen Vennor's voice warmed. "Oh, Tidsy. She's one of my best friends. Quite a character, as I'm sure you know. You must have met her on a train trip."

"Yes, I did. And she is certainly one of a kind."

After ending the call, Jill took the notebook back to her bedroom. Then she went downstairs, heading back to the kitchen, where Lora McLeod stood at the kitchen counter, with a colorful assortment of vegetables—yellow squash, red and green bell peppers, dark green cucumbers and bright orange carrots—arrayed near her wooden cutting board. Her mother was peeling the outer layer from a large yellow onion. That done, she set the onion on the board. The first cut released the pungent odor as she diced the onion, then swept the pieces into a large bowl.

"I made lemonade and iced tea. Both pitchers are in the fridge. Help yourself."

"Thanks, Mom." Jill filled a glass with ice and lemonade.

"How was your lunch with Mrs. Tidsdale?"

"Wonderful. We went to the Garden Court at the Palace Hotel. Very grand. I had salmon and Tidsy had roast beef."

Her mother smiled. "The Garden Court. How wonderful. Your father took me there once, for our anniversary. It was lovely, very special. If you had a big lunch, you might not have much appetite for this meatloaf I'm making." She opened the refrigerator door and took out a package of ground beef, setting it on the counter next to the bowl of onion bits.

"I'm sure I'll have a bite or two. How was your day?"

"Busy. I got all the laundry done, but there's still some ironing to do. By the way, your cousin Doug called." Mrs. McLeod opened the ground beef package and scooped the meat into the bowl that held the onions. She mixed the ingredients together, then rinsed her hands and dried them on a dish towel. Opening a cupboard, she took out several small tins and added spices to the mixture. "He and Pamela are coming to town next week, for a belated honeymoon, he says. They're staying at a hotel in the city because he wants to show her San Francisco. I invited them for dinner, on Thursday night. You'll be here, I hope."

"I don't know what my schedule is," Jill said. "I'll have to call and find out when I'm due for another run. It will be good to see Doug and Pam." Jill's cousin Douglas Cleary, the son of Lora McLeod's brother Sean, had married a young woman from Mississippi. They'd met four months earlier while on the *California Zephyr* and had married shortly after, living near Lake Tahoe, where Doug and a friend planned to open a ski resort. If ever there was a case of love at first sight, that was it, Jill thought, recalling the day when Doug and Pam had first encountered each other in the Vista-Dome. "Can I do anything to help with dinner?"

"I'd rather you talked with your brother." Her mother waved a spoon at the window that looked out to the backyard. Drew had finished washing his car and now he was out in the yard. He sat in one of the metal lawn chairs, pulled into the shade of the apple tree. He was hunkered over his guitar, not playing, looking out at nothing in particular. "See if you can figure out what's going on with him. He's been broody lately, like there's something on his mind."

"Okay. I'll do my best." Jill carried her lemonade outside. She kicked off her sandals and felt the blades of grass tickle her bare feet as she crossed the lawn. At the back of the lot, the neighbor's cat, a big ginger tom, walked across the top rail of the redwood fence, balancing on his paws like a tightrope walker.

Drew strummed chords on his guitar. He stopped and turned one of the pegs, tuning a string. Then he began playing, with a driving rhythm. Jill heard scraps of the lyrics. *"Crazy 'bout a Mercury, gonna buy me a Mercury… Cruise it up and down the road."*

"Are you singing about your car?" Jill asked, amused.

Her brother looked up. "Singing about somebody's Mercury. It's a song called 'Mercury Blues,' though I've heard it called 'Mercury Boogie.'"

"Who wrote it?"

"A couple of musicians in Oakland," Drew said. "K.C. Douglas and Bob Geddins." Drew reached for the bottle of Coke at his feet, taking a long swallow. "Geddins has a recording studio, Big Town Records, on Seventh Street."

Jill sat cross-legged on the grass, sipping her lemonade. "Got plans for this weekend?"

"We've got a gig," Drew said. "Me and the guys. We're playing Friday and Saturday nights, at a club called Ozzie's, near Slim Jenkins' place. Not as fancy, of course. Just a hole in the wall compared to Slim's." Seventh Street in West Oakland, near the rail yard, was a mecca for music lovers, lined with all sorts of clubs and nightspots. Of these, Slim Jenkins' supper club was well-known and frequently booked performers like Duke Ellington, Sarah Vaughan, and The Ink Spots. "You and Mike should come hear us."

"I know Mike likes all sorts of music," Jill said. "He'd probably be interested. Should we ask Lucy and Ethan if they'd like to join us?"

Drew made a face. "Lucy's taste in music runs to that doggie-in-the-window song," he said, talking about the Patti Page chart-topper that was ubiquitous on the radio earlier in the spring.

Jill laughed. "Lucy likes Kay Starr, Joni James, Dinah Shore *and* Patti Page. And Perry Como and Eddie Fisher."

"I'll bet she's never heard of Ma Rainey and Big Mama Thornton," Drew scoffed.

"Probably not. I know who they are, thanks to you." She took a sip of her lemonade. "Mom says you've been broody."

Drew played a chord on the guitar and smiled. "She sent you out here to find out what's going on."

"As a matter of fact. Is something going on?"

"What would you say if I told you I'm planning to drop out of school?"

Jill stared at him. Drew was nineteen and had just finished his freshman year at UC Berkeley. He hadn't yet declared a major, preferring to get the required courses out of the way. Maybe there was a reason for that.

"Why? Is it your grades? I thought you'd done well your first year. Or is it something else?"

Drew played a scrap of "Mercury Blues" on the guitar. "I'm not interested in getting a college degree. I just want to play music."

"Can you make a living at it?" Jill asked.

"Don't know. There's only one way to find out, and that's to do it." He crashed a chord on the guitar. "The band's been playing gigs here in the East Bay, almost every weekend. We're making decent money. Now we have a chance to go on the road, starting in August. That's about the time I'd be starting back to school. I'd rather go on the road with the guys than hit the books again."

"You've made money playing locally," Jill said, "and that's well and good, but you've been living at home, commuting to classes in Berkeley. If you go on the road, you'll have all sorts of expenses. Gas, food, places to stay."

"I know that," Drew said.

"How long would you be on the road?"

"Six, seven months, according to this agent we've been talking with. Gigs down the coast to Los Angeles and San Diego, then east to Nevada and Colorado."

Jill took another swallow of lemonade. "Dropping out of school, that is a big deal."

Drew strummed a chord on the guitar. "Yes, I know it is. Listen, I can always go back to school if things don't work out with my music. But I have to do this, Jill. Music is what I love. You're happy riding your trains and Lucy's all excited about getting married and having kids. Well, playing the guitar in the band is what excites me."

"Well," Jill said, getting to her feet. "You'd better talk with Mom and Dad. And do it sooner rather than later."

She went back to the house. Lucy and Ethan were still out on the front porch. She heard them talking, and then Lucy's laugh. The kitchen was empty. The oven was on and through the glass door Jill saw the casserole dish that contained the meatloaf her mother had constructed. She went through the dining room and then to the living room. Lora McLeod was taking a break from her household duties, stretched out comfortably in the armchair that turned the bay window into a pleasant reading nook. Her feet were propped up on an ottoman. On the table next to her was a glass of lemonade. She was reading the latest *Saturday Evening Post*. A stack of magazines was on her lap, including several issues of *Life*. One was a few months old, the cover showing Marilyn Monroe and Jane Russell, costumed in their roles for *Gentlemen Prefer Blondes*. Another cover showed a photo from the June coronation of Queen Elizabeth II.

"I have a bad habit of letting these magazines pile up," Mrs. McLeod said, reaching for her lemonade. "So I'm catching up on my reading while dinner cooks. Join me."

"I will." Jill set her lemonade on the coffee table and reached for the latest issue of *Life*, the one with the cover picture of that senator from Massachusetts, John F. Kennedy, and his fiancée, Jacqueline Bouvier. They were posed on a sailboat and the caption read SENATOR KENNEDY GOES A-COURTING.

Before she could sit down, though, the phone rang. Jill went to answer the downstairs extension, which was on a narrow table in the front hallway. She reached for the receiver and sat on the chair next to the table.

"Jill, it's Mike."

"Hi. How goes it with school?"

"I'm almost done with summer classes. I have one more final, tomorrow morning. Then I'll have a break until fall classes start."

Mike, Jill's steady boyfriend for the past few months, was studying geology at the university, sharing an apartment near the Berkeley campus with another student. When he wasn't going to classes, he worked part-time at a company near the Berkeley waterfront. "I called to check with you about plans for this weekend. And also about a short trip. Since I'll be done with classes and I have a few days off from my job next week, I want to go up to Oroville to see Grandpa. He's spending the summer with Aunt Adalina. Would you like to come with me?"

Most of the time Mike's paternal grandfather lived with Mike's mother and father in their home on Vallejo Street in North Beach, San Francisco's "Little Italy." The old man was confined to a wheelchair due to injuries suffered in a car accident several years earlier. From time to time, he would visit one of his daughters, who lived with her husband in Oroville, a town on the Feather River, where the *California Zephyr* stopped before heading up the scenic canyon to Portola.

"I'd love to meet your aunt," Jill said. "Your grandfather talks about her a lot. When were you thinking of going?"

"Leave Monday, come back Wednesday. Would that work?"

"It should," Jill said. "I'll call Western Pacific to find out when I'm scheduled for my next run. About this weekend. We talked about going to a movie, but I have another suggestion." She told him about Drew's band playing at the club in West Oakland.

"Let's go Friday night," Mike said. "And take in the movie on Saturday."

They talked a while longer, then ended the call. "Dinner as soon as your father gets home," Lora McLeod called, from the kitchen. "Lucy's setting the table."

Jill got up from the chair. Then the phone rang and Jill picked up the receiver. "May I speak with Miss McLeod?"

"This is Jill McLeod."

"This is Margaret Vennor. I'm returning your call."

"Thank you for getting back to me," Jill said. "I wonder if we could meet and talk."

Miss Vennor didn't respond at first. Then she said, "All right. The note my aunt left says you live in Alameda. I'll meet you at eleven tomorrow morning, at Lake Merritt, at the gazebo near Children's Fairyland."

Chapter Eight ———————————

L AKE MERRITT WASN'T actually a lake. It was a large tidal lagoon, connected by a channel to Oakland's Inner Harbor. Since 1870, it had been a wildlife refuge and the lake contained several artificial islands that were bird refuges. Lakeside Park was just off Grand Avenue, tucked between two arms of the lake. Jill turned off Grand onto Bellevue Avenue and parked the Ford near a curve in the road. The tall covered gazebo was located on the back side of the small amusement park called Children's Fairyland. She locked the car and followed a path down the slope toward the lake, the skirt of her pale blue sundress swirling around her legs.

A gaggle of Canada geese moseyed across the path ahead of Jill. They spread out on the lawn, feeding on the grass. Several mallard ducks waddled along the shoreline, the females brown and tan, the heads of the males iridescent green in the bright morning sunlight. Beyond that, half a dozen white pelicans splashed to a landing in the water, then paddled toward the middle of the lake. A great egret stood in shallow water, head and long neck extended as it searched for food. Then it struck quickly, coming up from the water with a wriggling fish in its beak. Jill watched as the egret swallowed the fish.

Two women in summery dresses and low-heeled shoes strolled along another path, heading toward the amusement park. One woman pushed a stroller and the other walked slowly, hand-in-hand with a toddler. Two boys, about ten years old, raced up and down the steps of the gazebo. A man called to them and they ran to join him, heading up the slope toward the street.

Jill circled the gazebo, moving counterclockwise. When she reached the other side, she saw a dark-haired woman seated on the steps, dressed in pale green cotton printed with bright yellow sunflowers. The woman was reading, her head bent, her right hand turning the pages of a book.

"Miss Vennor? I'm Jill McLeod."

The woman looked up. "I recognize you. Please, call me Margaret and I'll call you Jill. Miss Vennor and Miss McLeod sounds so formal."

"That suits me. What are you reading?" Jill asked.

Margaret held up the book so Jill could see the title, *The Nine Tailors*. "I like mysteries, especially Dorothy L. Sayers. And this one is my favorite."

"So do I. Agatha Christie is my favorite. I love the Miss Marple stories. But I have read some of Sayers's books."

Margaret tucked the book into her shoulder bag. She stood, brushing the full skirt of her dress, which had a scooped neckline. The diamond engagement ring Jill had seen on her left hand that day at the Oakland Mole now dangled from a thin gold chain around her neck. Jill had done the same thing with her own engagement ring after her fiancé died, until she decided to tuck it away in her jewelry box.

"Let's walk, shall we?" Margaret said. They strolled away from the gazebo, taking the path that hugged the lake shore along the smaller arm of the lake, with downtown Oakland visible on the other side. "How long have you been a Zephyrette? And why? It's an interesting career choice. Though I suppose if one likes to travel, it makes sense."

"I've been a Zephyrette for over two years," Jill said. "As for why, it wasn't my first choice. I have a degree in history from Cal as well as some education credits. I was going to teach school and get married. But my fiancé was killed in Korea, in December of nineteen-fifty. A few months later, someone suggested I might like being a Zephyrette, so I signed on. And I do enjoy it, very much."

Margaret nodded, a somber look on her face. "I lost my father in nineteen forty-two. He was in the Navy, on the *Yorktown* when it was sunk at the Battle of Midway. I was fifteen years old. My mother abandoned me and my father when I was ten. I lived with my Grandmother Vennor in Berkeley until she had a stroke, which was about the time Dad died. That's when I came to live with my aunt and uncle here in Oakland."

Margaret's story reminded Jill of Emily Charleton, the nine-year-old girl who had been traveling with Tidsy last December. Emily's mother was dead and her father had been killed in Korea. Tidsy, a friend of Emily's uncle, had escorted the child to Denver to live with her grandmother.

"I was going to teach school, too," Margaret said. "After I got married. Now I don't know what to do."

"You'll figure it out."

"I hope so. I don't think the life of a Zephyrette is for me." Margaret's steps slowed as they neared a park bench. "Why did you want to talk with me? To tell me that you'd lost your fiancé? Because I lost mine?"

"That's part of it." Jill felt tongue-tied. How could she mention that silly story about the ghost? "I know how it feels to lose someone you love. And I know your fiancé's death was a horrible shock. It's so unexpected for someone that young to die of heart failure."

"Who told you Kevin died of heart failure?" Margaret's voice was hard and sharp as a steel blade.

Jill was taken aback. "When the doctor arrived at the Pullman car, he examined the body and said the death appeared to be natural causes. He also said it was possible that the cause might be Mr. Randall's heart, given the fact that I found a prescription bottle in the roomette. It was for Digoxin, which is a drug people use for heart conditions."

"Kevin did have a heart condition," Margaret said. "He took Digoxin. His heart indeed failed, but it wasn't due to natural causes. He was murdered."

Jill stared at her. "How? Why?"

"I don't know who did it, or how. But I intend to find out."

Jill recalled Mr. Doolin's words when she had talked with him about the ghost he swore was haunting roomette four. "'That man's spirit ain't resting easy.'"

Margaret reached for her arm, eyes narrowed. "What did you say?"

Belatedly, Jill realized she'd spoken the words aloud. The cat was clawing its way out of the bag. "There's a story going around, about a ghost that haunts roomette four on the Silver Gorge. Mr. Randall was traveling on that particular sleeper car, in roomette four, when he died."

"A ghost? Because Kevin died on the train?" Margaret shook her head. "Not surprising, I guess, that a death on the train would lead to stories and superstition. However, I don't believe in ghosts."

"I don't believe in ghosts either," Jill said. "But in this case, something actually did go bump in the night."

Margaret sat down on the park bench. "You're serious. Did you see something?"

"Yes, and I heard something, too." Jill joined her on the bench. "It happened last week. I was on an eastbound run, heading for Chicago. On the first night out, I was walking back to my quarters late at night. When I came through the Silver Gorge I saw a strange light ahead of me. It appeared to be just outside roomette four."

"A trick of the light, perhaps?" Margaret suggested.

"That's what I told myself at the time. The light moved. And I could see through it. I was in the passageway and the light was in front of me. Then it seemed to float into the roomette. I knew the roomette was unoccupied, so I went inside. There was no one there, of course, and the light had disappeared. But the roomette was chilly. It kept getting colder. Then I heard a sound. Well, four of them. Four knocks, like this." Jill reached out and rapped the park bench seat. "It was unnerving. I left the roomette and headed back to my quarters. Evidently I had a startled look on my face, because when I went through to the next sleeper, the porter asked if I was all right. I told him what had happened. He said I must have seen the ghost. Then he told me that he had seen it twice, when he was working in that car. He's the one who said, 'That man's spirit ain't resting easy.'"

"I don't imagine Kevin is resting easy. I know I'm not." Margaret stared out at the water, where several mallards skimmed the surface. A pond turtle sunned itself on a rock just offshore.

"There was a new passenger in roomette four the second night out," Jill said. "The next morning, she told me she had trouble sleeping, because she heard voices during the night. She said it sounded like two men arguing. I supposed it could have been two passengers. But the porter didn't hear anyone, and the people in the roomettes around her were woman."

Margaret's eyes sparked with interest. "Could she hear what those voices were saying?"

"No. But they were loud enough to wake her." Jill shook her head. "The more I tell you, the crazier it sounds. But I saw and heard something strange and eerie. Something I can't explain."

"Ghost stories," Margaret said. "How very odd."

They sat in silence for a moment as a man and a woman approached, walking slowly along the path, holding hands and laughing at some joke shared just between themselves. Margaret looked at them, as though seeing two other people, herself and Kevin Randall. When they had passed, she reached into her handbag and pulled out a small photo album bound in honey-colored leather. She didn't open it right away. "Let me tell you about Kevin. He was born right here in Oakland and he went to school at the university in Berkeley. Just as you and I did. Yes, I went to Cal, the same time as you did, since I suspect we're the same age."

"I'm twenty-six," Jill said. "Class of nineteen fifty. I have a degree in history."

"Same here, but I majored in English literature. So we were on campus at the same time," Margaret said. "Kevin majored in business at Cal. He would have graduated in nineteen forty-four, if it hadn't been for the war. He finished his degree in 'forty-seven and went to work for a company in San Francisco. Then three years ago, he took a job in the financial department of my uncle's company. We met two years ago this month. Every summer, Aunt Helen and Uncle Dan give a party. They invite their friends and Uncle Dan invites people from his company. Kevin was there. We talked and discovered that we had so much in common. He asked me out that afternoon. We dated for a year, and last fall he asked me to marry him. Our plan was to get married this summer," Margaret added, her face shadowed.

"Mr. Randall was thirty-one, according to his driver's license," Jill said. "That's very young for someone to have a heart condition."

Margaret nodded. "Kevin had rheumatic fever when he was a child. It weakened his heart. He was four-F during the war, because of it. Although he served in other ways. He worked in the Red Cross Administration Corps during the war, and didn't go back to college until the war was over."

"Who else knew about his heart?" Jill asked. "If he was murdered, whoever did it had to know about his heart condition."

"He never made a secret of it. But he didn't broadcast it either. He told me about it, not long after we met. Here, I'll show you some pictures of Kevin." Margaret opened the album that she had been holding in her lap. Her index finger traced a line around the edge of the first photo. "My friend Alice took this picture. The four of us—Alice and her husband, Will, Kevin and I—were on a picnic at Tilden Park, near the Botanic Gardens," she added, mentioning the large regional park in the hills above Berkeley.

Jill leaned closer and looked at the snapshot. She remembered Kevin Randall as she'd seen him on the train two months ago, in a gray pinstriped business suit, white shirt and tie. Here he wore dungarees and a short-sleeved shirt, his arm around Margaret, who was dressed in a blouse and full skirt. They sat at a table that had been spread with a checked cloth, a basket at one end of the table. Margaret turned the page. The next picture showed Margaret and Kevin in more formal dress, standing with an older couple on a patio that had been decorated with flowers and streamers.

"That's my Aunt Helen and my Uncle Dan," Margaret said. "Uncle Dan is my father's younger brother."

She kept flipping through the photographs in the album, pointing out her cousins, Chuck and Betty, who were younger, still in their teens. Most of the pictures, though, showed Margaret, Kevin, or the couple together. Here were several shots taken at Margaret's engagement party, held at the nearby Bellevue Club, which looked out at Lake Merritt. In the photo, Margaret wore a deep pink taffeta dress with a draped neckline and a bow at her waist.

"He gave me an engagement ring last fall," Margaret said,

touching the ring that now hung from the chain on her neck. Margaret lingered over the photos of the party, then she turned the page. Here was a picture of the engaged couple standing arm in arm at the end of a *California Zephyr* dome-observation car.

"That's the Silver Solarium," Jill said.

"Yes, it is. We rode the *Zephyr* to Colorado last year, with Uncle Dan and Aunt Helen. They have friends in Glenwood Springs. We stayed at that beautiful old Hotel Colorado, the big sandstone building that overlooks the hot springs and the river. A few months later, we took the *City of San Francisco* to Truckee. Kevin loved trains. He particularly liked the *Coast Daylight*, because it runs with steam engines instead of diesel."

"Then he'd know train signals," Jill said, a speculative look on her face.

"You mean the warning whistles the engineer blows? Yes, he did. He explained them to me."

"How about Morse Code?"

"Yes, he did. He mentioned it once. Said he learned it in the Boy Scouts. Why do you ask?"

"Those four taps that I heard in roomette four," Jill said. "I was talking with a friend yesterday, about the possible ghost. I wondered about those four taps I heard. I told her it might be a train signal. Four short blasts on the whistle means a request for a signal to be given, or repeated."

Margaret tapped her finger on the photo album. "What would four short taps be in Morse Code?"

"I looked it up. It's the letter H."

"That's very interesting."

"Did Kevin know someone whose first or last name started with an H?" Jill asked.

"I expect he did. We all know someone with an H in their name."

"You must have some theories about who killed Kevin. Tell me what you know."

"I don't know much," Margaret said. "I just have suspicions. Right before he died, Kevin seemed preoccupied, worried. When I asked him what was wrong, he put me off. He said it was business and he'd sort it out himself. He'd gotten a promotion a few months before, more responsibility. He was very conscientious and always wanted to do his best."

"What exactly did he do for your uncle's company?"

"My uncle's firm is growing," Margaret said. "Over the past couple of years, he has been buying smaller companies. All sorts of companies, manufacturing, retail, shipping. Once they are under the big company umbrella, Uncle Dan and his executives go over their operations. Kevin's job involved reviewing business procedures and finances for several of those companies. When he went out of town, as he did a few times a month, he'd go to wherever that company was headquartered, to meet with the people in charge. He would look at their books, make recommendations, then report back to his supervisor. He traveled all over this part of California."

Jill thought for a moment. "He got on the train in Portola and told me he was on a business trip. He must have been visiting a company in Plumas County. I wonder, what sort of company, and where it's located? In that part of the Sierra Nevada, it could be mining, I suppose, or lumber. And it's a big county. Did Kevin ever mention any details? My theory is that something was going on with one of those companies. He never told you anything more specific about what was bothering him?"

Margaret shook her head. "No. I wish he had. That would give me something to go on. All I remember is Kevin saying he needed to have a serious talk with Uncle Dan when he got back from this particular trip. Instead, you found him dead in his roomette. Jill, I'm sure he found something off at that company, wherever and whatever it was. He must have been killed to prevent him from revealing whatever he found out."

Jill leaned back on the park bench. "If that's true, how do we prove it?"

Margaret shut the photo album and put it in her bag. "I'll start riding the train back and forth to Portola," she said, her voice frustrated. "If Kevin's ghost is haunting the *California Zephyr*, maybe he'll tell me what happened."

"You might have to ride the train farther than Portola," Jill said, "if the ghost only haunts the roomette at night. And if it only haunts roomette four on the Silver Gorge, you'd have to made sure that car is on the consist, traveling on that particular train. Seriously, Margaret, doing something like that makes people think you're unable to get past Kevin's death, that you're taking grief too far."

Margaret tightened her lips. "I *am* having a hard time getting over Kevin's death. My aunt and uncle are understanding, of course, but other friends and relatives tell me I have to move on and stop dwelling on it. I know they mean well, but I have difficulty with that. I have to grieve in my own way, and in my own good time. I know he was murdered. I don't tell people that, of course. I'm sure they'd look at me like I'm crazy. But you don't. You believe me, don't you?"

Jill nodded. "I do."

"So I don't really care what people think. I can't move on until I find out who killed him."

"I understand," Jill said, remembering those weeks after her fiancé had died. "There's always a séance." Suddenly Tidsy's crazy idea of the day before sounded as though it might be useful. "It's not really my idea. A friend of mine came up with it, when she and I were having lunch yesterday. Grace Tidsdale. She knows your aunt."

"She does. My aunt calls her Tidsy. They've known each other since college, according to Aunt Helen. A séance?" Now Margaret looked thoughtful as she considered the idea.

"I told her yesterday I thought it sounded ridiculous."

"Maybe not," Margaret said. "At this point, I'm willing to try anything, if it will help me find out who killed Kevin."

Chapter Nine

WHEN JILL RETURNED HOME after her meeting with Margaret Vennor, she changed clothes, hanging the sundress in the closet. She put on an older shirt and a comfortable pair of worn dungarees, suitable for digging in the dirt. She had promised to help her mother, who was pulling weeds in the backyard garden. First, though, she called Tidsy, from the upstairs phone extension, just in case someone might overhear.

"So she's amenable to a séance," Tidsy said. "Good. I say we go ahead and do it. I'll scout around and find a medium. Today's Thursday. It might take a few days to set this up. What does your schedule look like over the next week or so?"

Jill twisted the phone cord around her fingers. "I'm going out with Mike, Friday and Saturday nights. Then we're going to Oroville on Monday, to visit his relatives up there. We'll be back Wednesday."

"Keep Sunday evening open," Tidsy said. "I'll get to work and let you know. And I'll call Margaret myself. By the way, four taps in Morse Code is the letter H."

"I know. I looked it up, too."

After Tidsy hung up, Jill got her address book and called the Western Pacific Railroad office in San Francisco to find out when she was due to leave on an eastbound run. Next Friday, according to the schedule. She made a note on her desktop calendar. Then she went downstairs and out to the garden. She and her mother spent an hour pulling weeds that had sprung up between the tomato plants and the other vegetables. They also picked ripe tomatoes and squash. Finally Mrs. McLeod took off the straw hat she'd been wearing and wiped her sleeve across her face, which was damp with sweat. "That's enough for now," she said. "I'm hungry. Let's get some lunch."

They left their garden tools and hats on a bench outside the back door and carried their garden bounty into the house, washing up at the kitchen sink. Mrs. McLeod made a batch of tuna salad. Jill set out bread and condiments. They constructed sandwiches and poured glasses of lemonade from the pitcher in the refrigerator, then sat at the kitchen table to eat.

"Delicious," Jill said after she swallowed a mouthful. "And these bread-and-butter pickles you canned last summer are just perfect."

"Not bad if I do say so myself," Lora McLeod said. "I do love pickles, and these turned out so well. I hope we have a good crop of pickling cucumbers this year. Your sister baked sugar cookies yesterday. I think there are still some in the cookie jar, if your brother hasn't eaten them all."

"That's a distinct possibility." Jill wiped her hands on a napkin and got up. The cookie jar was shaped like a fat cat, painted to resemble a gray-and-white tabby. She carried it back to the table and took off the lid. "There are still cookies."

"Good. Speaking of your brother," her mother said, "when you talked with him yesterday, did he say anything about what's been going on with him?"

"He did. But he's going to have to tell you himself." Jill took two cookies from the jar, one for each of them.

"I wish he'd get on with it, then." Mrs. McLeod took another bite of her sandwich.

The phone rang. Jill went to the hallway to answer it.

"Jill, it's Big Milly. I need a favor."

Big Milly, a fellow Zephyrette, was really Angie Miller. Shortly after Angie, all five foot ten of her, had been hired, another young woman, Annette Miller, joined the dozen or so Zephyrettes riding the rails between the Bay Area and Chicago. Annette was only five two, so Jill and her coworkers bestowed nicknames, calling the pair Big Milly and Little Milly.

"What kind of a favor?" Jill asked.

"I need to trade runs with you," Big Milly said. "You're scheduled Friday, a week from tomorrow, and I'm scheduled the Sunday after that. I've got a family event that I really want to go to, but it's happening during the time I'm supposed to be gone. If I could take the earlier run, I would be home earlier. That way, I can go to my family thing, and everything would all be copacetic."

"I'm okay with that."

"Great. I'll call the office and take care of it on that end. Thanks, Jill, I really appreciate it."

Jill hung up the phone. She went upstairs to note the change of schedule on her calendar, then came back down, joining her mother in the kitchen. "Good news. I get an extra couple of days at home before I have to go out again."

Her mother smiled. "I'm always glad to have you home. That way I can get more work out of you, unlike your sister, who always seems to be out these days." The last was said with a twinkle in Mrs. McLeod's eyes. They both knew she was kidding. "Now, finish your sandwich. We have to deadhead roses and weed that border next to the house."

———

It was just after four o'clock when Dr. Amos McLeod came through the front door of the house on Union Street. He was in his mid-fifties, a fit man who walked to and from his medical office located at the Alameda Hospital, a few blocks away on Clinton Street. His brown hair had grayed at the temples and he had laugh lines on his face around his pleasant blue eyes. He took off his suit jacket and draped it on the back of the chair next to the hall table, where the day's mail had been left on a painted wooden tray, next to the telephone and the bowl that held car keys. He loosened his tie and sorted through the envelopes, pulling out three addressed to him, along with a medical journal.

"You're home early." Jill had been in the kitchen with her mother, spreading frosting on the chocolate cake she had baked after they'd finished with their garden tasks. She greeted her father with a hug.

He smiled at his elder daughter and kissed her on the forehead.

"I had a couple of canceled appointments and I was caught up on my paperwork. So I decided to get an early start on my evening."

He walked down the hall to his study. Jill followed, watching as her father stood behind his desk, using a letter opener to slit the envelopes.

"Dad, is it true that someone who has had rheumatic fever has a weak heart?"

Dr. McLeod looked up from the envelopes. "What prompts that question?"

"It's about Mr. Randall, the young man whose body I found on the train, back in May. I'm not sure what caused his death, though the doctor who looked at his body there at the train said it might be natural causes. I found a prescription bottle for Digoxin near the body. Today I talked with his fiancée, a young woman named Margaret. She told me he'd had rheumatic fever and that it damaged his heart."

Dr. McLeod didn't ask why Jill had been conversing with Margaret, though a curious look flickered over his face. He set down the letter opener and moved to one of the upholstered chairs near the bookcase, motioning for Jill to join him. She took the other chair, leaning forward to listen as her father began to talk.

"Rheumatic fever can develop as a complication of strep throat or scarlet fever," he said. "Both of those diseases are caused by an infection with streptococcus bacteria. The fever can have serious effects on the heart, including damaged valves and heart failure. How old was the young man who died?"

"He was thirty-one. Margaret said he'd had the fever as a child."

"Rheumatic fever is common in children ages five to fifteen, or thereabouts," the doctor said. "Though it can develop in younger children and even young adults. Do you remember my cousin Lorena, the one who lived in Fort Collins? You were about ten years old when she died."

Jill nodded. "I do. We drove up there for the funeral. I remember Mom saying she had a bad heart. At that age, I wasn't sure what she meant. So Cousin Lorena had rheumatic fever?"

"She did," the doctor said. "Lorena was a few years younger

than me. When she was fourteen, she got a serious case of scarlet fever, and it turned into rheumatic fever. It left her with a badly damaged heart. She was in her early forties when she died. She also took Digoxin, as I recall. What happened with the man on the train is probably a similar situation. We military doctors saw a lot of recruits during the war who'd had scarlet fever and sometimes rheumatic fever. Scarlet fever is not as common now as it was before the war, thanks to some of the new antibiotics. And I'm certainly hoping this new Salk vaccine has the same effect on polio."

"Thanks." Jill leaned back in the chair. "I wonder if there's any way to get a look at Mr. Randall's autopsy results. Do you know someone who works at the Alameda County Coroner's Office?"

Her father fixed her with a stern look. "Since December, you have encountered three dead bodies, and two murderers, all on the train. That's more than your share, Jill, unless you're a police officer. I'm beginning to wonder if this Zephyrette job is a bit too adventurous for a daughter of mine. Are you sure you don't want to come back to work for your old dad, as his office receptionist?"

"I should think your current receptionist would have something to say about that." Jill's voice took on a placating tone. "Now, Dad, you're exaggerating. I just happened to be the one who discovered those bodies. It's coincidence, nothing more than the luck of the draw."

"A strange sort of luck." He sounded skeptical. "I wonder what your cousin Doug, the gambler, would say about your luck, and those odds."

"You can ask him next Thursday. He and Pamela will be here for dinner. Besides, strange things happen on the trains all the time. I could tell you stories." She smiled, thinking about the director who wanted to make his film noir on the train.

"I'm sure you could. And I would feel a whole lot better if those strange things and stories didn't involve homicide. Let's get back to your question about the autopsy results. I know you're naturally curious. You have a sense of justice, as well as a good head on your shoulders. Nevertheless, it would be better if you left any investigating to the proper authorities."

"What if the authorities think Mr. Randall's death was due to natural causes?" Jill argued. "In that case, they're not investigating anything."

"Why would you think his death was anything other than natural causes? Or an accident due to an overdose of his own prescription medication? Which happens frequently, by the way."

"Margaret thinks he was murdered."

"His fiancée, the young woman you met this morning? I wondered why you were talking with her. I assume she has her reasons for thinking Mr. Randall's death was homicide."

"She does," Jill said, though she wasn't sure her father would think Margaret's suspicions credible. As for ghosts, the less said about that, the better.

Dr. McLeod sighed. "As it happens, I do know someone who works at the Alameda County Coroner's Office. He's an old Navy buddy."

Jill straightened in the chair and looked at her father, eagerness in her eyes. "Will you ask him about the autopsy results? Or take a look at them yourself?"

Her father held up his hand. "I'm not making any promises, Jill. But I will think about it."

"Thanks, Dad." Jill looked up as her mother appeared in the doorway.

"I thought I heard you come in," Lora McLeod said to her husband. "Just as well. We're eating early tonight."

"Why is that?" he said as he got up from the chair.

"Because Drew has to leave. He's rehearsing with his band. They're playing in Oakland on Friday and Saturday."

"That's right," Jill said. "Mike and I are going to hear him play on Friday."

"Where's that?" her father asked.

"A place called Ozzie's, in West Oakland."

"I see. Well, I'll go upstairs and change out of this suit." Amos McLeod left the study and retrieved his suit jacket, then paused at the foot of the stairs to talk with his wife. "It's all well and good that Drew is interested in music, but I really would like to see him concentrate more on his studies. He hasn't declared a major. I can't pin him down as to what he wants to do with his life."

"Give him time," Lora McLeod said. "He's only nineteen and he just finished his freshman year. I'm sure he'll settle into college soon."

Jill knew from her earlier talk with her mother that Drew had not yet told their parents about his plans to drop out of school and tour with the band. That will be an interesting conversation, she thought as her father went up the stairs.

She followed her mother to the kitchen, inhaling the enticing smell wafting from the oven. "Mmm, that smells wonderful."

"It does," her mother said. "Just roast chicken. I stuffed the cavity with garlic cloves and a lemon before I put it in the oven. We'll have salad made with the lettuce, cucumbers and tomatoes we picked earlier in the afternoon. Thanks for making that chocolate cake. It looks delicious."

Jill rinsed the lettuce and the other vegetables in the sink, setting them aside to drain while she washed the bowl and mixer she'd used to make the cake frosting. Lucy arrived home then, after a shopping trip to Oakland with friends. "Did you buy out the stores?" Jill asked as she tore lettuce for the salad.

"Not exactly. But I found a great dress on sale at Kahn's." Lucy took her bags upstairs and then returned, setting the table in the dining room for dinner.

Later that evening, Tidsy called. "The séance is on. I talked with Margaret this morning and she's agreed to do it. I also found a medium. Madame Latour," she added, her voice taking on a dramatic trill. "The madame does advertise in the *Chronicle*. Be at my place at eight on Sunday."

A séance, Jill thought as she hung up the phone. I can't believe I'm actually going to a séance. She went back to the living room.

"Who was that?" her mother asked from the sofa, where she was sitting with a book in her lap.

"Tidsy. She invited me to her house Sunday evening." Better leave it at that.

She sat down in the bay window armchair and put her feet on the ottoman. Sophie jumped onto her lap, turning in a circle before settling down to sleep. Jill stroked her cat, then reached for the copy of *The Uninvited* that she had checked out of the library the day before. She turned the pages to chapter one, and was soon drawn into the tale of a haunted house on the Devon coast. After reading a passage about a room that was unnaturally cold, Jill shivered and looked up from the page. She recalled what had happened on the train—the light she'd seen, the cold she felt in roomette four, and the odd knocking sounds she'd heard.

Could there really be a ghost? Was it possible that Kevin Randall's untimely death was murder?

She thought back to May, when she'd met Kevin Randall on the train, before she'd found his body at the end of the journey.

Chapter Ten

May 1953

THE WESTBOUND *CALIFORNIA ZEPHYR* arrived in Portola, California just after eight in the morning. The train slowed as it neared the railroad town nestled on the eastern side of the Sierra Nevada. The middle fork of the Feather River was to the north, swollen with spring snow melt, flowing swiftly as it paralleled the tracks.

Jill stood in the Silver Gorge's vestibule with Frank Nathan, the porter. To the south, she saw the backs of buildings along Commercial Street. Two people stood on the platform outside the small Portola station. When the *CZ* stopped, the porter unlocked the vestibule door, lowered the stairs and set down his step box. He got off the train, followed by Jill. The last time she'd gotten off the train was in Salt Lake City, late last night. Now she wanted to take advantage of this brief stop to stretch her legs and get some fresh air.

One of the passengers, a gray-haired woman in a plaid dress, walked toward the third chair car, the Silver Saddle, carrying a handbag and a small suitcase. The other passenger, a man, moved toward the Silver Gorge. He wore a gray suit and had dark hair and brown eyes behind his black horn-rimmed glasses. His suitcase and briefcase were the color of honey, the soft leather scuffed and scarred with years of use. As he reached the car, Jill greeted him. "Good morning, sir. Are you traveling on this car?"

The man nodded. "Yes, I have a roomette. Number four."

Frank Nathan reached for the man's suitcase. "I'll take your bag, sir. The roomette is just down the passageway."

The passenger climbed into the vestibule. He disappeared from view, the porter right behind him. Jill remained on the platform, watching as two other men rounded the corner. They must have been waiting on the other side of the station. The first man had a bulky frame and a big stomach, his shoulders straining the jacket of his dark suit. The other man was tall and balding, wearing serviceable khaki work clothes and boots. He was smoking a cigarette. Now he pitched the butt to the platform and ground it out with the toe of his boot. Both men walked toward the second chair car, the Silver Pony. As the man in the suit boarded the train, the tall man turned and looked right at Jill. He had a pencil-thin mustache, a thin sliver of brown on his weathered face.

The conductor and brakeman stood talking near the baggage car. Then the brakeman climbed onto the train. The conductor turned and began walking down the length of the train, calling, "All aboard."

Jill boarded the train as the porter appeared in the vestibule. The whistle sounded and the *California Zephyr* pulled out of the station, leaving Portola behind. For the next three hours, the train would wind down the rugged, scenic Feather River Canyon. Then the train, and the river, would leave the mountains for California's broad Central Valley, stopping at 11:25 A.M., in Oroville.

As the train picked up speed, Jill walked down the corridor to roomette four, where the new passenger had set his suitcase and briefcase on the floor below the window. "Good morning. I'm Jill McLeod, the Zephyrette. Where are you bound for today?"

"I'm Kevin Randall," he told her. "I'm going to Oakland."

"Let me know if you need anything."

Mr. Randall nodded. "Thank you, I will. Right now, I could use some coffee and breakfast."

"The dining car will be open for a while longer." Jill consulted her watch. "At least until nine, maybe later."

"Good. I hope they're serving French toast. It's my favorite."

Jill smiled. "Mine, too. I had some earlier today."

Mr. Randall took his briefcase with him as he left the roomette. It must contain something important, Jill thought, watching him walk in the direction of the dining car. Another passenger called to her from a nearby roomette and Jill stopped to answer a question.

A short time later, Jill entered the dining car, on this trip the Silver Restaurant. The *CZ* was approaching the Clio Trestle. The railroad bridge, one of the many sights along this scenic route, was over a thousand feet long, towering a hundred and seventy-two feet above Willow Creek. It was time for her to make her first announcement of the day, describing what the passengers would see in the Feather River Canyon. She picked up the mike on the public address system near the center of the car. After she had made the announcement, she walked through the car, where Mr. Randall sat at a table for four, drinking coffee as he consumed his plate of French toast. A few tables away, Jill noticed the tall man who'd boarded in Portola. He, too, was drinking coffee, though he seemed to be staring at Mr. Randall. As Jill passed his table, he lowered his gaze to a plate of scrambled eggs.

The train continued its journey down the canyon, passing the Keddie Wye, an impressive structure that towered high above Spanish Creek, with two legs on bridges and a closing track that ran into a tunnel. *Wye* was the term used to denote a triangular junction of tracks. The *California Zephyr* ran on what was called the mainline, while one set of tracks headed north through the steep, forested slopes to connect with the Great Northern Railroad. The wye was named after Arthur W. Keddie, the man who in the 1860s had surveyed the Feather River route, one of the lowest in elevation to cross the Sierra Nevada. Construction of the railroad through the rugged canyon began in 1905 and was completed in 1909, with the "Last Spike" ceremony taking place on November 1, 1909, right here at the wye.

As she walked through the Silver Gorge, she saw that Mr. Randall was in his roomette, unlike the other passengers on the *California Zephyr*, many of whom were in the Vista-Domes, admiring the scenery in the rocky canyon. He had removed his suit coat and loosened his tie, and his briefcase was open at his feet. He had turned the lid that covered the toilet seat into a small desk that held a blue-and-purple device covered with number keys. The legend at the bottom read MARCHANT FIGUREMATIC. It was a mechanical calculator, Jill realized. On Mr. Randall's lap was a book bound in brown leather, open to show ledger pages covered with figures. He had a lined legal pad as well. He was scribbling notes on the yellow pages, in a spiky, slanted hand.

He looked up at her and smiled. "My trip to Portola was business. I still have a lot to do before we get to Oakland."

"Then I'll leave you to it," Jill said.

She continued her walk through the train, all the way back to the dome-observation car. The bulky man who had boarded the train in Portola was there, standing at the table that held various newspapers. She began climbing the steps to the upper-level Vista-Dome, wondering briefly why the man, who was a passenger in the chair cars at the front of the train, was back in a section of the train normally used by sleeping car passengers. As she reached the dome, she was bombarded with questions by a trio of children who were traveling with their parents to Sacramento. She talked with them about the sights they were seeing, the rugged, rocky canyon carved by the river, and the Pulga and Tobin bridges, where the tracks and State Highway 70 crossed each other.

When she returned to the lower level, the man was no longer in the lounge. Jill walked forward through the transcontinental sleeper and the sixteen-section sleeper to the Silver Gorge. Two men were standing in the vestibule. One was Mr. Randall, who held the ledger and the legal pad. The other was the man she'd seen earlier. They talked in low urgent tones, keeping their voices down. Something about their body language told Jill they were arguing.

"The figures don't add up," Mr. Randall said, brandishing the ledger in his right hand. "And you know it. I have to—" He looked up and saw Jill in the vestibule.

"Excuse me," Jill said. "I didn't mean to interrupt you."

Mr. Randall rearranged his face from a frown to a tight smile. "It's all right."

The other man was ten or fifteen years older than Mr. Randall, and probably thirty pounds heavier. He loomed over the younger man, as though trying to intimidate him. Under his dark hair, slicked back with hair cream, he had a sallow face with large pores and a long nose. There were bags underneath the pale blue eyes that seemed to look through Jill.

She stepped past the two men, heading into the passageway that separated the roomettes. As she moved away, they began talking again. Mr. Randall's voice had a note of strain and urgency. "You should have told me you were coming to Portola."

"Just hear me out." The other man's voice was a low, insistent rumble.

"I know what you want me to do and I can't do it," Mr. Randall said. "Wait—"

The other man interrupted. Jill couldn't make out what he was saying. She entered the car and headed down the passageway between the roomettes. "I wonder what that was about," she said aloud, just as Frank Nathan stepped out of roomette nine.

"You wonder what?" he asked.

"I saw Mr. Randall in the vestibule with another man. I think they were having words."

"A big man with a long nose?" the porter asked. "Yes, I saw him earlier. He came through the car looking for Mr. Randall. I told him to check roomette four. Then they were having words, like you said, and they went out to the vestibule. I don't know what it was about. But they're still at it?"

"Yes," Jill said. She kept going and didn't think any more about what she'd seen, or heard, until her return trip through the train, about an hour later. As she walked down the passageway between the roomettes in the Silver Gorge, she saw another man standing outside roomette four. He was tall, dressed in khaki work clothes, and when he turned, she saw a weathered face with a thin mustache and lines around the man's brown eyes. It was the man she'd seen earlier, boarding the train.

"May I help you?" she asked.

His voice had a deep Western twang. He smiled. "Just looking for a fella. He doesn't seem to be here."

Jill glanced inside the roomette, which was empty. "If I see Mr. Randall, I'll tell him you were looking for him."

"No matter. I'll catch up with him later." The man stepped past her and walked forward, in the direction of the dining car.

Something odd about that, Jill thought, but she couldn't put her finger on why it seemed so. She walked forward and rounded the corner, looking out the window. The train was coming out of the mountains that had bracketed the Feather River, and North Table Mountain was visible in the distance. The flat-topped mesa was a few miles north of Oroville, the train's next scheduled stop at 11:25 A.M. As she walked up the corridor toward the next car, she encountered Mr. Randall, coming in the opposite direction. He was carrying the briefcase she'd seen earlier.

"There was a man looking for you," Jill said after she greeted him. "A tall man with thinning hair, and a mustache. He got on the train in Portola, same as you."

Mr. Randall looked down at the briefcase he carried and when he looked up again, his brown eyes took on a guarded expression. "Was he in my roomette?"

"No, standing in the doorway. He said he would catch up with you later." When he didn't say anything, Jill added, "Is something wrong, Mr. Randall?"

He shook his head. "No. No, everything is fine. Thanks for letting me know, Miss McLeod." He stepped past her and continued back toward the roomettes. By now the train was descending into the wide terrain of the great Central Valley. From the window, Jill glimpsed the outskirts of Oroville.

She had breakfasted early that morning, so now she was ready for lunch. She reached the dining car as the train pulled into the station. The steward pointed her toward a nearby table for four, where two people were already seated. Jill introduced herself.

"Ella Talbot," the older woman said. "And this is my husband, Carl. We're from Salt Lake City and we're going to Oakland to visit our daughter. She and her husband moved there last year. I'm so looking forward to seeing the grandchildren."

"I'm sure you are," Jill said. As she looked at the luncheon menu, the train left the Oroville station, moving slowly through town and picking up speed as it reached the countryside. The next stop, in Marysville, was barely twenty minutes away. Jill marked her meal check, ordering iced tea, a bacon, lettuce and tomato sandwich with potato salad, and chocolate pudding for dessert.

The waiter had just delivered her beverage when the fourth chair at the table was taken by Mr. Randall. He had put on his suit coat and straightened his tie. His briefcase was in his right hand. Now he set it on the floor at his feet.

"Hello," he said. "Kevin Randall, from Oakland, California."

"You're on your way home, then," Carl Talbot said. "That's our destination. Going to see family there."

The waiter delivered the Talbots' orders as well as Jill's sandwich. He set the dishes in front of them and looked at Mr. Randall. "Have you made your choice, sir?"

Mr. Randall had been studying the menu. Now he took a meal check from the stand and marked it. "I'll have the tomato salad and a cup of Navy bean soup. And iced tea, please."

The waiter took the meal check and departed. The Talbots tucked into their meals, short ribs for him and fish for his wife. Jill took a bite of her sandwich and listened as the Talbots talked. He was a retired tailor and his wife had taught school for many years. When his soup and salad were delivered, Mr. Randall picked up his spoon and dipped it into the soup. In response to a question from Mr. Talbot, he told them he was an accountant, working at a firm in Oakland.

As was the case with many passengers, the Talbots were curious about Jill's life as a Zephyrette, eager to hear about her day-to-day duties. She answered their questions with a friendly smile. "Yes, I've been a Zephyrette for over two years now. I make two or three runs a month, on average. It's two and half days to Chicago, then I lay over there for a couple of days, and come back. So I'm at the end of a run, looking forward to seeing my family and having some time at home."

"It sounds like an interesting way to live," Mrs. Talbot said. "Traveling around and meeting all sorts of people. Just the thing for a girl your age. But I'm sure some day you'll want to settle down and get married. There must be some nice young man at home, or perhaps someone you've met on the train."

There was indeed, but Jill wasn't going to talk about him. She was accustomed to passengers and their personal questions. Sometimes those questions were annoying. But she was the Zephyrette, always ready with a smile. She deflected Mrs. Talbot by taking a sip from her glass rather than responding to the older woman's curiosity about her marital status.

"Now, don't be so nosy, Mother," Mr. Talbot said.

"I'm just making conversation. What about you, Mr. Randall? Is there a young lady waiting for you in Oakland?"

Mr. Randall colored slightly, smiled and said, "As a matter of fact, there is. We're engaged to be married later this year. She is picking me up at the Oakland Mole."

"Well, congratulations to you both," Mrs. Talbot said. "And what on earth is the Oakland Mole?"

Jill laughed and explained. "It's a big train shed at the western terminus of the railroad line. Passengers from what we call the East Bay, the eastern side of San Francisco Bay, can get off the train there. Passengers going to San Francisco catch the ferry at the Mole and go across the bay to the Ferry Building."

They talked for a while longer, then the older couple left the table, their dishes collected by the waiter. Jill lingered, finishing her chocolate pudding.

Across the table from her, Mr. Randall set down his soup spoon and leaned toward her. "I'm glad I have the opportunity to talk with you alone, Miss McLeod. Would you be kind enough to do me a favor."

"Certainly. What is it?"

"We're due into Sacramento about one o'clock, aren't we?"

Jill nodded. "About twenty minutes, at twelve fifty-five. It's a longer stop, so we'll be in the station for a while."

"I wonder if you could mail a letter for me when we reach the station. I know the Zephyrettes do that, mail letters and send wires."

"Of course. I'd be happy to. I have stamps in my pocket if you need them."

"I have stamps in my briefcase," he said. "I've already put several on the envelope. It's rather thick so I'm sure it will require additional postage."

He leaned down, picked up his briefcase, and placed it on his lap, opening the metal fastener. The envelope he pulled out was a

California Zephyr envelope, a rectangle with a printed legend at the top of the flap that read ABOARD THE VISTA-DOME in small capital letters, followed by a larger CALIFORNIA ZEPHYR in a different typeface. He must have obtained it from the writing desk back in the dome-observation car, which was stocked with stationery and envelopes for the use of the passengers. Jill took the sealed envelope from Mr. Randall, noting how thick it felt in her hand, as though there were several sheets of paper inside. She glanced at the front of the envelope, seeing several stamps in the upper right corner, as well as a name and an Oakland address.

She slipped the letter into her skirt pocket. He thanked her and got to his feet, leaving the dining car. Jill took the last bite of her chocolate pudding and set down the spoon. Interesting, she thought as she took one more sip of iced tea, that Mr. Randall wanted her to mail a letter to Oakland. The *California Zephyr* would arrive at the Oakland Mole later in the afternoon. It would take the letter a day or so to get to its destination.

The Silver Lady was on time into the red brick station in downtown Sacramento. Before arriving, Jill had walked through the train asking passengers if they had anything to mail or wires to send. There were no telegrams, but she had several postcards in her pockets, along with Mr. Randall's envelope. She got off the train as soon as the porter opened the vestibule and crossed the platform to the station. There was a round-topped metal box there, marked U.S. MAIL. She dropped the stamped postcards, and Mr. Randall's letter, through the slot.

The train left Sacramento and made its stop in Stockton an hour later. Jill walked through the train and paused in the Silver Club. She saw Mr. Randall at a table for four, with the two men who had boarded the train in Portola. All three were drinking coffee and they appeared to be deep in conversation.

Jill turned to the bar, where the waiter, Alonzo Griggs, was washing cups and saucers. He stopped and dried his hands on a towel. Then he took a photograph from his pocket. "You asked about my daughter, Miss McLeod. Here's the latest picture. Her name's Emma and she's taking ballet lessons."

Jill took the snapshot and admired the little girl, about eight, who was posing at a barre, attempting to stand *en pointe*. "What a beautiful girl. How long has she been taking lessons?"

"About a year now," he said. "She says she wants to be a ballerina."

Jill handed the photograph back to Mr. Griggs. Then she heard raised voices behind her and turned, looking for the source.

Mr. Randall was getting up from the table where he'd been sitting. He looked around, realizing that others in the lounge were staring at him. He lowered his voice as he addressed his companions. "There's no point in discussing it any further." Then he stepped past Jill, holding his briefcase in front of him like a shield, and left the lounge, heading toward the back of the car.

Jill watched him go. She exchanged glances with Mr. Griggs, who didn't say anything and went back to washing dishes. Then Jill turned and looked at the two men who still sat at the table. The man with the mustache was lighting another cigarette, a frown on his face. The bulky man with the long nose glared at her. "What are you staring at?"

"I'm sorry," Jill said, with a polite smile. "I didn't mean to intrude."

What was that about? With a nod to Mr. Griggs, she left the lounge and walked back through the train. Mr. Randall was in his roomette. He had removed his suit coat again. It was folded neatly and tucked into the open briefcase on the floor near his feet. The mechanical calculator was on the toilet lid, and so were the brown ledger and the legal pad covered with his handwriting and columns of figures.

"Are you all right?" she asked him. "I couldn't help overhearing what happened in the lounge."

His face took on a rueful expression as he pushed his glasses up his nose. "I'm fine, Miss McLeod. It's just that those men would like me to do something I am not willing or able to do. I've explained to them—" He smiled. "It's not your concern so I won't burden you with it. I'll sort things out when I get back to Oakland."

"I see." Jill nodded and continued on through the train, wondering if this had something to do with Mr. Randall's letter, the one she'd mailed in Sacramento. She rode in the Vista-Dome of the dome-observation car as the *California Zephyr* climbed Altamont Pass, heading into the Bay Area. The train crossed the Livermore Valley, making a brief stop in Pleasanton. As she came back through the Silver Gorge, Mr. Randall was still in his roomette, but this time he had removed his glasses. He looked somehow vulnerable without them. He rubbed his temples and winced, as though he had a headache. She had aspirin in the first-aid kit in her quarters. She was just about to say she'd fetch it, then stopped as Mr. Randall took a small bottle from his pocket. He removed the cap and shook a couple of pills into the palm of his hand. He quickly popped them into his mouth and swallowed.

When he set his glasses on his nose, he looked up, surprised to see her. "I didn't see you standing there, Miss McLeod. I'm as blind as a bat without my glasses."

"Can I get you anything?" she asked.

He shook his head. "No, thanks. Just a little tired. I've had a couple of long days on this trip. I'll be glad to get home." He reached for the yellow legal pad. "I've got to finish these notes, though." He glanced out the window. "Where are we now?"

"Sunol. We go through the canyon, then we'll stop in Niles and head up to Oakland."

The train went through the little hamlet of Sunol without stopping. Then it wound through Niles Canyon, where the tracks and nearby highway twisted and turned through the East Bay hills, following the route carved by Alameda Creek.

"They used to make movies in Niles," he said.

"Yes, silent movies. The Essenay company was formed by Broncho Billy Anderson and George Spoor. I understand Charlie Chaplin's *The Tramp* was filmed right here in Niles Canyon."

He smiled. "That's right. I like silent movies. My father worked at the old Liberty Theater in Fresno, right after World War One, before he met my mother. He used to talk about the silent era and all those movies. Dustin and William Farnum were favorites of his. He liked Colleen Moore and Mabel Normand, too."

"My father always like Fatty Arbuckle," Jill said. "Buster Keaton and Laurel and Hardy."

Jill excused herself and walked forward. When she reached

the Silver Club, she decided it was time for coffee. She was tired after this run, and she usually did need a boost in the middle of the afternoon. The caffeine helped. The two men were still there, at the table, talking. They glanced at her as she got a cup of coffee from Mr. Griggs and sat down at one of the lounge tables. Then the large man with the long nose left, followed a few minutes later by the man with the mustache. She was halfway through her coffee when the attendant from the third chair car came looking for her. "Need you and your first-aid kit, Miss McLeod," he said. "A youngster fell coming down the stairs from the Vista-Dome."

"I'll be right there." Jill took one last swallow and set the cup on the counter as she left the lounge, heading for her quarters to fetch the kit.

The last time she saw Mr. Randall was after the train's brief stop in Niles, where two passengers from the first sleeper car got off the train. As the Silver Lady headed toward Oakland on the last leg of its westbound journey, Jill walked the length of the train. When she passed through the Silver Gorge, she glanced into roomette four and saw Mr. Randall. It looked as though his business trip and the long days he'd mentioned had caught up with him. He was asleep.

Or he looked as though he was asleep. When the train got to Oakland an hour or so later, she discovered she was wrong.

Chapter Eleven

MIKE SCOLARI JOINED the McLeod family for dinner on Friday. Jill had met the Army Air Corps veteran in December, when he and his grandfather had boarded the train in Oroville, heading for Denver. She had liked the young man immediately, and the attraction was mutual. They had been dating ever since. He was twenty-nine, three years older than Jill, a few inches taller, with a wiry frame. His eyes were a deep brown in his olive-skinned face and he had a head of curly dark hair.

He arrived a little before six, neatly dressed in blue slacks and a short-sleeved checked shirt, bearing a bouquet of flowers for Mrs. McLeod and a bottle of wine for Dr. McLeod. It was just the four of them for dinner. Lucy had gone on a date with Ethan, and Drew left the house early, saying he'd grab something to eat at the club where he and his band were playing. After Lora McLeod thanked Mike for the flowers, she told Jill she didn't need her help in the kitchen and shooed her out. "Show Mike the roses in the backyard."

Jill wasn't fooled. She knew her parents liked Mike, a lot. As her mother had made clear during their conversation a few days ago, she hoped eventually Jill would give up riding the rails and marry Mike. To that end, she was taking every opportunity to see that the two young people spent time alone together.

"We're supposed to look at the roses." Jill led Mike to the fence on the left side of the yard, where a vigorous yellow climber called the Lady Banks rose perfumed the air. "My mother has matchmaking on her mind."

"Does she?" Mike smiled at her. "How do you feel about that?"

"Not quite ready."

"That's an honest answer."

"I like you a lot," Jill said. "You know that. But we've only known each other for seven months. I'd like to get to know you better before we talk about any long-term plans. Besides, I'm not ready to give up being a Zephyrette."

He nodded. "Fair enough. I like you a lot, too. And like you, I'm not quite ready to take things to the next level. I have another couple of years before I finish my degree. After that, I need to get a job and establish myself as a geologist." He leaned over, plucked a bloom from the rose bush and handed it to her. "Let's just agree to think about things."

"That's fine." Jill held the rose to her face and breathed in the fragrance. "So you're finished with summer classes. How did it go with your last exam?"

"I think I did all right. It will be nice to have a break before the fall classes start." He took her hand as they strolled along the fence, pausing at another rose bush, this one called Black Magic, with deep red blossoms.

"I can go to Oroville with you on Monday," Jill said. "I have the whole week off. I leave for Chicago the following Sunday."

"Great." He squeezed her hand. "I'll call Aunt Adalina and tell her we're coming. I was thinking about taking the train instead of driving. I know you make your living riding trains, but I figured you might enjoy just being a passenger for a change."

She smiled. "I'd like that. It will be fun to sit and relax instead of doing walk-throughs and making announcements. Since I've met some of your San Francisco family, I'm looking forward to meeting the Oroville branch. I'll see you at the Oakland Mole Monday morning."

Dr. McLeod appeared at the back door, calling to them. "Dinner's ready."

After a dinner of salmon and salad, with peach pie for dessert, Jill and Mike left the house. Dusk had gradually given way to darkness. Though it was summer, the fog had cooled things off and Jill was glad she had slipped on her blue cardigan sweater. After leaving military service, Mike had bought a car from one of his many cousins. It was a 1948 Hudson Commodore two-door sedan, dark blue with white trim, and he kept it shined with the kind of attention that Drew lavished on his Mercury. When they reached the curb, Mike opened the door for her. Jill slid into the passenger seat, the full skirt of her blue cotton dress spilling around her. He got behind the wheel and started the car.

In Oakland Mike turned left on Seventh Street and headed west through Oakland's Chinatown, past Broadway and into West Oakland. This was one of the city's oldest neighborhoods, where the land met the bay, where ferries plied the water. In 1869 it became the terminus of the transcontinental railroad, its population swelling with railroad workers. Since the 1890s West Oakland had been home to people of all races and it had a thriving Negro community, with jazz and blues clubs lining the end of Seventh Street near the rail yard and the port. On this Saturday night, the street was full of cars and people thronged the sidewalks. Jill saw the bright neon sign that read SLIM JENKINS, OPEN NIGHTLY, DINE AND DANCE. So this was the famous Slim Jenkins Nightclub and Café her brother had told her about, where stars like Nat King Cole had played.

Mike turned right on Wood Street. Jill spotted a smaller sign that read OZZIE'S and pointed. "That's the place."

"I see it," Mike said. On the next block, he backed the Hudson into a parking place. They walked back toward Seventh Street.

With big plate glass windows on either side of the front door, Ozzie's looked as though it had once been a store. There was a large chalkboard on the sidewalk, saying that Drew's band, the Blues Timers, would be playing at 9 o'clock. Inside the club, the air was heavy with cigarette smoke and the yeasty smell of beer. The crowd was mixed, with Negro, white and Asian faces among the clientele. Drew had told Jill that the music scene on Seventh attracted people from all over the Bay Area, regardless of race.

To the left of the front door was an elevated platform where the band had set up. Drew was there, strumming the strings and fiddling with the tuning machines at the end of his guitar's neck. There were two other men in the band, a bass guitarist and a drummer. Both were Negroes. Drew had said nothing to his family about his fellow band members, only that he'd met them playing various clubs in Oakland. She waved to her brother and he gave her a quick nod, then turned to his band mates.

A bar made of scarred and stained oak extended along the left wall. Benches ranged along the right wall, and there were small round tables set up on the right side of the room. The space between the bar and the raised platform served as a dance floor, Jill guessed. There was a lot of noise in the club, even though the music hadn't yet started, with customers' voices competing with the clink of glasses and bottles.

Mike steered Jill toward a small table with two vacant chairs. They sat down and Jill draped her cardigan over the back of her chair. Mike asked Jill what she would like to drink.

"A beer would be fine," she said. Then she looked past him and smiled at the young couple who were sitting at the next table. "Hello, Mr. Nathan. I almost didn't recognize you in civilian clothes."

Frank Nathan did look different out of his porter's uniform, dressed tonight in a dark brown pinstriped suit with a white shirt and a blue bow tie. "I thought that was you when you walked in, Miss McLeod," he said. "I wondered if you might be here tonight. I heard someone say the guitarist's name was McLeod and I remembered that your brother likes this kind of music." He nodded in the direction of the stage.

"Yes, the guitarist is my brother. His name is Drew."

The woman sitting next to him was about Jill's age, with short dark hair and a round face. She wore a rose pink cotton dress with white eyelet trim. Frank Nathan made the introductions. "This is my friend, Bea Simmons. This is Miss McLeod. She's one of the Zephyrettes on the train."

"It's nice to meet you, Miss Simmons," Jill said.

The young woman waved at her from the other side of the table. "Likewise. I know about Zephyrettes. My uncle is a railroad cook. He travels on the *California Zephyr* all the time."

"No doubt I've eaten some of his cooking. What do you do, Miss Simmons?"

"I'm studying to be a nurse, at the Kaiser Foundation school over on Piedmont Avenue. I just finished my first year."

Mike introduced himself to the other couple. "Mike Scolari. I was a passenger on the train last December, when we had that memorable incident in the canyon."

"How could I forget," Frank Nathan said. "That was a mess for sure."

"Do you come here a lot?" Jill asked.

"I know the owner, Mr. Osgood." He pointed at a gray-haired man behind the bar. "He and my father are friends."

"I'm going to get our beers," Mike said. He headed for the bar.

"How is your mother?" Jill asked. The porter's mother was a housekeeper, working for Navy families who lived in officers' quarters at the Naval Air Station in Alameda.

Frank smiled. "She is just fine and keeping busy."

Mike returned a few minutes later with two bottles of cold beer, no glasses. Jill took a sip. She preferred wine, but every now and then she liked a beer. They talked for a few minutes, Jill checking her watch. It was after nine. Finally the band started, appropriately enough playing "Mercury Blues," the song Drew had been playing a couple of days before. The music was loud, driving, with Drew, his mouth close to the microphone, providing the vocal.

"He sounds good," she told Mike.

"Yes, he does. The whole band is good. C'mon, let's dance." Mike stood up and held out his hand.

They maneuvered their way onto the crowded dance floor, swinging into a Lindy Hop. They danced through several songs Jill didn't know, but she did recognize "Night Train." After that, the music slowed into a bluesy version of "Cry." With so many people packed together on the floor, the room got very warm.

"Let's sit down," she said, fanning herself with her palm.

Frank and his girlfriend had also returned to their table. As Jill and Mike sat down, Bea stood up and waved to someone out on the sidewalk, visible through the bar's grimy front window. "I see Wanda outside," she told Frank. "I'm going to say hello. I need to talk with her about something."

Mike pushed his chair back from the table and stood. "I'm

The Ghost in Roomette Four

going to the men's room. I'll be back in a minute. Do you want another beer?"

"I'm still not finished with this one," Jill told him. She had been nursing the beer all evening. After Mike had left, heading toward the back of the bar, Jill turned to Frank Nathan. "Do you remember that day in May when we got into the Oakland Mole and I found Mr. Randall dead in roomette four on the Silver Gorge?"

"Of course I do." He hesitated, his hand wrapped around the beer bottle in front of him. "That's the third body you've found on the train."

"I know. My father reminded me of that fact last night. He thinks it's getting to be a habit, but I'm sure it's just a strange coincidence. Yesterday I spoke with Mr. Randall's fiancée, Miss Vennor."

"The young lady that came to meet the train that day. You talked with her outside the car."

"I had to tell her he was dead," Jill said. "When I talked with her yesterday, she told me that she's convinced Mr. Randall was murdered."

He frowned, considering this. "I heard, second or third hand, that he died of some kind of heart condition. He was awfully young to die that way."

"I wonder what else you might have heard."

"I'm not sure what you mean." He looked past her, out the window where Bea stood on the sidewalk, talking with her friend.

"The ghost," she prompted.

He looked at her and took his time answering. "You know about the ghost?"

"I saw—and heard—something odd, on my last run. It was late and I was walking through the Silver Gorge on the way to my quarters. I saw a strange light in the passageway. It seemed to float into the roomette, which was empty at the time. When I went inside, it was very cold, and it got colder. Then I heard a rapping sound, four distinct knocks. I didn't know what to think. When I went through the next car, I ran into the porter, Darius Doolin. He told me about the ghost. That was the first I'd heard of it. I'm not sure I believe in it, though Mr. Doolin told me several of the porters have seen things." When Frank didn't say anything, she added, "Have you?"

He nodded. "Seen it, and heard it. But my experience was different from yours. It happened about three weeks after Mr. Randall died. I was on a run from Chicago to Oakland and the Silver Gorge was on the consist. It was late on the first night out, and I'd just settled down to see if I could get some sleep. Then the porter call bell from roomette four rang. I knew there was no passenger traveling in that roomette. I thought somebody was playing a trick on me. I went to check, though. Nothing there. So I turned around to leave, to go back to my quarters. Then I heard that noise. It sounded like you say, someone knocking on the wall. When I turned back to look, I saw a light, outside the roomette door. I thought it must have been a trick of the light."

"That's what I thought," Jill said.

"I went into the roomette," he continued. "And I felt that chill. Just then another porter call bell rang. This time it was a real passenger, in another roomette. I just figured my imagination was playing tricks on me, so I let it go out of my mind. Until now."

"Getting back to the sounds you heard, did it sound like four short knocks?"

"I didn't count the knocks," Frank said. "Short knocks? Are you thinking Morse Code?"

"Yes. I heard four short knocks. That's the letter H in Morse Code. Of course, four blasts on a train whistle means—"

"A request for a signal to be given, or repeated," Frank said.

"Or four taps meaning roomette four." Jill sighed. "Maybe it means nothing at all. Maybe I'm imagining things." She took a sip of her beer and looked around for Mike. He'd returned from the rest rooms at the back of the club and now he stood at the bar, talking with another man.

"Would both of us be imagining the same thing?" Frank asked. "You mentioned Mr. Doolin. I talked with him, and some of the other porters. People told me several porters have seen things on that car, ever since Mr. Randall died a couple of months ago. Miss McLeod, I don't believe in ghosts. But something strange is going on."

"There must be a logical explanation," Jill said. "It's possible Mr. Randall died of an overdose of that prescription medicine. You know I found a bottle of Digoxin next to the body. He could have taken too many pills. Or someone could have given him the pills. Who would be able to get close enough to him to administer something like that?"

"Somebody he knew?" Frank asked.

Jill nodded. "There were two other men who got on the train in Portola, the same time as Mr. Randall. Both of them boarded the chair cars. One was big and bulky, with a long nose. The other was tall, with a mustache."

"I saw both of them," Frank said. "The one with the mustache was outside the roomette. It was while we were in the Feather River Canyon, before we got to Oroville. I asked if he was looking for Mr. Randall. He said no, he just wanted to see what a roomette looked like. Then he left the car."

"I also saw him outside the roomette. But when I spoke with him, he implied he was looking for Mr. Randall." So the man with the mustache had lied to Frank. "As for the other man, he was back in the Silver Gorge, too. I came upon him with Mr. Randall, in the vestibule. They were having words. An argument, I'm sure of it."

"I remember that," Frank said. "I was in roomette three, across the hall, making up the bed back into a seat for a passenger that got up late that morning. That big man in the suit, he showed up, standing in the doorway of roomette four, talking to Mr. Randall. I agree with you, it was definitely an argument. As they talked, they got louder and louder. So much so that the lady who was traveling in number five stuck her head out of the roomette and asked them to either quiet down or take their conversation somewhere else. At that point, Mr. Randall apologized to her, and he and the other man went out to the vestibule."

"I'd give anything to know what they were talking about," Jill said. "I saw them briefly while I was walking through the vestibule, but I didn't hear much. Did you hear anything when they were in the roomette?"

"A bit." Frank thought about it, as though trying to reconstruct the fragment of conversation he'd overheard. "I heard something about figures, and Mr. Randall saying, 'I can't do it.' But that's all. What did you hear?"

"When I came upon them in the vestibule, Mr. Randall was saying something like, 'The figures don't add up.' And I'm sure he said, 'I know what you want me to do and I can't do it.' I wonder what the other man wanted him to do." And whether it got Mr. Randall killed, she thought, recalling the night she'd seen the light in roomette four. At the time the roomette had been unoccupied, but later in the run a passenger had boarded, traveling in that roomette. The passenger had told her the next morning that her sleep had been disturbed by voices, two men arguing, she'd said. Two men. Mr. Randall's ghost and—?

She looked up as Bea Simmons came back inside the bar, heading for the table where Frank sat. "Wanda invited us to a picnic next weekend," she said. "Are you going to be in town?"

Frank shook his head. "I'm leaving on a run this coming Wednesday, so I won't be back from Chicago till after the weekend."

"I was afraid of that," Bea said. "But you're a traveling man. I understand that."

Drew's band swung into a hard-driving rhythm and Bea took Frank's hand, leading him to the dance floor. Mike returned to the table, carrying his second beer. "Ran into a guy I know and got to talking."

"I know, I saw you."

"You and Frank Nathan were having quite a conversation. What about?"

"A ghost. I promise I'll tell you about it later. Come on, let's dance."

Chapter Twelve

"WELCOME. COME IN." Tidsy stood in the doorway of her apartment, opening the door wide for Jill and Margaret.

Jill walked through the living room to the window. It faced north, toward Russian Hill, North Beach and Fisherman's Wharf. Sunlight would soon give way to darkness on this summer evening. But there was enough light so that Jill could see, far below, a cable car making its way along Mason Street, heading for the wharf. In the distance, the dark blue water of San Francisco Bay glinted with gold as the sun made its descent to the west.

"Your apartment is beautiful," Margaret told Tidsy, who wore a dress in what was for her a subdued color, a deep burgundy red.

"I agree," Jill said. "What a terrific view."

Tidsy laughed, glancing around her home. "Yes, I've been fortunate. Little Gracie Ballew, the kid who grew up in a flat above a bakery on Guerrero Street in the Mission, living in a joint like this. Who would have thought it?"

The apartment was at the top of Nob Hill, on the seventh floor of the Brocklebank Apartments, a ten-story building that had been constructed in the 1920s, at the corner of Mason and Sacramento streets. The building's near neighbors were the Pacific Union Club and the Fairmont Hotel, both structures that had survived the 1906 earthquake that left much of the neighborhood in rubble and flames.

Tidsy's living room was simply furnished, with soft beige carpet, walls painted a light cream. Grouped around a coffee table were a comfortable high-backed sofa and two wingback chairs, all upholstered in a coppery fabric that complemented the russet drapes. The small dining area had a round oak table covered with a white lace cloth with scalloped edges, a crystal bowl in the middle.

"Let me take your jackets," she said.

The day had been warm, but as the sun went down, San Francisco had developed its usual chill. Both the living room and dining room windows were open slightly, a breeze coming through the screens, billowing the edge of the draperies. Jill had worn a lightweight blue jacket over her pastel blue cotton dress. Margaret, too, wore a jacket, pale green to go with her green-and-white shirt-waist. Now they removed their wraps and handed them to Tidsy, who hung them in the coat closet near the front door.

"How about drinks?" Tidsy asked. "Booze, or not?"

Jill shook her head. "Nothing alcoholic for me. If we're going to communicate with ghosts, I need to keep my wits about me."

"I second that," Margaret added.

"I figured as much. So I made a pitcher of tea. Go on, sit down, both of you." Tidsy waved her hand in the direction of the sofa and chairs, then headed for the kitchen.

Jill sat down in one of the armchairs, while Margaret took the other. A moment later, Tidsy returned from the kitchen, carrying two tall glasses filled with ice and tea, each garnished with a slice of lemon. Jill took a sip and set the glass on the nearby end table, making sure to put it on the round coaster.

Tidsy reached for her own glass, which contained ice cubes and a thin residue of golden-brown liquor. "I will have another drink. My wits are just fine, even better when lubricated with good scotch." She went to the bar in the corner of the dining area and poured another shot over the ice.

After taking a sip of her tea, Margaret asked, "What time will the medium arrive?"

"I told her eight-thirty." Tidsy glanced at the small brass carriage clock on a nearby bookcase. It was ten minutes after eight. Outside, the sky had darkened to blue-black, sprinkled with stars and city lights. "This time of year, it's not going to be dark until about then. I suppose the optimum time to hold a séance would be midnight or thereabouts. But I couldn't very well schedule it that late in the evening. I imagine you girls had to tiptoe around the truth as to why you were coming to the city tonight. Explaining a midnight visit to San Francisco would be more difficult. Anyway, Madame Latour said the timing of the séance wouldn't be a problem."

"I told my family I was driving over to the city tonight to see you. I didn't tell them why." Jill had an excellent relationship with her parents, which was why, for the time being, she continued to live at home. They were fine with her going to Oroville with Mike tomorrow, since she would be staying with his relatives there. But she had the feeling eyebrows would be raised at the mention of séances and mediums.

"As far as Aunt Helen knows," Margaret said, "I am meeting friends. By the way, Jill, you are invited to our party next Saturday. Tidsy will be there."

"I wouldn't miss it." Tidsy sipped her scotch, then set the glass on the coffee table. She picked up a pack, shook out a cigarette, and lighted it.

"Is there an occasion for this party?" Jill asked. "And may I bring Mike, the man I've been seeing? He and I are taking the *CZ* to Oroville tomorrow to visit his relatives, but we'll be back on Wednesday."

"By all means, bring Mike. I look forward to meeting him," Margaret said. "As for the reason for the party, it's an annual thing my aunt and uncle do. Every summer they invite their friends and people from my uncle's company, an open house sort of thing. They set up tables on the patio and lawn and a catering company provides the food. Aunt Helen has been planning it for months now."

"Helen and Dan throw quite a shindig, with lots of booze and good food," Tidsy said. "Speaking of food, do you kids want anything to eat? I've had dinner, but if you're peckish, I've got cheese and crackers."

Margaret shook her head. "Nothing for me, thanks. I had dinner not long ago."

"None for me, either." Jill took a sip of iced tea. "Before the medium gets here, I should tell you that since I spoke with both of you last week, I've been making an effort to remember more about the trip, that day when Mr. Randall, Kevin, was on the train. I've gone over it in my head and I also went through my notes. I have to file a trip report at the end of each run, so I keep a small notebook of things that go on during the days that we're out. I didn't find much that was useful in my notes, except that I did write down what happened after I found the body. What I was hoping to dredge up were some details about what went on between the time Kevin boarded the train and our arrival at the Oakland Mole. And I did recall a few things."

Tidsy leaned forward, interest sparking in her eyes. "What did you remember?"

"In addition to Kevin, two other men boarded the train in Portola. Both of them were traveling in the chair cars, while Kevin had the roomette back in the sleeper car."

Margaret nodded. "He always got the roomette when he traveled on business, even if the trip wasn't very far. He liked the privacy, so he could work."

"I saw both of those men later, back in the sleeper section of the train," Jill said. "I thought it was unusual, because most of the time, the coach passengers stay in those three chair cars, because each car has a Vista-Dome. They go to the dining car or the buffet-lounge car, but not that often are they back in the sleepers."

"What did these guys look like?" Tidsy asked.

"One of them was a tall man. He was losing his hair and he had one of those pencil-thin mustaches. His face was weathered, as though he'd spent a good deal of time outdoors. And he was dressed in working man's clothes, khaki pants and jacket, boots—not wearing a suit like a businessman. Shortly after we left Portola, Kevin went to the dining car for breakfast. And I saw this man in the dining car at the same time. He was at another table, staring at Kevin. Later, when I went back through the sleepers, the same man was standing outside roomette four. He told me he was looking for Kevin. I've also talked with the porter who was on that run. He says that he also saw this man outside the roomette. But he told the porter he just wanted to look at a roomette."

"So he lied to you, or he lied to the porter." Margaret shook her head. "Your description of the first man, it doesn't sound like anyone I know, or that I've seen. It's possible Kevin knew him, from the business trip to Portola. What about the second man?"

"He definitely had contact with Kevin," Jill said. "I saw them together, in the vestibule of the Silver Gorge. I came upon them when I was doing a walk-through, heading from one car to another. They were arguing about something. I heard a bit of it, and so did the porter. This particular man was dressed in a business suit. He had a big, bulky frame, and his face was sallow, with jowls and a long nose. His eyes were light blue, and very cold."

"A long nose?" Margaret asked. "And blue eyes? I have seen that man before. I think he works at my uncle's company. Uncle Dan hosts these company functions and sometimes the family goes. I'm sure I've seen him there. But right now, I can't put a name to the face."

"There must be a way we can find out who this guy is." Tidsy swirled her glass, rattling the ice cubes.

"The party on Saturday," Margaret said. "A lot of people from Uncle Dan's company will be there. Maybe this man with the long nose will be there, too."

Tidsy leaned back on the sofa and sipped her drink, then she set down the glass and reached for the cigarette, smoldering in the ashtray. "Jill, you and the porter overheard some of the argument in the vestibule. What did you hear?"

"I heard Kevin say, 'The figures don't add up.' He also said, 'I know what you want me to do and I can't do it.' That's all I heard. The porter heard something similar."

"Figures that don't add up?" Tidsy waved her cigarette. "That means numbers and money."

Margaret tapped her finger on the edge of her glass. "This must have something to do with Kevin's job. He worked in the financial department of my uncle's firm. He looked at the books of companies that Uncle Dan bought. When he traveled on business, that's what he did. In fact, before he left for Portola, he told me that was the reason for the trip."

"I remembered something else," Jill said. "Before we got to Sacramento, Kevin asked me to mail an envelope for him when we got to the station. Which I did. Try as I might, I can't recall the name on the envelope. But I do remember that it was an Oakland address. Margaret, I wondered if the letter might have been addressed to you."

Margaret furrowed her brow. "I don't remember receiving anything like that. I suppose it could have been sent to anyone. Maybe it had something to do with Kevin's job. In that case, he would have sent it to the office. I can call the secretary who used to work for him."

"That would be helpful."

"Listen, I have another plan in the works," Margaret said. "I have a friend… Well, I guess you could say he's a former boyfriend. He works for the freight department at Western Pacific. After I talked with Jill on Thursday, I called him. I wanted to find out when the Silver Gorge would be on the *California Zephyr* again. He checked and called me back yesterday." She smiled, a glint in her eyes. "It will be on the train tomorrow. So will I. After he called, I phoned Western Pacific and booked roomette four, all the way to Salt Lake City."

"You were lucky to get it," Jill said. "It's summer and people are traveling. The trains are full."

"I know. There had been a last-minute cancellation," Margaret said. "And I'm sure the ticket agent must have been wondering about me, since I insisted on having roomette four on the Silver Gorge, and none other."

The phone rang. Tidsy stubbed out her cigarette in the ashtray. She got up and walked to the bookcase that held the phone, picking up the receiver. "Yes, I'm expecting her. Please send her up." She hung up the phone and turned to face her two guests. "That was the doorman. Madame Latour has arrived. Get ready, girls. It's show time."

Jill had never attended a séance before. As a history student, and a woman who considered herself well-read, Jill was aware of the popularity of Spiritualism in the nineteenth century and its continuation into the twentieth, even as recently as the 1920s. She knew that Mary Todd Lincoln, grieving the loss of her young son Willie in 1862, had held séances in the White House, hoping to contact Willie and another son who had died young, years before. Arthur Conan Doyle, the creator of Sherlock Holmes, had been an adherent of Spiritualism, while the famed illusion-ist Houdini was a skeptic, believing attempts to contact spirits of the dead to be a fraud, and those who conducted séances, charlatans.

The role of the medium, she gathered, was to receive messages from the dead and whatever spirits might be floating around. She wasn't quite sure what to expect. Would the medium fall into a trance? What would she look like? Would she wear long, flowing robes? A turban and elaborate jewelry, carrying a crystal ball? Or a Ouija board?

Madame Latour, while not in the least ordinary, didn't look particularly exotic, either. With piercing blue eyes, she was tall and thin, to the point of being cadaverous. Her stylish silk dress, in a shade that Jill would have called pewter, had draped sleeves and a gored skirt that fell below her knees. Her hair was gray as well, though more silver than iron. She wore no watch or bracelet, just a plain gold ring on her right hand. Her only other ornaments were a pair of jet earrings dangling from prominent earlobes, and a jet brooch pinned just below the garment's scooped neckline. Her slim leather handbag, black like her shoes, wasn't large enough to hold a Ouija board or a crystal ball.

When she spoke, Madame Latour's accent held a vague hint of France. She declined Tidsy's offer of a drink, asking only for a glass of water. When she was settled on one end of the sofa, sipping her water, the medium said, her voice low and throaty, "Madame Tidsdale has told me of what happened. That Mademoi-selle Vennor's fiancé, Monsieur Randall, died on the train and that Mademoiselle McLeod was the one to find his body. Since then there have been ...manifestations, indications that a spirit wishes to communicate with the living. The porters on the train have seen and heard things, and so have you, Mademoiselle McLeod. Now, I wish to hear your firsthand account. Please, tell me what you saw and heard on your recent train journey, in as much detail as you can remember. Take your time."

Jill shifted in the armchair and took a sip of her iced tea. She took a deep breath. Then she began, describing the shimmering light she had seen and how it moved from the corridor, into roomette four. She shivered a bit, remembering the cold that had chilled her when she went inside. And she heard again the four knocks that might have been a Morse Code signal, spelling the letter H.

The medium probed, asking questions, pausing to consider, her long-fingered hands tented in front of her. Finally, she nodded and rose to her feet. "The word séance comes from the French. It means 'to sit.' In English, it has come to mean a gathering of people who wish to communicate with the spirits of those who have passed on. If the spirits wish to speak with us, they may do so through me. I may remain conscious, or I may go into a trance. In past séances, I have done both. If there is communication, more often than not I remember what has been said. In this case, tonight, you wish to communicate with the spirit of Monsieur Randall, should his spirit grace us with his presence. Take a moment, each of you to think of questions you wish to ask him. Madamoiselle Vennor, you have a photograph of Monsieur Randall?"

"I do." Margaret opened her purse and took out a snapshot of Kevin.

"Good." The medium took the photograph from her and gazed at it, as though committing the face to memory. Then she returned it to Margaret. She gestured at the round dining room table. "We will sit around this table. Madame Tidsdale, will you please remove the bowl? Do you have candles? Four would be good. And matches, of course."

"I do." Tidsy went to the kitchen and opened a cupboard. She returned with two pairs of candlesticks, one set made of polished brass, the other set etched crystal. She set these on the table and went back to the kitchen, fetching a box of white candles and a smaller box of kitchen safety matches. These, too, she set on the table.

Madame Latour put a candle in each candlestick. She positioned them around the table, forming a square. Then she glided to the window. By now it was dark, but the city lights twinkled. She pulled the drapes closed, shutting out the light. "We must make the room as dark as possible." The medium drew the drapes closed over the dining area window, while Jill did the same in the living room.

"There's a window in the kitchen. But it doesn't have curtains. I'll just shut the door." Tidsy turned and drew a pocket door from the wall, closing off the kitchen. "Margaret, would you turn off that light by the front door? Jill, get the hall light and close the bedroom door."

Jill and Margaret complied with her requests. Then they rejoined the others at the dining table.

"Now, let us begin," Madame Latour said. "Madame Tidsdale, will you turn off the lights, please? Then I will light the candles."

Tidsy reached for the nearby light switch, turning it off. The living room and dining area were plunged into darkness. Jill's eyes were adjusting to the gloom when she heard a match scraping against the matchbox. A flame leapt to life. Jill saw Madame Latour's face, looking eerie and strange in the contrast between light and shadow. The medium used the match to light each of the candles. She pinched out the flame and set the burnt match on the rim of one of the candlesticks. Now that the flames danced above the candles, the dining table was bathed in soft light.

"Sit down, please," Madame Latour said. "We will hold hands, making a circle. We will close our eyes. Think deeply about the spirits of those who have departed. Open yourself to connection with those who have passed on. I will say a prayer to begin. The prayer will cleanse this place and make it more receptive. Then each one of us will concentrate on the spirits we wish to summon. I will ask them to join us, especially the spirit of Monsieur Randall, to provide us with signs of their presence."

In silence, they gathered around the table, pulling out chairs. Tidsy sat to Jill's right, with Margaret across the table. Jill felt Tidsy's chunky garnet ring as she took the older woman's hand. Then she held out her hand to Madame Latour. The medium's right hand, with its plain gold ring, felt slightly cold to the touch, though the skin was soft and smooth. They sat quietly for a few minutes.

Jill took slow, deep breaths, and imagined she could hear the others breathing as well. She did as the medium had instructed, focusing her thoughts on Kevin Randall and his death two months earlier. But other thoughts intruded.

The purpose of the séance was to contact Kevin's spirit. But the medium had mentioned other spirits. Would the séance bring forth the ghosts of those who might hover over the women gathered around the table? What about the spirit of Steve Haggerty, Jill's fiancé, who had died in Korea? What about Tidsy's husband, Rick, who had died in distant China? Perhaps the places where they'd died were too far away, their spirits unable to cross the vast expanse of the Pacific Ocean to appear in a San Francisco living room high above Nob Hill.

Madame Latour began to speak. "We greet you tonight, spirits, and pray that any evil ones among you will pass us by. We gather here tonight with the hope that we shall receive a sign of your presence. Please feel welcome in our circle and join us when you are ready."

They waited. Nothing happened. Seconds lengthened into minutes.

Madame Latour repeated her earlier phrase, asking the spirits to join the circle. After another period of silence, she said. "If you are there, spirits, please provide us with a sign."

What sort of a sign? Jill wondered. Knocks, like those she'd heard in the roomette? She kept her eyes closed and breathed. She didn't hear anything that sounded like a spirit trying to communicate, but she heard people talking out in the hall. Tidsy's neighbors, no doubt. A woman laughed, and then a door slammed. Then it became quiet again.

"Kevin Randall," Madame Latour said again, "we gather tonight, hoping that we shall receive a sign of your presence. You are welcome in our circle. Please join us when you are ready." She paused, then went on. "If you are there, spirit, please give us a sign."

Still nothing happened. It appeared that Kevin Randall, if his spirit was abroad in San Francisco, wasn't interested in communicating tonight.

"I sense that someone in the room is resistant," Madame Latour said.

"What does that mean?" Tidsy asked, her voice sharp.

The medium's French accent became more pronounced, with a hint of annoyance. "It means that there is some blockage here. Something preventing the spirits from making contact. It is possible that the spirits do not come because they sense that some, or all of you, do not believe in them." Her lips compressed into a tight line as she surveyed them. In the shadows of the flickering candles, Jill felt like squirming. She didn't believe in ghosts or spirits, so it might be her fault that the spirits had made themselves scarce. "It is also possible," the medium added, with a Gallic shrug, "that the spirits do not wish to have an intermediary, such as myself. I will break the circle now." Madame Latour released the hands she'd been holding.

Tidsy stood and turned on the light fixture above the dining table. "Perhaps we'll try this another time."

She escorted Madame Latour to the front door and paid her with a roll of bills from her purse. When the medium had departed, Tidsy detoured to the coffee table to retrieve her scotch. She returned to the dining area, where she poured herself another shot at the bar. Jill and Margaret had pushed their chairs away from the table, though they still sat there. Tidsy pulled out the chair where she had been sitting, sat down and sighed. "Well, that was a bust. What can you expect from a medium who advertises in the *San Francisco Chronicle*? Next time I'll ask for references."

"Madame Latour, indeed," Margaret scoffed. "Her real name's probably Elsie Jones and I'll bet she's from Bakersfield."

Tidsy tilted her head to one side, her expression thoughtful. "I'm not so sure. The French accent sounded authentic. But who knows?"

Jill's only experience with French accents were those of the passengers she had encountered on the *California Zephyr*. She supposed that Tidsy might have come in contact with French nationals during her time in Washington, D.C.

Tidsy raised her glass in salute. "Better luck next time?"

"Will there be a next time?" Jill countered. "I must admit that I'm not a believer. Although if you get me in that roomette again, with the light and knocks, I might change my mind."

Margaret sighed and ran her fingers through her dark hair. "But you did see and hear something. And you're not the only one. The porters have seen it. As for me, I'm skeptical, too. Torn between wanting to believe that Kevin is trying to contact me, and taking the whole thing with several grains of salt."

"It was worth a shot." Tidsy fired up another cigarette. "I don't believe in ghosts or spirits, but there are a lot of things in this life that can't be explained. Was the woman a charlatan? A good actress? She certainly had all the right moves and set the atmosphere. I'll give her that."

Jill shrugged. "If she was a fraud, why didn't she just fake the so-called communication from the spirits? After all, I told her about what I'd seen. She knew we think it's possible Kevin was murdered. And she knew what he looked like, from the picture that Margaret brought. What if—?" Jill paused, considering the thought that was circling in her mind. "What if Kevin's spirit is stuck on the train, because that's where he was killed."

"In that case," Tidsy declared, "we'd have to hold the séance on the train, and that roomette's not big enough for a medium, and the three of us."

Margaret smiled. "It's a good thing I'm traveling in that roomette tomorrow, then. Maybe I'll have something to report when I get back."

"Speaking of traveling," Jill said, "we should go. It's after nine, and we're both taking the train tomorrow."

She set her hand on the edge of the table, preparing to get up. The light above the table flickered. So did the candles, which were still burning. Suddenly the curtains on the dining room window billowed out, as though a gust of wind had blown them.

"Is that window still open?" Tidsy got up and moved to the window. She lowered the sash and flipped the lock.

Jill shivered. She felt cold. But it wasn't like the cold, damp chill of a San Francisco night. It felt exactly like the cold Jill had felt in roomette four.

"It's not the window."

"I feel it, too," Margaret said, her voice nearly a whisper.

The lights flickered again, and the candle flames fluttered. Tidsy's glass moved, ever so slightly, toward the center of the table. Then they heard it, four sharp knocks, followed by a muttering sound that ebbed and flowed, indistinct, as though someone was talking.

Chapter Thirteen ———————

T HANKS FOR THE RIDE." Jill opened the passenger-side door and got out of the Ford. She carried her purse and a small case, packed with enough clothing and toiletries for her two nights away in Oroville.

"I should think you'd be tired of train travel," Lucy said. "You just got back from a run last week."

Jill smiled. "This is different. I'm not wearing a uniform, I don't have to take dinner reservations, make announcements, or provide first-aid to passengers with motion sickness or kids with scraped knees. And I'm not filing a trip report when I get back."

"Okay, okay." Lucy laughed. "Have fun. I'll pick you up Wednesday afternoon. Tell me again, what time will the train be here?"

"A quarter after four. I'll see you then." Jill shut the car door and waved as her sister drove away.

She was meeting Mike here at the Oakland Mole. After so many trips in her Zephyrette uniform, it felt different to be traveling as a passenger, instead of part of the train crew. This Monday morning in late July was beautiful, no fog for a change, with San Francisco visible in the distance over the sparkling waters of the bay. Jill wore a flared skirt with a palm frond print in blue, gold and tangerine and a blue short-sleeved blouse, and she carried a blue cardigan sweater. The skirt swirled around her legs as she walked toward the Mole.

On this warm, sunny morning, it was easy to dismiss what had

happened last night at Tidsy's apartment. Easy to scoff at that penetrating chill, the flickering lights, the way Tidsy's glass of scotch
seemed to move, of its own volition. The sharp rapping knocks
that made all three of them jump. And the voice, if that's what it
was, muttering. It hadn't gone on for long. But it had happened,
and they'd all seen and heard it. Perhaps Madame Latour had been
correct when she'd said the spirits didn't want an intermediary
such as a medium interfering with their lines of communication.

Jill shook herself, willing the memory to go away. It was daylight now, no spirits lurking here at the Mole.

The morning sun glittered on the shiny stainless steel cars that
gave the train its nickname, the Silver Lady. Each of the cars in the
consist had the legend CALIFORNIA ZEPHYR centered over the
windows. Below the windows was the name of the car.

Many passengers were already here on the platform or inside
the Mole, checking their baggage, or queuing at the ticket office.
To her left, a man and his wife, surrounded by four children, talked
all at once as they sorted through their luggage, putting larger
suitcases on a baggage cart. Then they gave their smaller bags to
a Red Cap, one of the railroad station porters whose bright red
headgear gave them the name. More Red Caps clustered inside
and outside the Mole, waiting for the ferry from San Francisco,
which would disgorge dozens of travelers needing assistance with
their luggage. In the distance, Jill saw the boat plowing through
the sparkling waters of San Francisco Bay, dwarfed by the pilings
of the Bay Bridge.

The train was due to leave in half an hour. Had Jill been working as a Zephyrette on this eastbound run, she would have arrived
at the Mole far earlier, going through her pre-departure routine.
The dining car crew had arrived before dawn, transferring the food
and supplies necessary to feed the train's passengers from the com-
missary building into the diner while still in the rail yard, before
the train was moved into position at the Mole.

She and Mike planned to rendezvous near the office, where
Mike would buy a ticket. Jill, as an employee of the Western Pacific
Railroad, had a pass which enabled her to travel for free. Now
she walked into the Mole, looking around for Mike. She saw him

standing to one side of the ticket office, casually dressed in gray gabardine slacks and a checked shirt, a jacket draped over one arm, a small bag at his feet. He waved to her and she quickened her step. He greeted her with a kiss on the cheek. Together they got in line. A few minutes later, they took their turn at the window. Jill showed her pass and obtained a round-trip ticket to Oroville.

"You're on the Silver Sage," the ticket agent told them as he collected money for Mike's ticket. "Third chair car."

Tickets in hand, Jill and Mike strolled toward the rounded end of the dome-observation car, where a small rectangular sign read CALIFORNIA ZEPHYR, in yellow neon letters against an orange background showing an outline of the Golden Gate Bridge. On the car's side was its name, the Silver Penthouse. The Pullman conductor stood nearby, greeting passengers and directing them to their cars. With him was one of Jill's fellow Zephyrettes, Sally Hastings, in her teal uniform skirt and jacket, the garrison cap perched on her carroty red hair. She smiled. "Hey, there. Nice to see you. Traveling as a civilian this trip?"

"A short trip to Oroville, with a friend," Jill said. She introduced Mike and Sally, then said hello to the Pullman conductor. She and Mike moved on, walking alongside the train, in the direction of the engines. Out of habit, Jill ticked off the cars by configuration. In front of the dome-observation car were the transcontinental sleeper and the sixteen-section sleeper. Then came the ten-six sleeper and the six-five sleeper. As Margaret had told her last night, the Silver Gorge was the ten-six on the consist for this eastbound run of the CZ. The porter who stood on the platform near the vestibule was Darius Doolin.

"This is the car," Jill said. "The Silver Gorge."

Mike looked at the sleeper. "The one with the purported ghost?"

Jill had told him about what she had seen and heard on the last trip. On Friday night, after they had returned from the club in West Oakland, they sat in the swing on the McLeods' front porch, holding hands as they rocked gently back and forth. Mike didn't believe in ghosts, either, but he was interested in her tale of strange lights and sounds, late at night in the darkened car. They had talked for quite a while before Mike kissed her good night and headed down the sidewalk to his car.

"I wonder if there's a passenger in that roomette for this run," Mike said.

"Yes, there will be." Before Jill could explain further, Mr. Doolin saw her and waved. "Good morning, Miss McLeod. I see that you're not wearing your Zephyrette uniform. Are you traveling with us for pleasure rather than business?"

"We are, Mr. Doolin. This is my friend, Mr. Scolari. I've told him all about my recent experience in this car."

"Have you?" A smile played on Mr. Doolin's lips. "We'll have to see if the passenger in roomette four has a quiet night. We have a full car this trip. Every space is taken. Where are you going today?"

"To Oroville," Mike said. "I have family up there."

A horn blared in the distance and Jill turned, looking back toward the water. The ferry from San Francisco had now docked. Passengers streamed off the upper and lower decks of the ferry, hurrying through the Mole toward the train. The Red Caps were busy, carrying suitcases and bags or piling them on luggage carts that would be pushed to the baggage car. People walked down the platform, looking for the cars in which they would be traveling.

Jill heard someone call her name. It was Margaret, her dark hair brushing the shoulders of her lightweight green linen suit. She carried a small tan leather suitcase and a white handbag looped over one arm, her train ticket in her hand.

"Well, here I go," Margaret said with a smile. "Heading off on my fishing expedition."

Mr. Doolin stepped forward. "Are you a passenger on this car, miss?"

"Yes, I'm going to Salt Lake City, in roomette four." Margaret handed her bag to the porter and showed him her ticket.

"I don't know that there's much fishing in the Great Salt Lake," Mr. Doolin told her.

Margaret laughed. "It's a different kind of fish."

Jill made the introductions. "Margaret, this is my friend, Mike Scolari. This is Margaret Vennor."

"I see." Mike shook Margaret's hand. "Jill has told me about you."

The conductor walked by, with his familiar cry. "Now boarding, the *California Zephyr*, destination Chicago, with stops in Stockton, Sacramento..."

"We need to find our car," Jill said. "Let's talk after the train leaves. Meet in the coffee shop?"

"Certainly," Margaret said. "Once we get rolling."

Mr. Doolin offered his arm to Margaret as she climbed into the vestibule. "Roomette four is just down the hallway, miss. You go ahead, and I'll follow along with your suitcase." He went inside the car, carrying Miss Vennor's bag.

Jill took Mike's arm and they walked past the six-five sleeper, coming alongside the dining car, which on this trip was the Silver Plate. Next was the dormitory-buffet-lounge car, the Silver Lounge. When they reached the Silver Sage, the third chair car, they boarded the train and located their seats, on the right side at the rear of the car. Mike lifted their bags into the overhead rack.

"Is Miss Vennor fishing for a ghost?" Mike asked.

"I know she is." Jill draped her cardigan over her shoulders and settled into the window seat. "She told me yesterday that she found out the Silver Gorge was going to be on the consist for this run. When she bought her ticket, she insisted on booking the same roomette where I found the body. And there's a reason she's going all the way to Salt Lake City. Doing that, she'll be traveling at night. She's hoping to experience whatever it is that I saw and heard."

He smiled. "You're sleuthing again, and she is, too. Trying to find out what really happened."

"What if I am? I'd just like to get answers to some questions."

"Go ahead. I wish you, and Miss Vennor, luck."

"Thanks," Jill said. "I think. In the meantime, let's relax and enjoy the journey."

She looked out at the platform. People hurried to board the train, or waved to someone who had already done so. A few minutes later, the conductor appeared at the side of the car, calling, "All aboard."

The engineer blew the horn twice, signaling that the train was moving. The *California Zephyr* pulled away from the platform. The train moved through the rail yard and the waterfront, past ships docked at the port. As it traveled, the engineer blew the customary warning that the train was approaching a crossing—two long whistles, one short and another long—for there were many intersections between streets and rails in this part of the city. Soon the *CZ* slowed, approaching the Western Pacific Station at Third and Washington Streets, signaling with one long blast on the whistle. It was a quick stop, taking on passengers. Then the train left the station, traveling past the fruit warehouses and meat packing plants, into the Fruitvale and East Oakland districts, neighborhoods full of canneries and factories. Once the train passed through the small community of San Leandro, famous for its cherry orchards, the next stop would be Niles. The small town was a flag station, which meant the train would stop only if there were passengers waiting to board.

A voice came on the train's public address system. Sally Hastings was making the Zephyrette's customary welcome-aboard announcement. Jill smiled and turned to Mike. "I can recite that from memory."

"After two years as a Zephyrette, I'll bet you can. Come on, I know you want to talk with Margaret. I'll go up to the Vista-Dome. You can meet me up there later."

Jill left her sweater in the seat. They walked to the buffet-lounge car, where the coffee shop was located. Margaret was already there, sitting at a small table, a cup in front of her. Mike kept walking and Jill sat down, ordering coffee from the nearby waiter.

"What did you tell your aunt and uncle?" Jill asked. "About this sudden trip to Salt Lake City?"

Margaret kept her voice low. "I just told them I felt the need to get away for a couple of days, on my own. Aunt Helen is distracted by preparations for the party this Saturday, so she didn't ask too many questions." She paused as the waiter delivered Jill's coffee. "Jill, after what happened last night... I might have been skeptical before, but we saw what we saw. And heard. That voice wasn't coming from outside Tidsy's apartment. It was inside. Right there in the room with us."

"I know. It was unnerving." Jill raised her coffee to her lips.

"If there's any possibility of making some connection with Kevin, I'm going to do it. That's why I agreed to go through with the séance. And that's why I'm taking the train, riding in the same roomette where Kevin died. Maybe I'll have the same experience you did, or something more." Margaret sighed. "I know people think I'm having a hard time getting over Kevin's death. But that's just the way it is. Finding out who killed the man I love is important to me."

"If only we could get a clearer picture of what he and that man were arguing about." Jill took another sip of her coffee. "Maybe riding the train will jog loose some more memories of that trip. And maybe I'll remember whose name was on the envelope I mailed. Let's finish our coffee and go up to the Vista-Dome. I'd like to look at the scenery as we go through Niles Canyon."

They paid for their coffee and walked back to the stairs that led to the upper-level dome. Mike was seated at the front and Jill joined him, Margaret taking a nearby seat. The *California Zephyr* slowed, the whistle blowing a grade-crossing warning as the train headed into Niles. There were passengers waiting to board at the little station. The *CZ* halted briefly, then began moving again, heading into the canyon, the tracks alongside Alameda Creek as both wound through the tree-covered slopes to the even smaller town of Sunol. After a stop in Pleasanton, the train headed across the Livermore Valley and climbed over Altamont Pass, dropping down into California's great Central Valley.

They stayed in the Vista-Dome, enjoying the 360-degree view from the windows. At this time of year, late July, the hillsides were golden-brown, since there had been no rain since May. In the distance were the Sierra Nevada Mountains, dark blue and green against the lighter blue sky, streaked with white clouds. The agricultural flatlands in the valley were a checkerboard of fields and orchards.

As the train approached Stockton, Margaret excused herself and went back to her roomette. "Let's meet for lunch, though."

"Noon in the dining car," Jill said. "That will give us plenty of time to eat before the train arrives in Oroville."

————

"That's the smallest mountain range in the world," Mike said, pointing out the window.

It was early afternoon. They'd had a pleasant lunch with Margaret in the diner and had returned to their car, the Silver Sage. Now they were seated up in the Vista-Dome, taking advantage of the scenery. The northern Sierra Nevada range towered to the east, but the mountains Mike was pointing at were to the west, where the flat plain of the Central Valley was broken by a much smaller patch of upraised rock.

"The Sutter Buttes? I've never heard them called a mountain range," Jill said. "They're so small and they don't spread for miles and miles like the Sierra Nevada or the Cascades."

"The buttes actually are a mountain range," he said. "And they're circular. The diameter's about ten miles and the mountains cover about seventy-five square miles. They're lava domes, from a volcano that's been dormant for over a million years. They used to call them the Marysville Buttes, but now they're called the Sutter Buttes, because they're in Sutter County. I've climbed South Butte. It's the highest one, over two thousand feet above sea level. Most of the land around there is privately owned, but I know a guy who knows a few of the owners."

"How did you become so interested in geology?" Jill asked. That was Mike's major at the university, where he spent most of his time in Bacon Hall, the mid-campus building where the Department of Geology was located.

He chuckled. "How could I not be interested in geology? I was born and raised in San Francisco. I have relatives who lived through the 1906 earthquake and the fire. They had to evacuate from North Beach and spend weeks camped out on the Presidio. I'm fascinated by the idea of how the landscape changes, with the faults lifting things up and moving them around. When I was a kid, my dad took me out to Point Reyes and showed me the earthquake fence."

"I've seen that," Jill said. "It used to be a straight line of pickets, and now there's a twenty-foot gap."

"When I was in the Army Air Corps, during and after the war, flying missions, I loved to look at the land I was flying over. The contours and the contrasts. It's fascinating." Mike gestured at the landscape visible through the curved windows of the Vista-Dome. "Back when I was growing up, we'd come up here to visit my aunt and uncle in Oroville. My cousins and I scrambled around the hills and hiked. You know, before they built all the dams and levees, the Sacramento Valley would turn into an inland sea."

"I've read about the flooding in eighteen sixty-two," Jill said. "The whole Central Valley was flooded, a lake three hundred miles long and about twenty miles wide."

"Right. It made an island out of the Buttes," Mike said. "I've read that the local Indians used to pack up and move to the mountains in the winter and spring. They knew about floods and flood plains. All that water, and those big floods, that's why this is such good farming land. My uncle says the state is talking about building a dam on the Feather River, up by Oroville. This part of the valley has some interesting archeology as well as geology. When my cousins and I went hiking, we'd always look for Indian artifacts, like stone tools and arrowheads. After all, this is where Ishi came out of the mountains."

Jill knew the story of Ishi, the last of the Yahi Indians, who had been wiped out during the late nineteenth and early twentieth century. Ishi had emerged from the mountains near Oroville in 1911. Hailed as the "last wild Indian," Ishi lived the remainder of his life with anthropologists from the University of California, until his death in 1916 in San Francisco.

The train made a brief stop in Marysville, then left the station. They would be in Oroville in half an hour. The farming community was in the foothills on the eastern rim of California's great Central Valley, where two large plateaus, North and South Table Mountains, loomed over the town. It was here that the Feather River spilled out of the Sierra Nevada Mountains onto the flat valley farmland. The town, founded in the Gold Rush days, was about seventy miles north of Sacramento. From here, it was another hundred miles or so up the scenic canyon to the *California Zephyr's* next stop, Portola.

As it reached the outskirts of Oroville, the train slowed, the whistle blowing frequent crossing warnings. Jill and Mike left the Vista-Dome and headed downstairs to collect their bags. Soon the *CZ* pulled into the station and stopped. They stepped down to the platform.

"Uncle Gaetano said he'd pick us up, but I don't see him," Mike said.

Jill looked toward the front of the train, where the conductor who had boarded the train in Oakland was greeting his replacement. Oroville was a crew change stop for the *CZ's* train and engine crews. The train crew, which included the conductor, brakeman and switchman, would be on board from Oroville to Winnemucca, Nevada. The engineer and fireman, who made up the engine crew, would ride the train to Gerlach, Nevada.

The new conductor turned, facing toward Jill, and she smiled. Pat Haggerty, her late fiancé's uncle, had been a Western Pacific conductor for years. He lived here in Oroville with his family. She had been hoping to see him while she was in town, but if he was about to leave on a run, this might be her only opportunity. She waved and walked toward Pat, looking trim in his uniform.

"This is a surprise," Pat said, catching sight of her. "Seems strange to see you out of uniform. What brings you to Oroville?"

Jill set her bag on the platform. "I'm here with a friend. Pat, this is Mike Scolari. And this is Pat Haggerty. Mike has family here."

"My aunt and uncle, Adalina and Gaetano Bianchi," Mike said, shaking hands.

"Bianchi," Pat said. "I know that name. They grow olives. And they've got a shop downtown, on Montgomery Street. I've been there. Good to meet you, Mike." Pat consulted his watch. "I have to leave in a couple of minutes. But I'll be back tomorrow. How long are you staying?"

"A couple of days," Jill said. "We're heading back to Oakland on Wednesday."

"I'll get in touch tomorrow, and we'll set up a time. We can have a cup of coffee and a piece of pie." Pat left them, walking along the platform with the familiar call, "Now boarding, the *California Zephyr*—"

Jill picked up her bag and they walked toward the station. Near the baggage office, an Asian man in work clothes was loading boxes onto a cart. He straightened and waved at Mike. The man was in his late thirties, Jill guessed, several years older than Mike. "Who is that?"

"His name's Kenzi Harada," Mike said. "We have a connection to the Harada family. Uncle Gaetano ran their farm during the war."

"When they were interned?" Jill asked.

"Yeah. When the order came, Uncle Gaetano said, That's not right. The Haradas have been here in Oroville since the eighteen-nineties. The Scolaris and Bianchis came over from Tuscany before World War One. A lot of those folks, they lost everything, had to sell their stores, their farms. Uncle Gaetano took over the Haradas' land. He farmed it, paid their taxes, and whatever money he got, he put it in a separate bank account for the family. When they came back after the war, he turned the money over to them. My uncle got some push-back from the locals, but I'm proud of him for doing that."

"I am, too. Why did your uncle decide to take a stand?"

"I told you my family came over from Italy before the big earthquake in nineteen-oh-six. They were from a little village near Siena. My Grandma Lucianna, she never became a citizen. So after Mussolini declared war on the States, right after Pearl Harbor, Grandma and other Italians who weren't citizens got declared enemy aliens. She even had an identity card. A couple of FBI agents came to the house, right there in North Beach. They took away a radio and told Grandma she was restricted, couldn't go more than five miles from home."

"That's terrible," Jill said.

"Yeah, but it was lots worse for the Haradas. The old people, the grandma and grandpa, they weren't citizens. But Kenzi was born here, and so were his brothers and sisters. Still, the government agents rounded them up and shipped them off to one of those concentration camps. There was all this panic on the West Coast and the politicians played right into it. People lost their farms, their houses and businesses. I've always thought it stemmed from the anti-Chinese feeling back in the nineteenth century."

"That's possible." From her history studies, Jill knew the Chinese Exclusion Act had been passed in 1882 and had only been repealed ten years ago, in 1943. "Things were somewhat different in Colorado."

When she was growing up in Denver, Jill had kept up with current events by reading the *Denver Post* and the *Rocky Mountain News*. That's how she knew that when the war started, Colorado Governor Ralph Carr, a Republican, opposed Executive Order 9066. As an attorney, he believed it was illegal to imprison American citizens without cause. Carr was the only western governor who was against the order and his stand cost him his political career, but he welcomed Japanese Americans to Colorado. Many already lived there, in Denver and in small farming communities, and others came to Colorado, even before forced removal from the West Coast began. Many of those Issei and Nisei were incarcerated in Colorado's only internment camp, Amache, which was located in the southeast corner of the state.

"There's Uncle Gaetano," Mike said.

The tall man walking briskly toward them had unruly gray hair atop a weathered face and a pot belly under his blue work shirt. The cuffs had been rolled up, showing ropy, muscled forearms. Faded denim pants and a pair of dusty work boots completed his outfit. Gaetano Bianchi waved at Kenzi Harada, then hurried toward Mike and Jill.

"Michele, sorry I'm late," he said in a raspy voice. He reached for Jill's hand, enveloping hers with his large, work-roughened palms. "So this is Jill. It's really good to meet you."

"I'm pleased to meet you, too, Mr. Bianchi."

"Gaetano, call me Gaetano." He took her suitcase. "Like I said, sorry I'm late. I got a few cases of olive oil to deliver to the store, if you don't mind us stopping there before we go out to the farm."

"Not at all," Mike said. "I'll help you unload."

The Oroville station was located where Oliver Street met High Street. Once Gaetano had loaded their suitcases into the back of his truck, the three of them got into the cab and he started the truck, heading down Oliver to Montgomery. He turned left and on the next block parked in front of a wood-framed building with a sign that read BIANCHI OLIVES. In back of the store, Jill saw trees along the banks of the Feather River.

A young man came out of the store and Jill was introduced to Mike's cousin Rinaldo. While the men unloaded the cases from the truck bed, carrying them into the store, Jill went inside to look around. The store was small, with shelves of green glass bottles of olive oil, all bearing labels that read BIANCHI. Other shelves contained jars of olives as well as jams and jellies.

After making the delivery, Uncle Gaetano drove them out to the farm, which was located four miles outside of Oroville, not far from the river. Jill had met Mike's father, and Aunt Adalina was his older sister. Olive orchards surrounded the two-story farmhouse and there was a large kitchen garden at the back of the house. As the pickup truck came up the drive and parked near the garden, Adalina came out to greet them, along with her two daughters, Lilianna and Donata. Both were in their teens, looking like younger versions of their mother.

Adalina hugged Mike, and when Jill held out her hand, she hugged Jill, too. Mike's grandfather, Salvatore Scolari, waved at her from the back porch. Jill had met him last December when he and Mike had boarded the train here in Oroville. They had been visiting Aunt Adalina and Uncle Gaetano and were headed to Denver to spend Christmas with Salvatore's younger daughter, Chiara, who lived there with her husband and children.

Jill leaned over to greet the old man and he kissed her on both cheeks. "I like seeing you with Mike," he said. "You and my grandson, you make a good team. I have been telling Adalina and Gaetano that maybe someday you'll be part of the family."

"We hope so," Adalina said. She kissed her nephew on the cheek. "It's time this one was married."

Jill smiled but didn't say anything. It seemed that everyone, including her mother and Mike's family, had expectations about her relationship with Mike. Why did everyone assume that just because she and Mike were dating that they were going to get married?

Adalina took over the handles of her father's wheelchair. Liliana held open the back door and Adalina wheeled the chair into the big kitchen. To the left a room off the kitchen, close to the downstairs bathroom, had been set up for Salvatore. A delicious smell wafted from the oven.

"Donata, make a fresh pot of coffee," Adalina said. "I have made a *pan forte* and we'll have some as soon as it's ready."

Chapter Fourteen

THE VISIT IN OROVILLE passed quickly for Jill and Mike. The younger Bianchi sister, Donata, had moved in temporarily with her older sister, Lilianna, so that Jill could have a room to herself. On Tuesday morning, after breakfast, Jill and Mike, dressed in dungarees and comfortable shoes, went for a long walk. They explored the olive groves on the Bianchi farm, where rows of trees with gnarled trunks and gray-green foliage were loaded with fruit that would be harvested in the fall. They hiked along the bank of a creek that ran through the property and had a picnic lunch on a rock overlooking a small waterfall. Later they toured the facility where the Bianchis pressed the olives they grew into oil and cured table olives, both processed for sale in their shop where, later that afternoon, Jill met Pat Haggerty, then walked down to a small café for coffee.

Now, late Wednesday morning, they waited on the station platform, Jill in the same outfit she'd worn on Monday. They were waiting to board the westbound *California Zephyr* for the trip to the Bay Area. As the train pulled into the station and stopped, Margaret Vennor was in the vestibule of her Pullman car. She waved urgently and called to Jill, who left Mike and Uncle Gaetano and walked over to the car.

"I have plenty to tell you," Margaret said. "Meet me in the dining car as soon as you get settled."

Jill nodded, then she returned to Mike, who was saying good-bye to his uncle. "Thanks for your hospitality," Jill told the older man. Despite Adalina's periodic hints that she hoped Jill would soon be Mike's fiancée, she had enjoyed spending time with Mike's relatives. They had quickly made her feel right at home.

"It was good to meet you," Gaetano said, kissing her on both cheeks. "You come back and see us again."

Jill and Mike climbed into the vestibule of the second chair car, the Silver Feather, as the conductor called, "Now boarding..." They located their seats and put their belongings in the overhead rack. Jill had an extra bag, containing two bottles, one of Bianchi olive oil and the other homemade Chianti, bottled by Uncle Gaetano. There was also a jar of olives and a package of Aunt Adalina's wonderful pastries.

The train pulled out of the station, moving through Oroville and its outskirts, heading south towards Marysville. They left their car and walked back to the diner, where Margaret waited at a table for four near the back of the car. It was not yet noon, so the car was half-full. They sat down, consulted the lunch menu and marked their meal checks, which were quickly collected by a white-coated waiter.

Margaret could barely contain her excitement. "I saw the shimmering light. And I heard things, too. The knocking sounds and the voices." At the look on Mike's face, she laughed. "Now, Mike, keep an open mind."

"I'm trying to." He poured himself a glass of water from the pitcher on the table and took a sip. "Go ahead, tell your story."

"On Monday night, I had the porter lower the bed at ten, but I was feeling restless, unable to sleep. I read for a while, then I turned out the light. It must have been around eleven o'clock. I didn't see anything right away. And then, gradually, this light appeared. It was similar to what you described, Jill. A shimmering light, near the ceiling." Margaret broke off her story as the waiter returned with glasses of iced tea for all three of them. "At first my reaction was, it must be some trick of the light. But it was the middle of the Nevada desert, so dark outside, with no light coming in the windows."

"Was the room cold?" Jill asked, remembering the chill she'd felt in the roomette during her own experience.

Margaret shook her head as she reached for her glass. "Not that

I could tell. Of course, I was in bed, covered with a blanket." She sipped her tea, then continued. "I lay there in bed, looking at the light, and it gradually disappeared. After that I must have dozed off. I woke up later because I heard—"

"The knocks," Jill said.

"No. Voices. Talking over one another. I couldn't understand what they were saying."

"It must have been someone in the corridor," Mike said. On Friday night, when Jill told him about the ghost, he had been skeptical about ghosts in general and the roomette ghost in particular.

"I got up and looked out in the corridor," Margaret said. "There was no one there. I really did see and hear something."

"Is that because Jill told you she saw and heard something?" he asked, taking on the role of devil's advocate. "You may have been predisposed to have an experience because of what she told you."

"It's possible," Margaret conceded reluctantly. "But I did hear something after I heard the voices. The taps."

Now the waiter returned with their lunches. Jill had ordered a ham sandwich, while Mike had opted for corned beef on rye, both with sides of potato salad. Margaret's choice was a chicken sandwich with tomato salad.

"The taps?" Jill picked up her sandwich and took a bite.

"The taps." Margaret speared a tomato with her fork. "Four short taps, just like you said." She glanced at Mike, but he kept his doubt off his face, working his way through a bite of corned beef. "Then, after a while, there were other taps. One short tap followed by a long one. Then after that, a short one, a long one, and a short one."

Jill reached for her handbag. Before leaving for Oroville, she had copied the Morse Code alphabet from her father's booklet onto a sheet of paper. Now she looked at her notes. She already knew that, in Morse Code, four short taps translated to the letter H. A short knock followed by a long was the letter A. Short-long-short was the letter R. Unlike the four short taps, there were no train signals that coincided with the other taps Margaret had described. What she and Margaret had heard must be Morse Code.

"If it's Morse Code, and I think it is," Jill said, "those taps are spelling out the letters H, A and R. But what does it mean? If it means anything at all, and I'm not convinced that it does."

"After what I saw and heard, I am," Margaret said.

"Is that because you want to be convinced?" Mike asked, wiping his hands on his napkin.

Margaret put her sandwich on the plate and looked at him. "Maybe I do. I got off the train in Salt Lake City early Tuesday morning, checked into a hotel and slept for a while. Then I got on this train very early this morning. I went right to bed and I didn't see or hear anything. Of course, the Pullman car I'm traveling in for this return trip is not the Silver Gorge. It's the Silver Palisade."

They looked up as an older man stopped and put his hand on the back of the empty chair at their table. "May I join you?"

That put an end to any talk of a ghost. Jill smiled at the newcomer and said, "Certainly. Please sit down."

———

The train arrived at the Oakland Mole on time. As she and Mike left the chair car and walked along the platform, Jill spotted the green-and-white Ford Victoria, with Lucy standing near the driver's-side door. Up ahead, Margaret had climbed down from the vestibule of her sleeper car. She tipped the porter and turned as Jill and Mike approached.

"I'll call you," Jill said. "Before the party on Saturday."

"Sure. We have plenty to talk about." Margaret walked to the line of taxis waiting to take passengers to their destinations.

They heard a car horn and then someone calling Mike's name. "There's my roommate." Mike waved, then he drew Jill into his arms and kissed her. "Call me, too, if we're going to this garden party on Saturday."

"I will." Jill watched him walk toward his car, then carried her suitcase to the waiting Ford.

"Welcome home," Lucy said as Jill put her belongings into the backseat. The sisters got into the car and Lucy started it. She put it into gear and drove away from the Mole. "Did you have fun?"

"I did. I really enjoyed meeting Mike's family. They're so warm, and welcoming."

"Wedding bells?" Lucy teased.

Jill felt a bit exasperated. "Not everyone is champing at the bit to get married."

"You were a few years ago. Before Steve died." Lucy piloted the car down Seventh Street, the thoroughfare looking as busy as it had last Saturday night when Jill and Mike had gone to Ozzie's. "Does it bother you that Ethan and I are getting married?"

"I already had this conversation with Mom." Jill glanced at Lucy. "Yes, with all your wedding preparations, I have been experiencing that what-might-have-been feeling. But I'm happy for you and Ethan. And I'm content with my life as it is right now. Mike's a nice guy and I like him a lot, but we've talked about it and we both have good reasons to wait before we make any decisions."

"Fair enough." Lucy drove through Oakland's Chinatown and made a right turn into the Tube that went under the estuary. Once on the Alameda side, she headed down Webster Street. When they arrived at home, Drew's Mercury was nowhere to be seen. "Baby brother sure has been moody these past few days. Do you know why?"

Jill sighed. "I do, but he has to be the one to tell all." And I hope he does it soon, she thought.

"Secrets between siblings?" Lucy laughed as she opened the driver's-side door and got out, tossing the keys in her hand. "Well, if you're sworn to secrecy, so be it."

They went inside the house and Lucy dropped the keys into the bowl on the hall table that held the downstairs telephone. Jill set down her suitcase and carried the bag containing the presents from the Bianchis back to the kitchen, where a pan of freshly baked gingerbread was cooling on a trivet near the store. Her mother was sprinkling spices on a rectangular Pyrex dish filled with chicken pieces.

"I'm home," Jill said, kissing her mother on the cheek. "And I had a good time."

"Good. Dinner will be about half an hour after I put this chicken into the oven. We'll have that, a big salad and French bread. I made gingerbread and I'm going to whip up a lemon sauce for it."

"I have some wine to go with it." Jill pulled a bottle from the bag. "Look, homemade Chianti, bottled by Mike's uncle. Also a big bottle of the olive oil that they sell and olives, of course. And some pastries that Mike's aunt baked. They're wonderful."

"Can't wait to try them. Your father will be home from work soon, but I don't know where your brother is. I'm looking forward to hearing all about your trip to Oroville."

Jill headed back to the hallway, where she looked through the envelopes and magazines on the wooden tray, but didn't see any letters addressed to her. She carried her suitcase upstairs. Sophie was curled up in the middle of the bed. The cat yawned and stretched, meowing as she demanded to be petted. Jill complied. "Home again, kitty, and I'll be here a few days before I leave again." She kicked off her shoes and changed clothes, putting on a pair of capri pants, a cotton blouse and her ballet flats. Then she unpacked her bag.

She walked to the head of the stairs and heard her mother and Lucy downstairs, talking. This seemed as good a time as any to call Tidsy, since the upstairs telephone, located in the hallway outside her parents' bedroom, was more private. She picked up the telephone receiver. When she heard the tone, she dialed Tidsy's number in San Francisco.

"I just got back from Oroville this afternoon," Jill said.

"Just so you know," Tidsy told her, "I have had no further manifestations from the spirit world. Although what happened Sunday night was quite an experience. I don't think I've ever had anything like that happen, and believe me, I've had some doozies."

"Margaret was on the train, both ways."

"Did she see the ghost?" Tidsy asked.

"The light, the voices, and the taps. But she heard more than just four short taps." Jill told her of the sequence of taps that Margaret had heard.

"H, A, R. I brushed up on my Morse Code after I talked with you," Tidsy added. "So the letters could be spelling someone's name?"

"Your guess is as good as mine. Maybe we can talk about it at the party on Saturday."

"Too many people," Tidsy said. "I have things to tell you, too. Let's get together before then, just you, Margaret and me. How about tomorrow? Or Friday?"

"I'm available both days," Jill said. "Although we do have company coming for dinner tomorrow evening and I'll need to help Mom get ready. I'll call Margaret and see whether she can meet with us either day."

When she disconnected the call, Jill wondered if it was too close to dinner time to call Margaret. Then she hear the front door open. Her father must be home from work. She went downstairs. Amos McLeod greeted his older daughter with a kiss on the cheek and glanced through the mail on the hall table, taking out several envelopes.

Lora McLeod appeared in the kitchen doorway, a dish towel in her hands. "Dinner will be ready soon. Drew's not home, though. He didn't say anything about being late."

"I'm sure he'll be along." As soon as Mrs. McLeod had gone back to the kitchen, Dr. McLeod beckoned to Jill. "Would you come into the study? There's something I want to discuss with you."

"Sure." Jill followed her father to his study at the back of the house. Dr. McLeod shut the door, then sat down in one of the upholstered chairs. Jill took the second chair.

"I did as you asked," Dr. McLeod said. "I spoke with my friend the pathologist who works for the Alameda County Coroner's Office. He let me have a look at Mr. Randall's autopsy results."

"What did you find out?"

"Mr. Randall did have a damaged heart valve, consistent with his having had rheumatic fever. Problems with heart valves that are associated with rheumatic fever include mitral stenosis, aortic stenosis, and aortic insufficiency, or any combination of those three. People with these heart valve problems often have a heart rhythm we call atrial fibrillation. That's an irregular heartbeat. I've had patients who've described it as feeling like a butterfly in the chest. Digoxin is a medicine containing digitalis and it's used to control the heartbeat. Mr. Randall died of valvular heart disease and digitalis toxicity, according to the autopsy results. Since the prescription bottle was found near the body, the medical examiner did check the Digoxin levels. They were elevated."

"An overdose," Jill said.

Her father nodded. "Mr. Randall took too many pills. Perhaps he mixed up his medicines, had an episode of atrial fibrillation and took too much, either all at once, or several incidents over several days. It happens frequently. I had a patient last year who over-dosed on Digoxin, though fortunately he didn't die. The excess of digitalis causes the heart rate to slow, leading to shock and death. It can also cause a dangerously rapid heartbeat, which also leads to death. There was something else. The medical examiner noticed some abrasions around Mr. Randall's mouth, and it appears at some point he bit his tongue. I'm not sure how that happened or what it means."

Jill sighed. "Thanks, Dad. I appreciate your taking the time to do this." Now she would have even more to tell Tidsy when they met.

There was a knock on the door, then Mrs. McLeod opened it. "Hey, you two. Dinner's ready. Drew still isn't home. We'll just start without him."

They sat down at the table, which held a big wooden salad bowl filled with greens from the garden, the baked chicken, and a tray bearing a loaf of bread. Dr. McLeod opened the Chianti and poured wine for all of them.

They had just started eating when Drew arrived. "Sorry I'm late," he called from the hallway. He detoured into the downstairs bathroom for a quick hand wash, then joined them at the table. "This looks great, Mom," he said, piling salad and chicken on his plate. "Hey, Sis, how was your trip to Oroville?"

Jill cut into a piece of chicken and launched into the tale of her travels. It was a typical evening meal for the McLeods. At least it was until after they'd eaten pieces of gingerbread topped with lemon sauce.

Then Drew took a deep breath and said, "Mom, Dad, there's something I want to tell you. I'm going to drop out of school."

Chapter Fifteen

THE DISCUSSION BETWEEN Drew and his parents, heated at times, went on long after Jill and Lucy cleared the dinner dishes from the dining room table and escaped to the kitchen, where Jill covered the remaining chicken with aluminum foil and found a space for it in the refrigerator. She scraped the rest of the salad into a container and set the salad bowl aside.

The McLeods had a Frigidaire Dishmobile, a dishwasher on wheels with a butcher block top. It had a hose and fitting that connected the kitchen sink faucet. Jill wheeled the dishwasher from its usual corner to the sink where Lucy was rinsing off the dishes.

"What do you think?" Lucy asked, a plate in her hands. "Our brother the bluesman?"

Jill opened the front of the dishwasher and pulled out the bottom rack. She began loading plates. "I think he should do what he wants."

"I thought he was already doing that, on weeknights and weekends." Lucy handed over more plates. "But to leave school and do it full time?"

"Have you ever heard him play?" Jill asked.

"Sure, here at home."

"I mean, at a club." Jill loaded forks and spoons into the dishwasher. "I have, last weekend when Mike and I went to West Oakland. Drew is really a talented musician. I can't blame him for wanting to see if he can make a go of it."

Lucy shook her head. "But dropping out of college to go

roaming around from town to town, playing music? Can he make a living doing that? Playing music for the rest of his life?"

"I don't think it's about making a living." Jill reached for a handful of table knives. "He's barely nineteen. I don't know that he's thinking of what to do for the rest of his life. Just what he wants to do for now. We don't know what the future holds, for any of us."

She thought of her other self, the one who had been engaged to marry Steve. That Jill thought she had all her plans in place. She was going to walk down the aisle with Steve, then teach school until she and Steve had babies. Then everything had changed in what seemed like the blink of an eye. That Jill was very different from the one who sported a uniform and rode the trains from Oakland to Chicago and back again. And this Jill, the one standing here in the kitchen with wet hands, knew that life must be lived now, not some time in the future.

They heard raised voices coming from the living room and looked at each other, then continued their kitchen cleanup in silence.

After the fallout of Drew's bombshell on Wednesday evening, Jill never did get around to calling Margaret. She did so Thursday morning after breakfast, while her mother and sister were still in the kitchen.

"I have several commitments today," Margaret said. "How about Friday for lunch? I'm going shopping that morning. I want to pick out a new dress for the party. How about one o'clock? At Thelma's Tea Room on Telegraph Avenue."

"That's fine. I'll call Tidsy and set it up." Jill disconnected the call and dialed Tidsy's phone number. "Lunch with Margaret tomorrow in Oakland. Margaret suggested one o'clock, but I think we should meet earlier. I have a lot to tell you, and I don't want to say it on the phone."

"All right," Tidsy said. "I'll meet you at twelve-thirty. That should give us time to talk. Where are we having lunch?"

"At Thelma's Tea Room. It's on Telegraph Avenue near Six-teenth Street."

"Tea?" Tidsy laughed. "I'm a scotch-on-the-rocks girl. I usually prefer something stronger than a pot of Darjeeling."

"I know that," Jill said. "But Margaret picked the place. She has some shopping to do downtown, and this is nearby."

"Oh, well," Tidsy said. "I can sling tea with the best of them. See you tomorrow."

Jill hung up the phone as her mother came out of the kitchen, carrying a basket that held cleaning rags and a bottle of furniture polish. She set this in the hallway near the front door and opened the hall closet, taking out the Hoover upright vacuum cleaner. She wheeled it into the living room. Jill picked up the basket and followed. The McLeods' home was usually quite presentable, but company was expected for dinner tonight. Besides, Jill suspected, her mother was taking refuge in housework after Drew's announcement and the subsequent discussion.

"What can I do to help?" Jill asked.

Mrs. McLeod unwound the vacuum cleaner cord and plugged it into the nearest electrical outlet. "I'll do the living room. I need something to occupy my mind. Would you and Lucy polish the good silver?"

"Sure." Jill headed for the kitchen and corralled her sister. "Mom wants us to polish the silver."

"My goodness, we're putting on the ritz." Lucy finished her coffee and set the cup in the sink. "It's just cousin Doug and his new wife."

"You know how Mom is with company. It's the first time she's met Pamela. I know she wants to make a good impression."

They went to the dining room and Jill opened the lower door on the sideboard, removing the wooden case that held the silverware. In Lora McLeod's house, stainless steel cutlery would suffice for everyday, but company meant the good silver and the special china. Lucy pulled out the polish and cloths and the sisters set to work, accompanied by the sound of the vacuum cleaner running in the living room.

"Was it love at first sight?" Lucy asked. "Doug and Pamela, I mean."

"Yes, I believe it was." Jill smiled at the memory. "I knew it the minute I introduced them."

Doug Cleary was the son of Lora McLeod's brother Sean, a retired Denver detective. He was nearly eight years older than Jill, who was the eldest of the three McLeod children. For years Doug had been something of a black sheep, at odds with his father, but the two were on better terms now. Growing up in Colorado, Doug was an avid skier, a member of the Rocky Mountain Branch of the National Ski Patrol. During World War II, he joined the Tenth Mountain Division and trained in winter survival and skiing at Camp Hale, then he'd gone to northern Italy, where he had been among the thousands of ski troopers who had been wounded in action.

Doug was also a skilled gambler, good enough to make a living at poker. Last April, he had been traveling to California on the *California Zephyr*. So had Pamela Larch, a Southern belle from Jackson, Mississippi, who had been on the lam from an engagement to a man she really didn't want to marry. When Jill introduced them in the Vista-Dome, sparks flew. Pamela had been heading for San Francisco, but she never got there. Instead, she left the train with Doug in Portola. Doug was meeting a friend there, to discuss plans to open a ski resort high in the Sierra Nevada. A short time later, Jill got a telegram announcing their marriage. They were living in South Lake Tahoe and this trip was a delayed honeymoon for the couple.

"I knew Ethan was the one for me," Lucy said now, polishing a serving spoon. "I went sailing with some friends and there he was. To think, I almost didn't go."

Jill smiled. "I wasn't sure about Steve. I met him at a mixer on campus. He asked me out twice before I finally said yes. Now, pass me that silver polish."

———

Pamela Cleary had a twinkle in her blue eyes as she declared, "Well, I finally made it to San Francisco. And I love it. What a wonderful city. I'm sure I'll enjoy finding out all about the history here in the Bay Area. We have lots of history in Mississippi, but it's different."

They were sitting on the patio in back of the McLeod house, drinks in hand, talking before dinner. Pamela's long blond hair was caught back in a loose ponytail. She wore a sundress made of crisp cotton, a blue background printed with tiny pink and yellow flowers. Her arms below the short puffy sleeves were tanned, indicating she'd spent some time in the sun recently. A white cardigan sweater was draped over her shoulders, just in case the tiny wisps of fog coming in from the bay lowered the temperature.

Doug, tall and blond, wore a short-sleeved checked shirt on this summer evening, showing the scar on his right arm. It ran all the way from his shoulder to his wrist, and it was the result of encounters with shrapnel and barbed wire during the war. "We're staying at the Chancellor Hotel near Union Square. We have quite an itinerary planned for the next few days. San Francisco, then down the coast to Monterey. Until today, Pamela had never seen the Pacific Ocean."

"It's different from the Gulf of Mexico," Pamela added. "The gulf can be rough during hurricane season, but the ocean, it's fierce, I would say."

"We have a saying here in California," Jill said. "Don't turn your back on the ocean. There are big waves called sneaker waves, that come up unexpectedly and sweep people off the shore, out to sea."

"And rip currents," Dr. McLeod said. "Even in shallow water, they can drag you out to sea."

"My goodness, how inhospitable." Pamela laughed. "I'll be afraid to stick my toe in the water. Doug is preparing me for winter up in the mountains. He tells me a train was stuck in a blizzard up there last year."

Jill nodded. "That was terrible. The train was the *City of San Francisco*, a Southern Pacific streamliner. That train travels on a route that's higher than the Feather River route and sometimes they have problems with the weather. The train was stuck for six days but they got the passengers out after three days."

The story had been all over the newspapers and newsreels in January 1952. A huge storm with fierce winds had piled drifts high. On January 13, the *City of San Francisco* rammed into a snow slide and was stranded at Yuba Pass, about twenty miles west of Donner Pass. Snow-clearing equipment and snow-blowing rotary plows were sent to reach the train, but they froze on the tracks near Emigrant Gap. With 196 passengers and twenty crew members aboard, a huge rescue effort began, with hundreds of railroad workers as well as volunteers. The Sixth Army sent vehicles that could travel over the snow, as well as soldiers trained in winter survival, while military doctors and nurses were dispatched to likely rescue locations. Rescuers worked to clear nearby Highway 40, in order to reach the train. Ski patrols ferried food and other supplies to those onboard. After thirty hours, the streamliner ran out of diesel fuel, plunging the train into cold darkness. Finally the rescuers were able to evacuate all those on board, moving them on foot along the tracks to vehicles that then carried them to safety. Those who were weak or sick after the ordeal had been carried out on toboggans. No one aboard the train died, but two rescuers did. It took three more days to extricate the train.

"It was scary," Jill said now, remembering the photographs she'd seen of the stranded train and the rescue. "I've never been in weather that severe, in the Sierra or the Rockies."

"I hope I can manage the winters," Pamela said. "Cold weather in Mississippi means rain. I told you before I'd never seen snow until a family visit to Wisconsin."

Doug gave his new wife a fond look. "We'll get you some good cold-weather clothes. Besides, I'm going to teach you to ski."

"How are things going with plans for the ski resort?" Dr. McLeod asked.

Doug, Pamela and Bud, Doug's friend from Plumas County, were now partners in the venture, along with several other investors. They had purchased a defunct ski resort near Lake Tahoe's north shore and were in the process of refurbishing it, hoping to open by the time ski season rolled around later that year. Doug told them about what he and the others were doing to upgrade the ski runs and lifts, while Pamela added, "I'm redecorating the insides of the buildings, the main lodge, the hotel rooms, the restaurant and ski shop. I'm having such a good time with all these plans. Doug, while we're here, I really do need to pay a visit to some restaurant supply stores. We've got to have new dishes and glassware, not to mention pots and pans."

"Speaking of pots and pans," Lora McLeod said, "I need to check on dinner."

"I'll do it, Mom." Jill stood and went up the back steps. In the kitchen she opened the oven door and pulled out the rack. A pork roast surrounded by apples and onions, glazed with spices and honey, sizzled in a pan. Jill used a meat thermometer to check the roast's temperature. It was nearly done. She put the roast back in the oven and surveyed the kitchen counter, which held a big green salad and a basket of rolls. Her mother had visited a friend in Sonoma County earlier in the week and had brought home a bushel of Gravenstein apples, the first flavorful apple of the season, so there was a freshly baked apple pie for dessert, the golden-brown lattice crust oozing apples sprinkled with cinnamon and other spices.

In the dining room, the table was set for seven—five McLeods, plus Doug and Pamela. Lucy was out on the patio with her parents but Drew wasn't home. He'd made himself scarce after breakfast, and Jill wondered if he would appear for dinner.

Just then, the front door opened and Drew came in, wearing the same frown on his face that he had last night and this morning.

"I wondered if you were coming home," she said.

He shrugged. "Got to be polite and put in an appearance. Where is everybody?"

"Out on the patio. Go wash up."

As Drew headed upstairs, Jill went to the back door to report. "Another five minutes is my guess."

"Then we'd better come inside," her mother said. "After we have dinner, we'll make the ice cream and talk. Maybe we can play some games."

"How about poker?" Doug said, with a laugh. For years he had made a decent living with his skills at the card table.

"With you?" Dr. McLeod shook his head. "No, thanks. I'll keep my money in my wallet, where it belongs."

As they went inside the house, Pamela reached for Doug's hand and he squeezed it. Jill was pleased to see her cousin and his new wife looking so happy.

In the kitchen, Lora McLeod leaned toward Jill and said, "Is your brother home?"

Jill nodded. "He's upstairs, getting cleaned up. Don't worry, Mom. Everything will work out."

"I hope you're right." Her mother sighed and opened the oven door.

Jill and Lucy carried food to the table and everyone ate their fill of the delicious meal. Pamela insisted on helping with cleanup as the men went outside to the patio, to start their contribution to dessert. The McLeods had a hand-cranked ice cream maker, a wooden tub with a metal can that fitted inside. Mrs. McLeod had made the mix earlier, with heavy cream, eggs, sugar and vanilla. Now she poured it into the cylindrical cream can and put in the large beater, which she called the dasher. She carried it out to the backyard, where Dr. McLeod had filled the tub with ice and rock salt. Now he, Drew and Doug took shifts at the crank, turning it until the liquid in the can turned into rich vanilla ice cream. In the meantime, Jill put on the coffee to perk, while Lucy and Pamela cut slices of pie and put them on trays, ready to take outside.

"Ice cream's done," her father called.

Outside, her father lifted the beater from the can. Jill took it from him. She couldn't resist swiping a finger along the edge of the beater, scooping up ice cream.

"Let me have a taste," Lucy said, reaching for the beater.

Jill held it out of her reach, then Drew relieved her of it. "I get the beater. After all, I cranked the handle for half an hour."

Doug laughed. "What about my contribution?"

"Let them have it," Dr. McLeod said, as he plopped a spoonful of ice cream atop a piece of apple pie. He handed it to his wife. "While the children are fighting over the beater, that just means more ice cream for the grownups."

Chapter Sixteen ─────────

THELMA'S TEA ROOM was located in downtown Oakland, on Telegraph Avenue, a narrow storefront restaurant in the middle of the block. Jill arrived first. She checked her reflection in the window, smoothing the full skirt of her flowered piqué dress.

She had driven to downtown Oakland in the Ford, parking near the tearoom. There were many more cars on the streets today than usual. The familiar Key System buses that usually filled the streets, moving passengers all over the East Bay, were gone. The employees had gone on strike a week earlier. That morning's newspapers had speculated how long the strike might last, and so did the passersby. The subject seemed to be on everyone's lips. Two women walked past and Jill overheard them talking. "My husband usually takes the bus to work and now he has to drive."

"Surely it will be over soon," the other woman said. "That strike back in nineteen forty-seven lasted eighteen days, the paper said."

"That's almost three weeks. I certainly hope this one doesn't last that long."

Tidsy sauntered around the corner in a white cotton dress decorated with red polka dots, a big leather purse swinging from her arm. She greeted Jill with a wave. "Lots more traffic today. I'm sure it's because of the strike."

"Yes, I noticed the same."

Tidsy opened the door and they went inside. The tea room looked as though it had been furnished from someone's attic, with tables of varying size, some small enough for just two people, while others were intended for larger parties. The tables were set with white cloths and napkins, a teacup and saucer at each place and a small vase of flowers on each table. Mismatched chairs were tucked under the tables. Cabinets and bookcases were arrayed against two walls, all holding an assortment of china teapots, cups and saucers. On the back wall was a counter with a cash register, and a display of items for sale, such as packaged teas and teapot cozies.

A waitress in a white uniform with black collar and cuffs greeted them. "Table for two, ladies?"

"There will be three of us," Tidsy said, as she pointed. "How about that table there, in the corner by the window?"

"Certainly, ma'am. Please follow me." The waitress showed them to the table.

Jill opened the menu. "Let's have tea while we're waiting. I'll have a pot of Earl Gray." She liked the distinctive taste and had read that the tea leaves were flavored with the oil of the bergamot orange fruit.

"Darjeeling," Tidsy said with a wink, reminding Jill of their conversation the previous afternoon.

The waitress nodded and left, returning a short time later with two pots of tea. Jill's pot was rounded, the white china decorated with blue flowers. Tidsy's pot had a squared shape, and it was pale yellow with red flowers.

Jill turned over her teacup, which was in the classic Blue Willow pattern. She set the silver strainer on top of her cup and poured. She didn't normally use sugar but today she decided to drink her tea as the English did, so she stirred in sugar and milk.

Tidsy took her tea straight. After swallowing a mouthful, she said, "How was your trip? Did you have a good time?"

"I did. I enjoyed visiting Oroville, and meeting Mike's family. They're nice. But..." Jill's voice trailed off.

Tidsy tilted her head and raised her eyebrows. "But? What?"

"Lately it feels as though lots of people are telling me what to do with my life. Namely get married and have babies. I get it from Mom. Which is to be expected, because she's my mother. I get it from various other family members. I even get it from passengers on the train. Usually in the form of 'It's nice that you're a Zephyrette, but sooner or later you'll want to settle down.' And on this trip to Oroville, I got it from Mike's family. I like them, but Mike's grandfather and aunt acted as though Mike and I are practically engaged, and all that's left is to set the date. The only person who doesn't make assumptions is Mike. I know he's thinking along the lines of us getting married, but we've talked about it and I've told him I'm not ready for that kind of commitment. Not yet. And he's fine with that."

"Society's expectations," Tidsy said. "We all get the party line, from family and those damned women's magazines, which are full of fantasy rather than reality. We're supposed to get married and have kids, defer to our husbands, be the support troops, not career women. Well, I got married. He died, and then I discovered I liked being a career woman just fine. Although I got put out to pasture after the war was over. Don't buy the party line, Jill. I know you'd like to scream and tell people to mind their own damn business. But sometimes you have to smile and move on."

Jill picked up her teacup. "That's what I have been doing. But it's good to be able to talk about it with someone who understands. My sister's getting married later this year, so right now she and my mother are occupied with wedding preparations. Marriage and family are in the air at the McLeod manse, and I admit to being a tiny bit weary of it. What about you, the career woman? I know you left your government job at the end of the war. And I get the feeling that you work from time to time."

"I do keep my hand in," Tidsy said.

"But you don't say at what." Suddenly Jill struck the table with her hand. "You'd make a great private investigator."

"Really?" A smile played on Tidsy's lips. "Tidsy on the case, hmm. Me and Sam Spade? I thought I was more the Brigid O'Shaughnessy femme fatale type."

"Femme fatale, maybe. But Sam Spade was interested in justice, while Brigid was just interested in the falcon. You're on the side of good, not evil." Jill checked her watch. "Margaret will be here soon. Before she gets here, I want to tell you about a conversation I had with my father, after I talked with you on Wednesday. He's a doctor, as you know. Last week, I told him about Kevin

Randall's death. I asked him about heart damage due to rheumatic fever. Dad said he knows someone in the coroner's office and he told me he'd see if he could get a look at Randall's autopsy results."

Tidsy's blue eyes sparked with interest. "Did he?"

"Yes. He told me Randall had a damaged heart valve that would cause something called atrial fibrillation, an irregular heartbeat. Digitalis is used to control the heartbeat. According to Dad, Randall's death was caused by valvular heart disease and what he called digitalis toxicity."

"An overdose of digitalis," Tidsy said.

Jill reached for the teapot and strainer, pouring more tea into her cup. "Randall had a prescription for Digoxin. I found the bottle near his body. It's one of several prescription medicines that contain digitalis. Dad thinks it's possible Randall took the overdose himself. He says it happens all the time, with patients who have an episode. So Randall could have taken too much Digoxin, or made a mistake about how much he'd taken earlier in the day, or over a few days."

Tidsy's look turned speculative. "But you don't think so."

"It's possible, yes." Jill added sugar and milk to her tea. "But Dad said there were abrasions around Randall's mouth and that he'd bitten his tongue. How did those injuries happen? Were they accidental? Could he have bitten his tongue when he was dying? Or did it happen while he was having lunch?"

"If Randall was murdered," Tidsy said, "someone gave him that overdose. Maybe that accounts for the abrasions, and tongue."

"Who would have access to Digoxin?" Jill asked. "And how would that person administer an overdose?"

"Digitalis is foxglove," Tidsy pointed out. "And foxglove is a very common ornamental plant. It grows everywhere. I understand the whole plant is toxic, right down to the roots and seeds. If the flowers have been in a vase, even the water is deadly. If someone gave Randall an overdose of pills, I'm guessing the killer has access to the drug, either a prescription for Digoxin, or a family member or friend who uses it. As for how, whether it was poisoned water, chopped-up foxglove or pills, the fatal dose could have been mixed with food or drink."

"Mr. Randall sat at my table during lunch," Jill said. "I didn't see him consume anything but coffee or tea the rest of the time. But that's not to say he didn't."

"The man you saw arguing with him would be a logical suspect," Tidsy said. "But would Randall have consumed anything he offered?"

"I doubt it." Jill had a thought just then, but it was fleeting, going out of her head. She wondered where Margaret was. They had agreed to meet at one o'clock, and it was after that now. Just then, she looked out and saw Margaret coming up the sidewalk, wearing a summery yellow shirtwaist.

Margaret entered the tea room, carrying bags from Capwell's and Kahn's, two of Oakland's larger department stores. She walked over to the table and sat down, putting the shopping bags on the floor at her feet. "I'm a bit late, I'm sorry. Hello, Mrs. Tidsdale. It's nice to see you again."

"Oh, call me Tidsy. Everyone does. Come on, girls, I'm hungry. Let's get this tea party on the road."

The waitress stopped at their table and Margaret chose a pot of English Breakfast tea. After the waitress returned with a third teapot, they ordered a full tea for three.

"I've been doing some research," Tidsy said. "Kevin's job involved reviewing the financials of companies under the Vennor Corporation umbrella. We know he was on a business trip to Plumas County, because that's what he told Jill on the train." Now Tidsy reached for her oversized handbag and took out a notepad and a thick sheaf of printed pages. "I got hold of a Dun and Bradstreet business information report for the Vennor company. It tells me a lot about the corporation, of course. Now, what I was looking for was in the history section of the report. That usually lists the names and business descriptions of affiliated companies. In this case, there are quite a few affiliates, since your Uncle Dan has been building a bigger empire." She flipped open the notepad, the first sheet covered with handwriting. "I went through the list of affiliated companies and looked for businesses in Plumas County. I made a list. There are five in all."

Jill took the list and scanned it. As she had speculated during her earlier conversation with Margaret, the companies in Plumas County were mining and lumber concerns. The Soda Ridge Mining Company had an address in Quincy, along with Tidsy's note saying the mine's operations were actually located in Belden, in the western part of the county. Sierra Lumber Mills was located in Chester, up by Lake Almanor in the north county. In the eastern part of the county, two mining companies, Grizzly Mountain and Penman Peak, had addresses in Portola, though the mines were located in Spring Valley and Blairsden, both west of Portola. The Mohawk Valley Lumber Company had a Portola address. Jill knew from her travels that the valley was between Portola and Blairsden.

"Not an H among them," Jill said, thinking of the four taps that she had heard, possibly Morse Code for the letter H. But Margaret had heard more taps, spelling different letters. "Of course, this doesn't tell us the names of the people who run these companies. Which would be helpful." She glanced at Margaret. "Once your uncle buys a company, does he leave the previous owners in charge?"

"I have no idea," Margaret shook her head as she read the list. "I've never heard of any of these companies. And I don't recall hearing Kevin mention them." She handed the list to Tidsy.

"It would make sense to leave the previous owners in charge of the day-to-day business operations. I'll dig deeper and see what I can find out." Tidsy put the report and list back in her handbag. "Now, Margaret, I understand you had an interesting encounter on the train. Tell me about it."

Just then the waitress arrived with their order, on a three-tiered tray, with sandwiches at the bottom, scones in the middle, and tiny pastries on the top. Tidsy inspected the sandwiches and wrinkled her nose. "Cucumber, I don't think so. Now, roast beef, that's for me." She picked up the sandwich and set it on her plate.

Jill had no problem with cucumber sandwiches. She took one of those, and added a scone.

Margaret chose a scone and a chicken salad sandwich. "Yes, I had a very interesting trip in roomette four. I saw the shimmering light. I heard voices, two voices, I think. But they were talking over one another and I couldn't make out any words. And I heard the taps. Four short taps, like the ones Jill heard, and the ones that we heard after the séance."

"I've been doing some reading," Tidsy said. "Those taps are quite common. The term for it is ghost knocking."

"But the taps aren't random," Margaret said. "They seem to be spelling out something and I think Jill's right, it's Morse Code. There were four short taps, then silence. Then one short tap followed by a long one. Another silence, followed by a short tap, a long tap, and a short tap."

"In Morse Code, that would be—" Jill began.

"The letters H, A and R," Tidsy said. "I see what you mean by that list of company names. Not an H among them. Neither do we have an A or an R. So what does it mean?"

They sat in silence for a moment, eating their scones and sandwiches. "I have an idea," Jill said. "About the séance."

"You mean hold another one?" Tidsy asked. "I suppose we could try holding it on the train, the next time the Silver Gorge is in the rail yard in Oakland."

Jill shook her head. "This is something we can do tomorrow at the party. We don't have to hold a séance. If our goal is to find out who killed Kevin Randall, we can get just as much mileage out of the threat of a séance."

Tidsy nodded as she finished off her sandwich. "I see where you're headed."

"I don't," Margaret said. "What do you mean?"

"We smoke out the killer," Tidsy said.

Jill elaborated on her plan. "The man I saw on the train the day Kevin died is big and bulky. He has a long nose and cold, unpleasant blue eyes. When I described him, Margaret, you told me you're certain you've seen him before, maybe because he works for your uncle's company. If that's the case, he might be at the party tomorrow afternoon. If this man is there, here's what I think we should do. Tidsy, you ask Margaret about her recent trip to Salt Lake City. That gives Margaret her opening. She brings up the reason she took the trip, to ride in the supposedly haunted roomette."

Tidsy laughed. "Perfect. Margaret, you announce that you're

certain Kevin was murdered and that his ghost is trying to contact you. Then I'll bring up the séance, saying that we ought to hold one and see if we can contact Kevin to find out more about his killer. That will knock everyone for a loop, especially the guilty party."

Margaret looked dubious, pushing aside the crust of her chicken salad sandwich. "I should say it will. I can just hear what my aunt will say."

"Helen will be all right with it," Tidsy predicted. "Jill, you watch and listen. Keep an eye on Long Nose to see how he reacts to all of this. But watch yourself. We don't want him realizing that he's seen you before because you were the Zephyrette on that run."

Jill nodded. "I figure if this man has taken all these steps to make Kevin's death look like natural causes, hearing that Margaret thinks it's murder should make him nervous. And nervous people make mistakes."

"Indeed they do," Tidsy said. "It should work, if Long Nose shows up."

"If he doesn't," Jill said, "it's back to the drawing board." She looked at the top of the three-tiered tray, at the little desserts assembled there. "Now I am going to have that lemon tart."

Chapter Seventeen

JILL DRESSED WITH CARE for the Vennors' garden party, in a short-sleeved dress, with pink rosebuds and blooms scattered on a white cotton background. The dress had a slim skirt and a V-neckline that showed off the gold chain she fastened around her neck. Her low-heeled, open-toed white shoes completed the ensemble. She carried a white straw handbag as she went down the stairs to the living room.

Her father had gone out after breakfast, to play tennis with a friend on the courts at a nearby city park. Drew had disappeared right after breakfast, saying he was going to West Oakland to rehearse with his band mates. Lucy, too, had left the house early. She and her fiancé had loaded up Ethan's car with beach gear and a packed picnic basket, then they headed for the coastal town of Half Moon Bay and a picnic with friends. Jill had eaten a light lunch with her mother earlier. Now she found Mrs. McLeod relaxing on the chair in the living room bay window, her feet on the ottoman, the cat on her lap. A glass of iced tea was on a nearby table, along with several books.

"We're all leaving you alone today," Jill said.

Her mother laughed. "I don't mind a bit. I'm going to sit here and read all afternoon." She stroked the cat, who shifted, stretched and circled into a tight ball, putting her paws over her nose. "Sophie and I will hold the fort. You look lovely. The weather's just right for an outdoor party. Blue skies and warm temperatures, but it's not too hot. What time is Mike picking you up?"

Jill looked at the clock above the mantel. It was nearly one o'clock. "He'll be here in a few minutes."

"I thought the party started at two," Lora McLeod said.

"It does. But I want to have plenty of time to find the address." That wasn't the only reason, though. During lunch on Friday, Jill and Tidsy had agreed to arrive early, to meet Margaret's aunt and uncle and, as Tidsy put it, get the lay of the land.

Mike came to the front door shortly before one, dressed in white shirt, tan slacks and lightweight sports coat. He greeted Jill with a quick kiss on the cheek and came inside to say hello to her mother.

"Have a wonderful time," Mrs. McLeod told them as she picked up a book. "I'll look forward to hearing all about the party."

They walked out to Mike's Hudson, which was parked in the driveway. Leaving Alameda, they traveled through the Tube to Oakland, then around Lake Merritt to Lakeshore Avenue. Jill consulted her handwritten note, the directions that Margaret had given her the day before. "Take Lakeshore to Trestle Glen Road, then turn left onto Sunnyhills Road and right onto Hillcroft Circle." As Mike approached the intersection of Sunnyhills and Hillcroft, Jill looked at the street sign. For some reason, Hillcroft sounded familiar. But she couldn't recall why. Maybe she had been here before. After Mike made the turn, she said, "It's the fifth house on the right, with a circular drive."

"I see it. I'll park on the street. Easier to make our getaway." He pulled the Hudson to the curb just before the driveway, which was marked by a large brass mailbox on a post, with black numbers denoting the address. They got out of the car. As they walked toward the drive, a horn blared behind them. Jill turned to see a bright red convertible pull up behind Mike's car, Tidsy at the wheel. They detoured to meet her.

Mike gave an admiring whistle as he ran a hand over the car's sleek hood. "That's the new Dodge Coronet. Great-looking car."

Tidsy opened the driver's-side door and stepped out of the car, wearing a red dress with a white geometric print, the crimson fabric very nearly the same shade as the car's paint job. "You like it? I bought it a few months ago. A V-eight, handles like a dream. Good to see you, Mike. You too, Jill." She reached into the car and snagged her purse, a red leather bag with brass buckles that went with her shoes. "So are we ready for this shindig?"

Ready as I'll ever be, Jill thought, thinking of the strategy she, Tidsy and Margaret had discussed yesterday.

They walked up the circular drive that led to the Vennors' two-story house, which was built in the Mediterranean style, with a white stucco exterior and a tile roof. Pale green trim surrounded the windows. Above the front door was an arch decorated with a half-circle relief of green leaves. Rose bushes clustered in front of the windows, with blooms of pink and yellow. On either side of the door, large ceramic pots glazed in the same shade of green held bright red geraniums. The front door was oak, with a large circular brass knocker and a doorbell on the right side.

Mike rang the bell. The door was opened by a Negro maid wearing a crisp white uniform. "Good afternoon, Mrs. Tidsdale."

"Hello, Agnes," Tidsy said. "All set for the party?"

The maid smiled. "Yes, ma'am, we certainly are. Come on into the living room and I'll let Mrs. Vennor know that you're here."

The maid ushered them into a central hallway and then to the living room on the right. The spacious room had cream-colored walls highlighting various paintings, mostly landscapes. A bright oriental rug in shades of blue, green and red covered most of the hardwood floor. Mossy green drapes hung on the front window, framing another view of the roses outside. French doors on the back wall stood open, leading to a patio. There was a fireplace on the long wall, with framed family photographs lining the mantel. The room was furnished with a low, modern sofa and two matching armchairs upholstered in a nubby green fabric.

Jill walked to the French doors and looked out. The patio was a semi-circle, paved in red and gold flagstones, with wide, shallow steps going down to the lawn. Several big ceramic pots were grouped here and there on the patio, displaying geraniums, with blooms in red, white, pink and coral. Colorful curved metal chairs, light green and blue, were arranged around small round tables. Beyond the patio, additional tables and chairs had been set up all around the wide lawn. Margaret had told Jill that the party was catered. Jill saw the door leading to the kitchen, and through this, maids and waiters were carrying platters of food out to the long buffet table at one end of the patio. At the other end of the patio was a full bar staffed by two bartenders.

"Tidsy! You and your friends are here. Welcome." Helen Vennor was a tall woman with short salt-and-pepper hair above a pleasant, round face. She wore a full-skirted dress of pale blue seersucker, covered with a pattern of tiny white flowers. Jill recognized her from that day at the Oakland Mole. Mrs. Vennor was a good head taller than Tidsy, the difference marked as she put her arm around the smaller woman. "Good to see you, old friend."

"Who are you calling old?" Tidsy cracked, in mock anger. "We have known each other a long time, I agree. Thirty years ago, Helen and I were flappers together, drinking bathtub hooch and dancing the Charleston. They used to call us Mutt and Jeff."

Jill laughed. "Tidsy, I can just picture you dancing the Charleston."

"I was damned good at it, too."

"Much better than I was." Mrs. Vennor extended her hand to Jill. "Miss McLeod, I remember you from that day at the Oakland Mole, when poor Kevin... It was so kind of you to call me, and to stay with Margaret until I arrived."

"Thank you for inviting me. This is my friend, Mike Scolari."

Mrs. Vennor shook their hands. "Margaret will be down soon. Here are Dan and the children."

She turned as a tall, well-built man joined them, followed by two teenagers. The man was in his fifties, dressed in a lightweight summer suit. This was Daniel Vennor, Margaret's uncle and the head of the Vennor Corporation, where Kevin Randall had worked. With him were the Vennors' two teenaged offspring, Charles and Elizabeth, otherwise known as Chuck and Betty. Chuck was seventeen, the older of the two, tall like his father, with his brown eyes and regular features. Betty, who was fourteen, had a round face and a gangly adolescent frame. She resembled her mother.

"I shut Skeeter in the bedroom, like you asked," Betty told her mother.

"Thank you. We have a dog, a rapscallion of a mutt," Helen Vennor said. "We love her but if we leave her out during the party, she'll be climbing in everyone's laps."

"Eating the canapés is more like it," her husband said.

"Now that we've all met," Tidsy declared, "point me to the bar. I need a drink."

Dan Vennor laughed. "Back this way, Tidsy. I have a new single malt scotch you should try." They all went out to the patio, where a bar had been set up. Mr. Vennor poured a scotch for Tidsy, then asked Jill and Mike what they wanted to drink.

"Nothing right now, thank you," Jill said. "Maybe later."

Mike took a beer. As Daniel Vennor and Tidsy discussed the merits of the scotch, Jill and Mike walked to the edge of the patio, looking out at the lawn. Roses and rhododendrons lined the redwood fences surrounding the backyard. A moment later, Margaret joined them, wearing a pale green linen dress that set off her dark hair. "Come on, I'll give you the tour." She led the way, showing them through the house.

The afternoon sun was warm when they returned to the patio. Other guests were arriving, some sitting in the living room, others heading out the French doors to the patio and the backyard. People greeted each other and mingled, moving from group to group, gathering at the bar and the buffet table. The noise level increased, a pleasant buzz of conversation mixed with the clink of silverware on plates and ice cubes in glasses. Jill heard scraps of conversation, weaving in and out, as people discussed baseball, movies and the two biggest news stories of the day, the Armistice in Korea and the Key System strike.

"It's quite a crowd," Jill said.

"My aunt and uncle know lots of people," Margaret said, pointing out the publisher of the *Oakland Tribune* and a member of the city council. "Those people near the bar are from Uncle Dan's company, and that woman in the yellow dress does volunteer work with Aunt Helen. I'm sure you've met important people on the train."

"I certainly have. Most recently Angelo Constanza, the opera singer, and Lydia Stafford, the writer."

Jill heard someone call her name and turned to see another Margaret, this one older and a familiar face. Benjamin and Margaret Finch had been passengers on the same train journey back in December, when she'd also met Mike and Tidsy. The same run, in fact, with the writer, the opera tenor, and his wife. Mr. Finch owned several canning factories located in Oakland's Fruitvale district and his wife was well-known in East Bay social circles. It wasn't surprising that they would know the Vennors. Jill and Mike talked with the Finches for a few minutes, with Jill asking after their two daughters, Nan and Cathy. Then the Finches moved away, to talk with other partygoers.

Jill turned to Mike. "I'll have that glass of wine now."

They walked to the bar, where the white-coated bartender poured a glass of Chardonnay for her. At the buffet table, they filled plates, choosing from a bountiful array of appetizers, everything from deviled eggs to mushroom caps to canapés spread with cheese or deviled ham and walnuts dotted with flavored cream cheese. One chafing dish was filled with Swedish meatballs, another with bacon wrapped around dates. Big bowls at each end of the table held melon balls and strawberries. Jill tried not to go overboard, but it all looked delicious and she had to sample a bit of everything. She nibbled on a puff pastry filled with shrimp and scanned the crowd, but she didn't see the bulky man who had been arguing with Kevin Randall on the train. Margaret had been sure the man worked for the Vennor Corporation. But Long Nose, as Tidsy referred to him, wasn't here now. Jill saw Tidsy across the table, a glass of scotch in one hand, a plate of canapés in the other. At the questioning look in Tidsy's eyes, Jill shook her head. She finished the puff pastry and set the plate on a nearby table that had collected glasses and plates. Mike was nearby, talking with another man who had also been in the Army Air Corps. Margaret was farther away, in a group of three young woman.

Jill took another sip of wine. Then, with a start, she saw the man she was looking for. The beefy man's frame was as big as ever inside his light gray suit. He had a bland expression on his sallow face and his pale blue eyes swept over the partygoers. He looked right at Jill, then his gaze moved on. Good. She was hoping he wouldn't recognize her as the Zephyrette who had been on the train that day. Most people saw the uniform, not the person wearing it. Still, she couldn't be sure.

Now the man walked over to Daniel and Helen Vennor, who greeted him with smiles and handshakes. Then Helen Vennor turned to speak to another guest. Jill moved closer, hoping to hear something of the conversation between Vennor and the newcomer.

"...should have that by the middle of the week," the man said.

Vennor nodded. "What about..." Jill couldn't hear the rest of what he said because he'd turned his head away. Then he moved his head again, and she heard him say, "...Plumas County. I have some concerns about that. We really need to finish it, and soon."

The big man nodded. "I agree. I'll go up there and talk with Pierson, later this week."

"Sounds fine," Vennor said. "Now, this is a party. Let's keep the shop talk to a minimum. Get yourself a drink, and something to eat."

"Of course," the big man said, with a smile. He headed for the bar, and Jill followed a few steps behind. She heard him order a gin and tonic.

Plumas County, she thought. And someone named Pierson. Who was Pierson? Did he have a connection with one of those affiliate companies in Plumas County?

Jill went looking for Margaret and found her talking with an older woman near the buffet table. At the look on Jill's face, Margaret excused herself and walked toward Jill. "What is it?"

Jill nodded in the direction of the newcomer. "The man at the end of the bar, the one in the light gray suit. That's him. The man I saw arguing with Kevin. Have you seen him before?"

Margaret turned and studied the man, speaking in a low voice. "Yes. When you said he had a long nose, I thought this might be him. His name is Wade Hardcastle. He was Kevin's supervisor."

Was he also Kevin's killer? Perhaps they would find out.

"Then we proceed as we discussed," Jill said. "Let's find Tidsy." She set down her wineglass and looked around. Tidsy was no longer at the buffet table. Then she heard a raucous laugh and followed the sound out to the lawn, where Tidsy was working her considerable charm on a silver-haired man who had been introduced earlier as a superior court judge. Margaret followed, a few steps behind.

Tidsy saw them and took the last swallow of scotch, then raised her empty glass, rattling the ice cubes. "Lovely talking with you, Judge. Now if you'll excuse me, I'm going in search of a refill." She stepped away from the man and turned to Jill and Margaret.

"He's here," Jill said. "On the patio near the bar."

Tidsy's sharp blue eyes took in the people on the patio. Hardcastle turned away from the bar. He crossed the buffet table, and began loading food onto a plate. "I see him. He really does have a long nose."

"I overheard him talking with Mr. Vennor. He mentioned Plumas County, and someone named Pierson."

Tidsy nodded. "Probably someone who's working for one of the businesses up there. Well, it's show time, girls. We all have our parts to play."

Margaret moved away first, heading for the patio. She stopped near Hardcastle. Tidsy headed for the bar. Jill followed a few steps behind her. Hardcastle, plate in hand, moved away from the buffet and back toward the bar. He sipped his drink and set it down on a table, then picked up a canapé, taking a bite. Tidsy stepped up to the bar and ordered a fresh scotch. She took a sip, winked at Jill, then turned to Margaret, speaking in a voice loud enough to draw attention. "Margaret, I hear you went to Salt Lake City. Were you visiting friends?"

Margaret followed Tidsy's lead. "I don't know anyone in Utah. I went for another reason. There's a car on the *California Zephyr*. It's called the Silver Gorge. That's the car my fiancé, Kevin Randall, was traveling in when he died. In roomette four. As it happened, the Silver Gorge was on the train when I went to Salt Lake City. And the trip was interesting in so many ways."

Jill hovered near the bar, watching Hardcastle. When he heard Kevin's name, he turned in Margaret's direction, alarm visible on his jowly face.

"Yes, I heard about your fiancé's death," Tidsy said, her voice sympathetic. "I'm so sorry for your loss. So this trip was some kind of pilgrimage?"

Margaret reached for the engagement ring that she now wore on the chain around her neck. "I suppose you could call it a pilgrimage. I've heard stories, from several sources, that roomette four on the Silver Gorge is haunted. By Kevin."

Her words fell like a stone in a pond, with ripples spreading outward as people stared at her. Helen Vennor put down the glass of wine she'd been holding and quickly walked to her niece, distress on her face. "Margaret, what an odd thing to say. You can't possibly believe—"

"Oh, but I do." Margaret looked positively beatific as she fingered the engagement ring like a talisman. "Kevin is trying to tell me something. You see, I don't believe he died of natural causes. I think he was murdered."

The color drained from Wade Hardcastle's face. He stared at Margaret in disbelief, then he frowned. He raised his glass to his lips, slamming down a large portion of his gin and tonic.

Now the whispers grew louder, as people stared at Margaret and then at the pained expressions on the faces of her aunt and uncle.

"A ghost?" Tidsy let loose with a laugh. "What a hoot." She sashayed over to Margaret, scotch in hand. "A ghost, huh? I've got a great idea. We'll hold a séance. Maybe we can even hold it on that rail car, the Silver Gorge. I know somebody at Western Pacific. I'll bet he could arrange to let us do that. Maybe that ghost can tell us what it wants us to know. I know this fabulous medium over in San Francisco, Madame Latour. She's very good. When it comes to communicating with the dead, she gets results. Why, once she even discovered the identity of a killer."

By now, Tidsy was drawing a crowd. Some people tittered nervously, others looked taken aback at this odd turn in the conversation. Jill kept her eyes on Wade Hardcastle, consternation visible on his face. He drank the rest of his gin and tonic and turned away, heading for the bar. He elbowed his way past a man and a woman standing there and ordered another drink.

In the meantime, Helen Vennor took Tidsy's arm and steered her away from the onlookers, speaking in a low, urgent voice. "Tidsy, what in the world are you thinking? A séance? For heaven's sake, Margaret is having a difficult time dealing with Kevin's death. This kind of talk just encourages her to hold on. I realize it's only been two months since he died, but she needs to move past it. All this talk of a ghost and a haunted railroad car and now a séance. It's nonsense. Please don't encourage her."

Tidsy looked unperturbed as she rattled the ice cubes in her scotch glass. "It will take more than a few months for Margaret to get over this loss. She needs to grieve in her own way, Helen. If that means a ghost and a séance, so be it. She is old enough to make up her own mind."

Helen tugged at Tidsy and they moved out of hearing range, conversing in whispers. Margaret walked over to Jill and so did Mike. He directed his words to Jill. "You knew that was going to happen, didn't you?"

"I did," Jill confessed, with a sidelong glance at Margaret. "Tidsy, Margaret and I planned it."

Mike frowned. "I wish you would have let me in on the secret. What was the purpose?"

"We wanted to get someone's attention," Jill said. "And we did. Besides, we already had a séance. On Sunday night, before we left for Oroville."

Mike narrowed his eyes. "And you didn't tell me?"

"Nothing happened during the séance. Not until after the medium left. Then we heard those taps."

"I haven't ruled out holding another one," Margaret added. "If it will help me find Kevin's killer, I'll call Madame Latour myself and set it up."

"So this very public announcement is a ruse?" Mike asked. "Whose attention did you get?"

Jill inclined her head. "See that man over by the bar? The big man in the gray suit, with the long nose?"

Mike scanned the people near the bar and nodded. "I see him. Who is he?"

"Wade Hardcastle," Margaret said. "He worked with Kevin."

"More importantly," Jill added, "he's the man I saw arguing with Kevin on the train."

Now Tidsy joined them, a thoroughly unrepentant look on her face. "Margaret, I'm afraid your aunt is upset with me. With you, too. You're going to hear from her later. Jill, how did our subject react?"

"He didn't like what he was hearing about ghosts and séances. He went white as a sheet."

Mike shook his head. "What are the three of you up to? Nothing good, I'll bet."

Tidsy took a pack of cigarettes from her purse, stuck one in her mouth and fired up her lighter. "We're trying to smoke out a killer. Let's see what he does next."

Chapter Eighteen ——————

WHAT HARDCASTLE DID NEXT was down another gin and tonic—and leave the party.

The bulky man with the long nose jostled his way to the bar after hearing Tidsy hold forth about the ghost and the séance. He swallowed his drink quickly, then sought out his host and spoke briefly to Daniel Vennor. Then he looked around, his gaze lighting on Margaret and then Tidsy. Jill shrank back, turning away so he couldn't see her face. In her peripheral vision she saw him go through the French doors to the living room.

"I'll make sure he's gone," Mike said. He followed and returned a moment later. "He went out the front door and down the street. So you've seen the last of this guy for now. I'll leave you ladies to your plotting. I'm going to get another beer." He walked toward the bar.

"We did indeed get his attention," Tidsy said.

"Now what?" Jill asked.

"We'll have to wait and see. Sometimes setting the wheels in motion is enough. As for now, I'd better make it up with Helen. She's not too happy with me."

Margaret nodded. "I know. I'll be extra nice to her the rest of the weekend. Let's go in the house. After our little scene, people have been staring at me and whispering."

"And I could use the bathroom," Jill said.

"I'll show you where it is." Margaret led the way into the house, directing Jill to the downstairs bathroom. When Jill came out a few minutes later, she paused in the hallway. Margaret was near the front door, talking with her cousin Betty, who was sitting on the bottom step of the staircase leading to the upper level. Judging from the conversation, Betty, bored with the party full of grownups, had left to go play with Skeeter the dog.

The front door opened and Agnes, the maid who had greeted them earlier, entered the house, carrying a handful of envelopes and several magazines. "The postman just went by. I saw him and got the mail."

"Anything for me?" Betty asked. "I'm expecting an invitation to a birthday party."

Agnes shook her head. "Nothing, Miss Betty." Betty sighed and headed in the direction of the kitchen. "But this letter is for you, Miss Margaret."

Margaret took the envelope addressed to her and glanced at the return address. "It's from a college friend." She turned the envelope over and stuck her little finger in the edge of the flap.

Jill stared at the writing on the front of the envelope. But she wasn't really seeing this envelope. It was another envelope she pictured. She reached out and stayed Margaret's hand. "Wait."

Margaret glanced at her. "What is it?"

"Let me look at that, please."

When Margaret handed her the envelope, Jill held it closer, examining the address written on the front. Jill called up an image of the envelope Kevin had given her. She remembered looking at it before she dropped it into the mailbox on the platform in Sacramento. That's why the Hillcroft Circle street sign had looked so familiar when she and Mike were driving to the party. She had seen that street name before.

"Hillcroft Circle," Jill said. "That's it. The address on the envelope that Kevin asked me to mail, that day on the train. It was addressed to you. He was going to see you later that day, when you met the train at the Oakland Mole. Why would he mail a letter to you? Unless there was something in it, something important. Something he didn't want his killer to find. What was in that envelope?"

Now Margaret looked distressed. "You told me this before, and I said I don't remember receiving anything from him. But—" Now she frowned. "Right after Kevin died, I was so upset. People sent me condolence cards and I didn't even open them. I still haven't. I shoved them in a drawer in my desk."

"We have to find that envelope."

"Come on." Margaret led the way upstairs to her bedroom, at one end of a long hallway. The room looked similar to Jill's own bedroom. A small teddy bear, its brown plush fabric worn in places, sat atop the pillows plumped against the oak headboard. A bookcase near the window held an assortment of books, and several framed photographs, including one of Margaret with Kevin. On the other side of the bed was a desk with three drawers on the right side. Margaret left the letter she'd just received on the desk top. She pulled out the bottom desk drawer and carried it to the bed, dumping the contents on the bedspread. The unopened envelopes must have numbered two dozen or more. Using both hands, Margaret spread the envelopes across the bed, turning each one over so the addresses were visible.

"There it is." Jill pointed. She recognized the envelope, thicker than the others, with its *California Zephyr* legend and the cluster of stamps in the upper right corner. The postmark over the stamps was smudged, but enough was visible to see that the envelope had been mailed from Sacramento. And she recognized the spiky slanted letters that spelled out "Miss Margaret Vennor" and the address of the house on Hillcroft Circle.

Margaret picked up the envelope, her voice subdued. "It's his handwriting." She reached for the cup on the desk and pulled out a small brass letter opener. She slit open the envelope and pulled out several folded sheets of paper. She unfolded them and spread them out on the bed, shoving the other envelopes out of the way. "This is what he mailed to me. But why? I don't understand what it is."

Jill looked at the sheets, some of them pale green, with lines covered with figures and ragged edges indicating they had been torn from a book. The other sheets were yellow and lined, legal-sized, also covered with figures, and notes in Randall's handwriting.

"I know why, at least I do now," Jill said. "He mailed these pages to get them away from someone who wanted them. These must be from the ledger and pad he was working on. We know he was up in Portola to look at the books of a company that your uncle's corporation had acquired, probably one of those companies on the list that Tidsy compiled. Kevin had one of those mechanical calculators with him in the roomette. My guess is that he was checking figures from the ledger. He found something that wasn't right, something that would be revealed by these papers. When he argued with the man on the train, he realized that he needed to hide them. So he put these in an envelope and asked me to mail them to you, thinking he would retrieve them later. When I found the body, the ledger and the legal pad weren't in the briefcase. Whoever killed him must have taken both. But they didn't know he'd torn sheets out of the ledger and the pad. Now we have them."

"We do. But what do they mean?" Margaret fingered the papers, looking at the figures written in small, neat lines. "It's like number soup. I don't understand any of this."

"I don't either," Jill said. "And I don't see anything that identifies the company. But I'll bet Tidsy can figure it out. Let's give these papers to her."

"Agreed." Margaret folded the sheets of paper and stuck them back in the envelope. Then she put the envelope in her dress pocket.

They went downstairs, looking for Tidsy. She was out on the patio, helping herself to food from the buffet, piling Swedish meatballs on her plate. "Did you taste these meatballs? They're delicious. I may have to take some home with me."

"We need to talk with you," Jill said.

Tidsy looked from Jill to Margaret, replaced the serving spoon in the chafing dish, and picked up her drink before stepping away from the table. She gestured with the hand that held the scotch. "What we need is a secluded corner, not that we're particularly secluded at this shindig. That corner, by that rose bush." They stepped off the patio, following Tidsy across the yard to the rose bush, which was covered with lush, dark red blooms that perfumed the air with their fragrance. The small table that had been set up nearby was vacant. Tidsy took a swallow of her drink and

set it on the table, then plunged a fork into one of the meatballs.
"What gives?"

"We found the letter I mailed for Kevin," Jill said. "It was
addressed to Margaret."

Margaret hastened to explain. "I didn't realize I had it, until
Jill remembered—"

Tidsy cut her off with a wave of her fork. "Never mind that.
You've got it now. What was inside?"

When Margaret pulled the envelope from her pocket, Tidsy set
her plate on the table and opened it. She studied the green and
yellow sheets while Jill explained her theory that Kevin had mailed
them to get them out of the killer's hands.

"Plausible," Tidsy said. "Quite plausible. Now, to figure out
just what was going on."

"Neither of us knows anything about accounting or keeping
books," Jill said. "But I have a feeling you can tell us what's going
on."

Tidsy smiled. She folded the papers and put them back in the
envelope. "I have some passing familiarity with numbers, gained
during my days in Washington." She frequently called herself a
"government girl," never giving any details of what she'd done
in the service of her country, but Jill knew that the older woman
had worked for the Office of Strategic Services, the OSS. She had
a feeling Tidsy's participation in the war effort had involved more
than typing and filing.

"I'm leaving on a run tomorrow," Jill said. "I'll be back from
Chicago next Saturday."

Tidsy put the letter in her red handbag and reached for her
scotch. "I'll look these over and we can confer when you get back."

Chapter Nineteen

THIS IS SILLY, JILL THOUGHT. I might as well go to bed.
She was sitting in roomette four of the Silver Gorge. It was
late Friday night, and the *California Zephyr* was somewhere in the
Nevada desert, moving west toward the next station stop in Elko.
Nothing had happened. In fact, she had dozed off twice and was
now fighting to stay awake.

So much for her experiment in communicating with a ghost.
Once again, she told herself she wasn't sure there even was a ghost.

Then she heard four taps, one right after the other.

Her heart began to pound.

Perhaps the experiment was working after all.

Jill had left the Bay Area on Sunday morning, the day after
the party. The *California Zephyr* had arrived in Chicago Tuesday
afternoon. The eastbound run of the Silver Lady had been routine.
She spent Tuesday and Wednesday nights in the Windy City, then
on Thursday afternoon she reported for the westbound run back
to the Bay Area. As she walked along the platform, she saw that
the Silver Gorge was on the consist. An idea began to take shape.

Lonnie Clark, a Chicago-based porter, stood near the vestibule,
and he waved at her. "Good to see you, Miss McLeod."

"Hello, Mr. Clark. Do you have a full car this trip?"

He nodded. "Leaving Chicago, anyways. I've got quite a few
people getting off in Omaha and Denver."

I wonder who is traveling in roomette four, Jill thought as she
hurried to her appointed spot. At Chicago's Union Station, the
Zephyrette stood with the Pullman conductor at the back of the

dome-observation car, on this trip the Silver Planet. There they greeted passengers, directing them to their cars, and Jill made dinner reservations for those passengers traveling in the sleeper cars.

Later, as the *California Zephyr* sped across Illinois, Jill made one of her periodic walks through the train. Stopping in the Silver Gorge, she introduced herself to the passenger who was traveling in roomette four. He was an older man with a shock of unruly gray hair, eager to talk. "Todd Saunders, from Evanston, Illinois. I'm going to Provo, Utah to see my daughter. She's married to a school-teacher and I have three grandkids. My wife went out there earlier in the month, but I couldn't get away from work until now."

"I know you're looking forward to seeing your family, Mr. Saunders. Enjoy your trip."

'I'm sure I will. I brought some books I've been meaning to read. And I hear the food in the dining car is really good."

"It is," Jill said, resuming her walk-through. She'd have to wait until tomorrow morning to see if anything supernatural paid Mr. Saunders a visit during the night.

The rest of the afternoon and evening was uneventful. Jill retired to her compartment early, working on her trip report before opening one of the Juanita Sheridan novels she'd brought to read. She rose early Friday morning, took her usual sink bath and put on her uniform. Then she left her quarters and headed for the Silver Café, the dining car for this run. She was drinking her first cup of coffee when she was joined by Mr. and Mrs. Greenleaf, a middle-aged couple from New York City, who were traveling all the way to San Francisco in the transcontinental sleeper.

"A second honeymoon," Mrs. Greenleaf said, smiling at her husband. "We're going to stay at the Saint Francis hotel, right on Union Square."

The Greenleafs marked their meal checks and handed them to the waiter. Jill was well into her usual breakfast of French toast and bacon, when Mr. Saunders sat down at the table. After intro-ducing himself and exchanging pleasantries, he poured his first cup of coffee from the pot on the table, then he looked over the menu. "I shouldn't be hungry after that excellent pot roast I had last night. But I am. Bacon and eggs for me, an English muffin and a glass of orange juice." He marked the meal check and the waiter took it.

Jill smiled at him. "Did you sleep well, Mr. Saunders?"

What she really wanted to know was whether he'd seen or heard anything during the night. A ghost perhaps?

"Indeed I did. I always sleep like a log, especially on trains. You could shoot a cannon down the corridor and I wouldn't hear it."

"So do we," Mrs. Greenleaf said. "There's nothing like sleeping on a train. It must be the motion, and that sound of the wheels on the rails. It lulls me to sleep every time. Where are you from, Mr. Saunders?"

"Evanston, Illinois. And you?"

"New York City."

"I've been there," Mr. Saunders said. As the waiter delivered his breakfast, he picked up his form and regaled the Greenleafs with his stories of visiting New York City while he was in the Navy during World War II.

Jill cut the corner off her French toast and dredged it through a puddle of melted butter and syrup. So much for that. The man was a sound sleeper. He didn't hear a thing in that supposedly haunted roomette.

The train arrived in Denver soon after, with passengers departing the train and others boarding. The *CZ* exchanged its Chicago, Burlington & Quincy locomotives for those of the Denver & Rio Grande Western, and the CB&Q crew gave way to D&RGW personnel. Then the train pulled slowly out of the Mile High City's Union Station, heading west. It climbed the S-curve at Big Ten and entered the canyons and forested slopes of the Rocky Mountains. As the *CZ* approached the Moffat Tunnel, Jill was up in the Vista-Dome of the Silver Planet, explaining that the long tunnel bored under the Continental Divide. The lower elevations were clear, but the highest peaks, towering above the tree line, showed their year-round cover of snow. After going through the tunnel, the train emerged on the western side of the divide, at the Winter Park ski resort, with bare slopes waiting for next winter's snowfall and skiers. The little town of Fraser and Fraser Canyon were next, then Granby, where the train joined the Colorado River, traveling through remote and beautiful canyons carved over millennia. Jill sat in the Vista-Domes of various cars, pointing out the landmarks, talking about Colorado history, and answering questions from the passengers who reveled in the scenery.

When the train reached Dotsero Canyon, Jill went downstairs to the Silver Club, where she asked Mr. Griggs for coffee. She was greeted by a chorus of *"Guten Tag, Fraulein* McLeod.*"*

She returned the greeting. *"Guten Tag."*

A boisterous quartet of Germans, college students on holiday in the United States, had boarded the train in Denver, traveling in the chair cars. They had been hiking in Rocky Mountain National Park, and now they were traveling to Grand Junction, planning to explore the Colorado National Monument. "We like taking the train," one student told her. "This part of your country is very different from where we live, near Bremen." In talking with the four young men, Jill had welcomed the opportunity to practice her German. During her two years as a Zephyrette, dealing with passengers from all over the world, she had picked up a smattering of different languages.

Jill took her coffee to a small table. At the next table were an older couple, about the age of Jill's parents, drinking coffee. As the students conversed in their native language, the man glanced at them, then looked away. Finally, when the students left the lounge, the man said, "Germans. Nine years ago I was coming ashore at Omaha Beach, Germans shooting at us like we were ducks at a shooting gallery."

"They're just kids," his wife said. "Nine years ago, they were probably in grade school."

The man kept his voice low. "Nine years ago, they were probably in the Hitler Youth."

The woman put a hand on his arm. "The war's over. It's water under the bridge."

"I know," he said. He took a sip of coffee. "Except when I ache from that shrapnel in my hip."

Nine years, Jill thought. A long time, and not so long. In 1944, she had still been in high school in Denver. She remembered the newspaper headlines heralding the D-Day landing where the man at the next table had come ashore, in Normandy.

She finished her coffee and took the cup back to Mr. Griggs. Then she went upstairs to the Vista-Dome above the Silver Club. She sat down in the only available seat, near the back, next to a young man named Mr. Martin, who had boarded the train in Denver. He was about the same age as the German students and he was traveling in roomette seven on the Silver Gorge. Earlier that day, he'd told Jill that he'd just graduated from the University of Colorado in Boulder, where he'd studied geology. "The man I've been seeing is studying geology, too," Jill told him. Mr. Martin looked a bit disappointed at this mention of a boyfriend. Which was why Jill had brought it up.

Now, as the train wound through Glenwood Canyon, he drew an audience of other passengers as he pointed out the geologic features and the various kinds of rock that made up the canyon's steep walls.

Jill said, *"Auf Wiedersehen"* to the German students when they got off the train in Grand Junction. The afternoon sun and the vibrant red sandstone put on a spectacular show as the train wound through Ruby Canyon. Jill had dinner in the dining car, lingering over coffee and talking with passengers as the train left Helper, Utah and climbed Soldier Summit.

It was after nine when the train stopped in Provo, Utah. Jill was in the vestibule of the Silver Gorge, watching as Mr. Saunders stepped off the train to the platform. His family was waiting for him, greeting him with hugs. The *California Zephyr* left the station a moment later.

Jill walked up the passageway and glanced into roomette four, which had just been vacated by Mr. Saunders. The roomette would be empty tonight. Why not? This would be an opportunity to see—and hear—whatever might be lurking there.

She usually stayed up until the train reached Salt Lake City. Then she would go to bed, sitting up in her pajamas as she worked on her trip report, perhaps reading her Juanita Sheridan novel before turning out the light. Tonight she went to her compartment in the Silver Club, the buffet-lounge car. She made notes of the day's activities for the report. The rhythm of the wheels changed and the engineer blew the warning signals as it approached a crossing. Jill glanced out the window and saw the lights of Salt Lake City. Soon the *California Zephyr* slowed and pulled to a stop in the Salt Lake City station.

She went through the dining car to the Silver Thrush, the first sleeper car, where the porter was assisting an elderly woman who was departing the train. Jill stepped down to the platform and looked around. Toward the rear of the train, four people were boarding the Silver Poplar, the sixteen-section sleeper. She turned and walked forward, past the diner and buffet-lounge cars. The three chair cars—the Silver Dollar, Silver Ranch and Silver Schooner—ranged behind the baggage car. Salt Lake City was another equipment and crew change stop, where the Denver & Rio Grande Western Railroad handed off the Silver Lady to their counterparts from the Western Pacific Railroad. The five D&RGW diesels that had pulled the train over the Rockies had already been uncoupled and moved to a siding. Now three WP locomotives backed up to the train and were locked in place.

The doors on the side of the baggage car were open, and several large boxes were being loaded from a wheeled cart. The baggage man signed for the cargo and the station baggage crew moved the cart back toward the station. Nearby, the new Western Pacific conductor, Bill Dutton, conferred with Gerald Carville, the Denver & Rio Grande Western conductor who had boarded in Grand Junction. Jill said hello to both men, waved at the new WP brakeman, then climbed back on the train at the nearest vestibule, the third chair car. The two conductors parted, with Mr. Carville walking toward the station as Mr. Dutton checked his watch. He straightened his cap and called, "Now boarding, the *California Zephyr...*" as he began walking alongside the train. A few minutes later, he came back this way. His call had changed to "All aboard."

Up in the front locomotive, the engineer blew the whistle, signaling that the train was about to leave. Then the *California Zephyr* pulled out of the station.

Jill stood at the vestibule window and watched as the lights of Salt Lake City receded. The world outside the window grew dark. She knew the train would travel along the Great Salt Lake's southern shore, crossing a small arm of the lake at Lakepoint. Somewhere to the north was the old beach resort called Saltair.

She walked through the Silver Club, where the coffee shop and lounge were empty. The waiters and cooks had long since gone to bed in the dormitory at the rear of the car, where bunks were stacked five high. She passed her own compartment and entered the deserted dining car. White tablecloths gave the car a ghostly air. Outside the windows, the darkness was pierced by an occasional light, showing the flat, otherworldly landscape of the Great Salt Desert. She moved quietly through the Silver Thrush, the six-five sleeper. Si Lovell, the porter, was asleep in his cramped little alcove. He didn't wake up as she walked past. It was just after eleven, according to her watch. She entered the Silver Gorge, walking quietly down the passageway outside the bedrooms. Most of the passengers had turned in for the night, though Jill heard voices coming from one of the bedrooms. She turned the corner near the soiled linen locker and heard snores coming from several roomettes. She'd reached the doorway of roomette four when the porter stepped into the passageway from his tiny compartment near the vestibule. He'd removed his cap and loosened his tie, in preparation for getting some sleep.

"Miss McLeod, I thought you'd turned in for the night," Lonnie Clark said. "Is something wrong?"

Jill felt as though she'd been caught with her hand in the cookie jar. Well, there was nothing for it but to tell him. She liked Mr. Clark and thought she could trust him to keep a secret. She headed for the vestibule, motioning for him to join her.

"Have you been a porter on this particular car before?" she asked. "And have you heard any stories?"

"The Silver Gorge? Yes, I have. We've got about twenty of these six-ten sleeper cars. With two trains a day, east and west, it stands to reason this car would rotate through the consist several times a month. As for stories, I've heard plenty of them." He paused and gave her a speculative look. "Are you talking about ghost stories, Miss McLeod? Yes, I've heard them. Mostly from Darius Doolin, who has a fanciful turn of mind. As for ghosts and spirits and what-not, I'm the practical sort. We've got enough going on in this life without paying attention to such tales."

"Ordinarily I would be inclined to agree with you, Mr. Clark." She sighed. "Someone died in roomette four back in May. I found the body shortly after we arrived in Oakland."

"I heard about that on the porter grapevine. But Miss McLeod, surely you don't believe in ghosts."

"Mr. Doolin is not the only person who claims to have seen a ghost. I saw and heard something in this car two weeks ago. I'm still not convinced it was a ghost, but it was certainly unusual. I saw a shimmering light in the passageway that moved into roomette four. When I went inside, I heard tapping sounds, like Morse Code." When she saw the skeptical look on Mr. Clark's face, she added, "I know it sounds far-fetched, but it seemed very real. I can't explain it. Other passengers who've traveled in that roomette have heard things, too. Although Mr. Saunders told me this morning that he hadn't heard a thing."

"The way that man was sawing logs last night, I'm not surprised." The porter's expression turned thoughtful. "So when you saw this car was on the consist, and you knew Mr. Saunders got off the train, you figured you'd come back here after everyone had gone to bed and pay a little visit to roomette four."

"That's about the size of it. I thought I'd sit there for a while and see if anything happens."

He shrugged. "Well, the roomette's empty. Go ahead. I'll be in my compartment, so if you need me, I'm nearby."

They left the vestibule and returned to the darkened corridor. Mr. Clark went into the porter's compartment and shut the door. Jill moved to the doorway of roomette four and stepped inside, sitting down on the bench seat. She leaned back, listening to the familiar clacking sound of wheels on rails. Nothing happened. In fact, she felt herself becoming drowsy. She looked at her watch as the train approached Wendover, Utah. She dozed off, and when she woke, her watch read nearly midnight. The train's next stop in Elko, Nevada was over two hours away. She fell asleep again and then woke as the train moved into a curve.

This is silly, she thought. I might as well go to bed. Nothing had happened, and she was fighting to stay awake.

So much for her experiment in communicating with a ghost. Once again, she told herself she wasn't sure there even was a ghost.

Then she heard four taps, one right after the other.

Her heart began to pound.

Perhaps the experiment was working after all.

"I'm here," she whispered, feeling foolish even as she said the words.

More taps, the sequence different. Then silence. Another series of taps. She remembered the Morse Code chart. H, followed by an A, then an R.

The letters H, A and R. It must mean Wade Hardcastle, she thought. She listened but heard only the wheels on the rails. No more letters. Nothing happened for the next few minutes. She felt so tired. It was time to go to bed. She put her hands on the seat, ready to push herself into a standing position. Then the roomette chilled, a penetrating cold that felt as though it was seeping into her bones. Something shimmered in front of her. The light.

It was too much, and too close. She scrambled to her feet and stepped out of the roomette.

"What the hell?" Lonnie Clark came out of the porter's compartment, wearing a white shirt unbuttoned part way, the tail flapping over his dark uniform pants. He stared at her in consternation, then he opened the door that led to the vestibule. "Nobody there. I could have sworn I heard voices. It was like people out on the vestibule. Talking over each other, like having an argument."

"I hear it, too." The noise coming from the vestibule was like a buzz, punctuated by sibilant noises, and she could just make out a few words.

"The figures don't add up."

"Hear me out."

"...want me to do..."

The very words she'd heard back in May, when Kevin Randall and Wade Hardcastle were arguing in the vestibule.

Now Lonnie Clark's eyes widened. He was looking past her. Jill turned as the shimmering light moved out of roomette four, into the passageway. The porter backed away from the apparition.

"What the hell is going on?"

Chapter Twenty ————————————

JILL DIDN'T ANSWER. She watched as the light glimmered, becoming brighter as it moved. Then the light faded and disappeared. The voices in the vestibule dwindled into a faint buzz. Then all was quiet, save for the steady *clackety-clack* of wheels on the tracks.

Lonnie Clark took a deep breath and let it out in a sigh. He kept his voice low, so as not to wake the passengers in the nearby roomettes. "That's the craziest damn thing I ever saw. And believe me, I've seen a thing or two."

They stood there for a moment but nothing else happened. Suddenly a series of loud, whistling snores rumbled from the occupant of roomette one.

Jill looked at her watch. "It's almost twelve-thirty. I'm exhausted. I'm going to bed."

The porter nodded. "I'd better do the same. I've got passengers getting off the train in Elko, and we'll be there in an hour and a half." With that, he stepped back into his compartment and shut the door.

Jill turned and walked forward through the train to her quarters in the buffet-lounge car, where she undressed, put on her pajamas, and washed her face. She pulled her bed down from the wall and climbed between the covers. As soon as her head hit the pillow, she fell into a deep sleep.

At this time of year, sunrise was early, about twenty minutes after five. Jill woke as the dawn's light peeked in the window of her compartment, edging the curtains in pale gold light. The

Silver Lady was in the western rim of the Great Basin, somewhere between the 4:17 A.M. stop in Winnemucca and the 5:53
A.M. stop in Gerlach. She stretched her arms over her head and
dozed off again, sleeping lightly until she woke. The train slowed
as it neared the Gerlach station. Soon the *CZ* would cross into
California, heading into the Sierra Nevada Mountains. Jill threw
back the covers and sat up in bed, ready to start her day. After a
quick wash, she put on her uniform, left her compartment and
crossed the vestibule into the dining car, walking along the passageway next to the kitchen. It was just after six, and when she
reached the dining car steward's counter, she saw a few early risers
sitting at the tables, perusing the breakfast menu. Winnemucca
was a crew change stop, so Mr. Dutton, the WP conductor, had
turned over the train to another conductor. Mr. Wylie was a tall
man in his mid-forties. His name was Arthur, but his rust-colored
hair had earned him the nickname Red. He and the brakeman, a man named Lee Bogardus, sat drinking coffee at a table
for two.

"Good morning, Miss McLeod," the conductor said. "Hope
you're keeping things quiet."

"Uneventful so far," Jill told him.

At least on the temporal plane. She saw no reason to mention
the supernatural.

She sat down at a table for four and soon the waiter set down
a silver pot. "Here's your coffee, Miss McLeod."

"Thank you. I really need it this morning." Jill had already
marked her meal check and now she handed it over.

The waiter smiled when he saw the check. "Your usual, I see.
French toast and bacon."

"Of course." Jill doctored her coffee with cream, then raised
the cup to her lips for the first restorative sip. She'd had a short
night, in terms of sleep, but the caffeine revived her.

And what a night it had been. Such a strange experience. Can
there really be a ghost? she thought. It would be easy to say she'd
been imagining things, but this was the second time on the train
she'd seen the light that moved and glowed, and heard the taps
that seemed to be Morse Code. And now the ghostly echoes of the

argument in the vestibule. What's more, Mr. Clark had seen and heard those things, too.

She thought back to May, when she came upon Kevin Randall and Wade Hardcastle in the vestibule. The men had been arguing, and Jill was sure it had something to do with their jobs. When Jill had walked through the vestibule, she'd heard Kevin say the same thing, "The figures don't add up." Then he'd said, "I know what you want me to do and I can't do it."

Do what? Figures implied numbers and Kevin worked in the financial department, as did Hardcastle. The books, Jill thought. Kevin Randall had been working in his roomette for most of the journey from Portola to Oakland, with that brown leather book, a ledger of some sort, and a mechanical calculator on the toilet lid in front of him. He had been scribbling notes on that yellow legal pad. The ledger and the pad were missing from the roomette when Jill found the body. Taken by the killer, no doubt. But Kevin had torn out those pages and mailed them to Margaret. The killer knew the pages were missing, but not where they were.

Jill took another sip of coffee, thinking about Kevin's business trip to Portola. He'd gone to audit books for one of the companies that was held by the Vennor Corporation. Hardcastle worked over Kevin in the financial department. Something must be amiss with the finances of that particular company. Both men knew it, but Hardcastle wanted Kevin to cover up the discrepancy. That was Jill's best guess. And Tidsy's task this week was to find out which company. There couldn't be that many companies located near Portola.

The waiter brought her breakfast. She spread butter on the French toast and poured syrup over the lot. Then she picked up her fork.

"Good morning, Miss McLeod. May we join you?" The middle-aged woman in the floral print dress was already pulling out one of the chairs on the other side of the table.

"Of course, Mrs. Hagedorn. You're up early."

"I always wake up early in the summer," the other woman said, sitting opposite Jill. "Because the sun's up. Now, in the winter when it's dark, I stay in bed. Particularly if the weather's bad. My husband should be along soon."

Mrs. Hagedorn pulled a breakfast menu from the stand and glanced at it. The waiter appeared and poured coffee for her. Then Mr. Hagedorn, in a lightweight summer suit, sat down next to his wife. Jill had met the Hagedorns yesterday, while making dinner reservations for the sleeping car passengers. They had boarded the train in Grand Junction, Colorado, traveling in bedroom E of the Silver Gorge, and were headed to Sacramento, where Mr. Hagedorn, an engineer, was interviewing for a job with the California Department of Transportation.

"I'm having the omelet, with ham," Mr. Hagedorn said as he marked his meal check.

His wife closed her menu and placed it back in the stand. "Poached eggs for me. I am so looking forward to seeing the Feather River Canyon, Miss McLeod. I've heard the scenery is marvelous."

"It is," Jill assured them. "Make sure you get seats in the Vista-Dome."

The waiter took the Hagedorns' meal checks. The dining car was filling up now, as passengers came in search of breakfast. Another passenger took the fourth place at the table. Jill had met him the day before when he boarded the train in Denver. He was wearing civilian clothes for this trip, but his military bearing marked him as an officer even before he introduced himself as Colonel Lusco.

"I hope you slept well." Jill smiled as she thought, he must have, because I could hear him. Colonel Lusco was the passenger in roomette one on the Silver Gorge, the one who had been snoring so loudly during the night.

"Oh, yes, very well, thank you." The colonel looked over the menu and marked his meal check. "I think I'll take a leaf from your book, Miss McLeod, and have the French toast."

"I was in the Army myself," Mr. Hagedorn said. "With the Seventh Infantry at Anzio."

"Twenty-first Infantry Regiment, in the Pacific Theater and then Korea," the colonel said.

"I'm really glad they've signed that Armistice in Korea," Mr. Hagedorn added. "Who would have thought we'd fight another war so soon after the last one."

"Indeed," the colonel said, pouring himself more coffee from the pitcher. "After the Twenty-first left Korea in January of 'fifty-two, I transferred to Camp Carson in Colorado Springs, training soldiers. Now I'm reporting for duty at the Presidio in San Francisco next week."

"Is your family with you?" Mrs. Hagedorn asked.

Colonel Lusco paused as the waiter delivered the Hagedorns' breakfast. He handed his meal check to the waiter and reached for his coffee. "No, I'm alone this trip. My wife is closing up our quarters at Camp Carson and coordinating the move, as she has done so many times before," he added with a smile. "She and the children—we have a son and two daughters—will be arriving in a few weeks."

"I was born in Denver and lived there until the war was over," Jill said. "And the Hagedorns are from Grand Junction."

They talked about Colorado while they ate, then the Hagedorns excused themselves. "I want to get up to the Vista-Dome," Mrs. Hagedorn said.

When they'd gone, Jill looked across the table at Colonel Lusco. "Was your regiment at Chosin?"

He put down his fork. "No. We fought in the battles at Osan and Chochiwon, and on the Naktong River. Why do you ask?"

Jill touched the rim of her coffee cup. "My fiancé was killed at Chosin."

"I'm sorry to hear that," he said. "We lost a lot of good men in Korea. I'm glad that war is over."

———

After breakfast, Jill left the dining car and went forward to the Silver Club, where Mr. Griggs presided over the coffee shop and lounge. She saw him delivering pastries and coffee to a party of two in the coffee shop section. She followed him back to the lower level in the middle of the car. She was planning to go up to the upper-level Vista-Dome, to ride as the train left Nevada for California. At the last minute, she turned and went down to the lounge.

Mr. Griggs was behind the counter, washing cups. Washing cups, Jill thought, as he had been back in May. That's right, Mr. Griggs had been on the *California Zephyr* for that westbound run.

"Good morning, Mr. Griggs. How are you today?"

"Just fine," the waiter said. "I'll be glad to get home this afternoon."

"So will I." Jill leaned on the counter. "Mr. Griggs, do you remember that run in May, when we talked about your daughter and her ballet lessons? You showed me her picture."

"Why, yes, Miss McLeod." Mr. Griggs set a cup in the dish drainer. "My Emma wants to be a ballerina, like Janet Collins."

"I've never heard of Janet Collins," Jill admitted.

"She's a dancer with the Metropolitan Ballet in New York City," he said. "The first Negro dancer they've had."

"Really? I'll look that up. About that run in May. That was when I found a man dead in his roomette back in the sleeper cars."

"I sure do remember hearing about that," he said. "What a shame. I understand he was a young man and it was something with his heart."

"His heart, yes." Jill frowned. She was remembering that day on the train, trying to bring things into sharper focus. "The man's name was Mr. Randall. That afternoon, he was here in the lounge with two other men. One of them had a mustache and the other was big and bulky. He had a long nose."

"His eyes were cold," Mr. Griggs said.

"They are," Jill said. She knew that very well after seeing Hardcastle at the Vennors' party on Saturday.

"And he was real unpleasant," the waiter continued. "He snapped at you. I remember it very well. The three of them were having words. They got loud and people noticed. Mr. Randall left, and that man was rude to you, because you were looking at him. Then you left, but you came back later."

"I went back to Mr. Randall's roomette, to see if he was all right," Jill said. "Then I came back here, to the lounge. And had some coffee. Those men were still here. And then—" She stopped and thought for a moment.

A movement caught her eye. The woman passenger who was seated near the bar had a glass of iced tea in front of her. She had just taken something out of her patent leather purse. It was an aspirin bottle. Jill recognized the familiar Bayer label, the rounded shape, the brown cap. The woman shook the bottle and the pills inside rattled against the glass. Then she removed the top and shook two aspirin tablets into her palm. She popped them in her mouth and washed down the pills with a swallow of tea.

An aspirin bottle, Jill thought.

That triggered a memory.

Chapter Twenty-One ———

May 1953

THE LITTLE GIRL IN THE PHOTOGRAPH was about eight years old. She wore tights and a pink tutu and posed at a barre, attempting to stand *en pointe*. She looked very much like her father, Alonzo Griggs, who was a waiter here in the Silver Club, the buffet-lounge car.

"What a beautiful girl," Jill said. "How long has she been taking ballet lessons?"

Her father smiled proudly. "About a year now. She says she wants to be a ballerina."

Jill handed the photograph back to Mr. Griggs. Then she heard raised voices behind her, and turned, as did other passengers in the lounge, to look at the source.

She had entered the lounge a few minutes earlier, after the train had left the Stockton station. Mr. Randall sat at a table for four, his back to Jill and the bar. Across the table from him were the two other men who had boarded the train in Portola. Each man had a coffee cup in front of him. The man with the mustache hunkered over an ashtray that contained a smoking cigarette. He said very little. The other man, big and bulky, with a long nose and pale blue eyes, was doing most of the talking. He was the one Jill had seen earlier, arguing with Mr. Randall in the vestibule of the Silver Gorge. He was talking, his voice getting louder, as Mr. Randall tried to interrupt him.

Finally Kevin Randall slid out of the seat, getting up from the table. He glanced at the other occupants of the lounge, who were staring at the group, and then his gaze moved back to the two men at the table. "There's no point in discussing it further."

He stepped past Jill, carrying his briefcase. Since he'd gotten on the train this morning, she had never seen him without it. Right now he held it in front of him, like a shield. Or perhaps he was protecting the case. He left the lounge and headed toward the rear of the train.

Jill looked at the two men still seated at the table. The man with a mustache was frowning. The cigarette in the ashtray had gone out. He shook another one from a pack and stuck it in his mouth, then thumbed a battered lighter and held the flame to the cigarette. The long-nosed man with the cold blue eyes glared at Jill. "What are you staring at?" he snapped.

"I'm sorry," Jill said, with a polite smile. "I didn't mean to intrude."

Though it was difficult not to look, or hear, when people made themselves objects of scrutiny, by their actions and the loudness of their voices.

She turned back to the bar. Behind it, Mr. Griggs was washing dishes. They traded looks, then Jill left the lounge.

What had caused the raised voices? There seemed to be a lot of tension between Mr. Randall and these men. She picked up on it every time she saw them. After stopping in her own quarters, Jill headed back through the train. In the Silver Gorge, Mr. Randall was in roomette four. The setup was as before, the briefcase open at his feet, with his suit coat inside, neatly folded. The mechanical calculator sat on the toilet lid. In his lap were the brown ledger book and yellow legal pad. "Mr. Randall, is everything all right? I couldn't help overhearing what happened in the lounge."

He pushed up the black, horn-rimmed glasses that had slid down his nose, his expression rueful. "I'm fine, Miss McLeod. It's just that those men would like me to do something I am not willing or able to do. I've explained it several times, but—" He stopped and smiled. "It's really none of your concern, though. I won't burden you with it. I'll sort everything out when I get back to Oakland." He picked up the legal pad. Jill glanced at the notes he'd scribbled there and caught sight of the words "Mohawk Valley."

She knew that was a valley west of Portola, near the little community of Blairsden.

As she walked back through the rest of the sleeper cars, Jill thought about that letter Mr. Randall had given her, the one she'd mailed at the station in Sacramento. She wondered if the contents of the envelope had something to do with those lines and columns of figures in that ledger book, and all those notes he was scribbling on the legal pad.

When Jill reached the dome-observation car, she climbed the steps to the Vista-Dome. The *California Zephyr* climbed Altamont Pass and she saw the welcome sight of the East Bay hills, knowing that San Francisco Bay, and home, were on the other side. She left the dome as the train crossed the Livermore valley. After the brief stop in the little town of Pleasanton, she walked back through the train. Mr. Randall was still in the roomette in the Silver Gorge. He had removed his glasses and his face looked very different without them. It appeared he had a headache, since he was rubbing his temples. He winced and Jill opened her mouth to offer aspirin from her first-aid kit. But Mr. Randall took a bottle from his trousers pocket, opened it and shook two pills into his palm. He swallowed them quickly, and put on his glasses.

Now he looked surprised. "Miss McLeod, I didn't see you there. I'm as blind as a bat without my glasses."

"Do you have a headache? Is there anything I can get for you?"

"I'm fine, thank you. Just tired after a couple of long days. I'll certainly be glad to get home. I've got to finish these notes," he added, fingering the yellow pad. He gestured toward the window, at the trees and hills visible outside. "Where are we now?"

"That little town, Sunol. We're just starting through the canyon to Niles, then we head up to Oakland. We'll both be home soon."

'Can't wait. I'll see my fiancée. By the way, did you know they used to make silent movies in Niles?"

Jill smiled. "Yes, I do. It was a company called Essenay, using the initials of the founders, George Spoor and Broncho Billy Anderson. They filmed that Charlie Chaplin movie, *The Tramp*, right here in Niles Canyon."

"My father worked at the Liberty Theater in Fresno, years ago, right after World War One. He liked those actors, Dustin and William Farnum, and Colleen Moore and Mabel Normand."

"My father likes Fatty Arbuckle, Buster Keaton and Laurel and Hardy," Jill said as the train wound into Niles Canyon, traveling alongside Alameda Creek. Then Jill excused herself and headed forward to the Silver Club. She had the urge for a cup of coffee. Sometimes she felt tired in the late afternoon, and the caffeine would give her enough of a boost to finish out the run.

The two men were still there, though one of them, the man with the mustache, had moved, sitting across from his companion instead of beside him. Both men looked at her, then glanced away.

Mr. Griggs was behind the bar. Jill leaned on the counter. "I'd love to have some coffee. It's the middle of the afternoon."

"And you need a jolt," he said with a smile. "Here you are." He set a cup on the counter and poured it full of strong black coffee. She doctored it with a generous dollop of cream and took a sip. Just right. She carried the cup to a vacant seat across from the table where the two men sat. After saying hello to the woman sitting next to her, she took another sip of coffee and watched the two men over the rim of the cup, hoping they wouldn't notice.

The man with the long nose and the unpleasant blue eyes tapped his fingers impatiently on the table. "Are you sure it will do the job?" he hissed in a low voice.

Across from him, the man with the mustache stared at the ashtray, where the cigarette he'd been smoking had turned into a stub. "If what you've told me about him is true, it will."

"We're almost to Niles," the first man said. "We have to do it soon, before we get to Oakland." When he didn't get a response, he made a disgusted snort. "Now is not the time to get squeamish. We both have something to lose."

He got up from the table and left the lounge, turning left, heading for the rear of the train. Jill glanced out the window, seeing Alameda Creek in the ravine below the tracks. When she looked again at the man who remained at the table, he was staring at the smoldering butt in the ashtray. He raised his head and looked out the window, his eyes a deep opaque brown in his weathered face.

Then he reached into his pocket and took out a Bayer aspirin bottle. She recognized it from the label, as well as the rounded shape and the brown cap. He unscrewed the cap and poured pills into his palm. More than a few, Jill thought, surprised. More like a handful. He must have quite a headache, if he's taking that many pills.

He didn't take them, though. He closed his hand over the pills and got up from the table. He walked past the counter and left the lounge, heading back toward the sleeper cars.

Jill took another sip of her coffee. Then she heard someone call her name. The attendant from the third chair car stood near the entrance to the lounge. "Need the first-aid kit," he said. "Got a rambunctious youngster who decided to jump down the Vista-Dome steps and he fell instead. He's got a cut on his hand."

"I'll be right there." Jill stood and carried her cup to the counter. Then she retrieved her first-aid kit from her quarters and headed for the chair car.

Chapter Twenty-Two

THE PILLS, JILL THOUGHT NOW.

She played the scene over again, seeing it in her head. The man with the mustache had most certainly pulled an aspirin bottle from his pocket. She had been close enough to see the shape, the brown cap, the label, buff and dark red, the word BAYER in white lettering.

But that didn't necessarily mean that the little glass bottle had contained aspirin. She hadn't gotten a good look at the pills the man had poured into his palm. Other than to think that it had been a lot of pills, far more than anyone would take for a mere headache.

Could the pills have been Digoxin? But where would he get that much Digoxin? Unless he, or someone he knew, had access to the drug.

Who was he? What was his connection with Hardcastle?

The woman who had just taken two aspirin got up, leaving her empty tea glass on the table. Mr. Griggs left the bar and came around the counter, collecting the glass and two empty coffee cups from another table.

"We're coming into Portola," he said.

The train slowed. Jill looked out the window and saw the outskirts of the town and the middle fork of the Feather River, just down the embankment. The river was lower now, in midsummer, than it had been in May. It had been hours since she'd gotten off the train in Salt Lake City. This would be a good opportunity to stretch her legs and get some fresh air. She headed forward, to the

Silver Schooner, the third chair car. When the train stopped, she stepped down to the platform and took a deep breath, rotating her shoulders to work out the kinks. She walked alongside the cars. An elderly woman was boarding the Silver Ranch, the second chair car. Someone else stood nearby, waiting to board, partially hidden by the car attendant. Then the attendant moved out of the way.

Jill stared. What was Wade Hardcastle doing here? Then she recalled the conversation she'd overheard at the garden party last Saturday. Hardcastle had been talking with his boss, Daniel Vennor. After Vennor had said something about Plumas County, and having some concerns, Hardcastle had said, "I'll go up there and talk with Pierson."

"Up there" must mean Portola. But who was Pierson? The person whose company was being audited?

Now Jill saw another man walking toward Hardcastle. The tall man with a mustache was dressed as he had been before, in serviceable work clothes and boots. The two men conferred briefly, then both men climbed aboard the Silver Ranch.

So that's Pierson, Jill thought. It has to be.

Mr. Wylie, the conductor, had been up by the locomotives, talking with the brakeman. Now he checked his pocket watch and turned, calling, "All aboard."

Jill boarded the train and the car attendant pulled up the steps and locked the door. The engineer blew the whistle and the train moved, slowly at first. Then it picked up speed, traveling along the river.

Jill walked back through the buffet-lounge car, where passengers crowded the coffee shop, and into the dining car, walking quickly along the passageway that ran alongside the kitchen. The public address system was located near the steward's counter. Normally she would have identified herself as Miss McLeod, the Zephyrette. Today she altered the familiar script she knew by heart. She wasn't sure if Hardcastle had heard her name mentioned at the Vennor party, but she wanted to play it safe.

She keyed the mike and began. "Good morning, this is the Zephyrette. We are now in the famous Feather River Canyon..."

When Jill finished speaking, she replaced the mike and turned, coming face to face with Wade Hardcastle, close enough to see his pale blue eyes and the long nose in his jowly face. She held her breath. Did he recognize her? No, she didn't think so. Hardcastle was more interested in breakfast. He looked past her at the dining car steward, who pointed him toward a spot at a nearby table. Jill stepped aside so he could pass. He sat down at the table and reached for the menu.

Jill turned away, heading up the passageway next to the kitchen. She went through to the next car, the Silver Club, stopped in her own compartment, then continued forward, past the crew dormitory. To her right, steps led to the upper-level Vista-Dome and down to the buffet-lounge below the dome. She went downstairs, passing the kitchen, and entered the lounge. The man with the mustache sat alone in the corner of the lounge, a cup of coffee on the table in front of him. He was taking a cigarette from a pack. He stuck it in his mouth and held the lighter to it.

"Can I get you anything?" Mr. Griggs asked her.

"I'll have a cup of coffee. With cream."

Mr. Griggs poured the coffee and Jill stirred in cream. She sat down near the man she guessed was Pierson, close enough to observe him and eavesdrop if Mr. Hardcastle came to join him.

Instead another passenger entered the lounge, the elderly woman she had seen boarding the train in Portola. She appeared to be in her seventies, hatchet-faced, with sharp eyes and white hair twisted into a bun at the nape of her neck. She wore a mustard-colored dress with green collar and cuffs and carried an oversized handbag. She walked over to where the man with the mustache sat and fixed him with a sharp gaze. Her voice grated on Jill's ears as she addressed the man in a loud, hectoring tone. "Harry Pierson, I saw you at the station. I waved at you, but I guess you didn't see me."

Jill took a quick inward breath. As she suspected, this was Pierson, the man Hardcastle had been talking about with Daniel Vennor at the party last weekend. The man whose company had been acquired by Vennor and whose books were being audited by Kevin Randall. And his first name was Harry. Wade Hardcastle,

Harry Pierson. Both had names starting with the letters H, A, R. Jill felt frustration bubbling in her chest. Which man was guilty, and of what?

She sipped her coffee and glanced to her right. The look on Pierson's face told her he didn't like the old woman. She wondered if he'd been avoiding the woman earlier, in Portola.

He took a drag from his cigarette and blew out smoke before speaking in a rumbling voice that went with his weathered face. "Mrs. Bowman. No, I didn't see you at the station."

"I'm surprised you didn't," the woman said, her voice sounding aggrieved. "It's small enough."

Pierson drew in smoke, his finger absently stroking his thin mustache. "Are you going to Stockton to visit your son?"

"I certainly am. I want to see Walter and my grandchildren, even if I don't much care for that woman he's married to." Mrs. Bowman sat down between Jill and Pierson, crowding Jill to the left as she set down her handbag. She waved her hand at Mr. Griggs, behind the bar. "You, boy. Get me some coffee. With sugar and cream."

The waiter nodded, his face impassive. "Certainly, ma'am. Coming right up."

Now Jill eavesdropped shamelessly as Mrs. Bowman buttonholed Mr. Pierson, asking where he was going and why. "Where are you headed today? The Bay Area? On business? Things must be good at the lumber mill if you can go to the Bay Area all the time. Weren't you there last month?"

Pierson's mouth tightened as he replied, "No, it was the month before."

"Oh, right. May, wasn't it? Around the time of your father's birthday."

He puffed on his cigarette, blowing out smoke, an edge to his voice. "That's right. The week before Memorial Day."

Mrs. Bowman stopped talking as the waiter delivered her coffee, with a cream pitcher and sugar bowl. She dumped in two spoonfuls of sugar and a generous pour of cream. "What's this I heard about your business having problems? Georgia Markley said she heard you and your sisters were having a difference of opinion about the way the business is run. I shouldn't think you'd be having money troubles, especially after you sold out to that company in the Bay Area."

Pierson's face darkened. It seemed to Jill that he was having difficulty containing his temper, but he was reluctant to make a scene because there were others around. "Mrs. Markley is talking out of turn."

Mrs. Bowman looked affronted. "Well, it's none of my business but—"

"You're right, it isn't," Pierson snapped.

Mrs. Bowman gave him a sour look. "If you feel that way, then we won't talk about it. I'm just being neighborly. How is your father? I know he had another episode with his heart."

Pierson bit off the words. "He's fine."

"He takes Digoxin to control it. I saw your sister at the pharmacy, filling his prescription." He gave her a look that would have quelled a less nosy woman, and she went on, a bit defensive. "Well, I couldn't help reading the label, could I? My husband takes Digoxin, too. You have to be careful with it, of course. He took too much last year and very nearly died of heart failure."

Now Pierson dropped his gaze, concentrating instead on the ashtray as he ground out his cigarette butt. "I heard about that."

Digoxin. Kevin Randall took the drug and it was possible he'd died of an overdose. She thought back to May, and the pills that Pierson had poured into his hand. What Jill had just heard confirmed that Pierson had access to Digoxin. Since his father was taking it, no doubt he had knowledge of the overdose effects as well.

Hardcastle and Pierson. They were in this together.

Speak of the devil, she thought, as Hardcastle walked into the lounge. He looked first at Pierson, then his gaze swept over Mrs. Bowman and then lingered on Jill. Her coffee cup was halfway to her mouth. She raised it and drank the last of the coffee. Once again she wondered if Hardcastle recognized her. Before, he had looked right through her. Now his gaze had lengthened. Perhaps it had occurred to him that he'd seen her before, and more than once. But what, if anything, would he do about it?

He sat down near Jill, at the table with seating for four. Pierson got up, without a word, and carried his coffee to the table where Hardcastle sat, slipping into the seat across the table. Mrs. Bowman sniffed, offended at Pierson's open rudeness. She got up and swept out of the lounge.

Time to leave, Jill thought. She would catch up with Mrs. Bowman later, hoping to pump the old woman for more information about Pierson and his family business. She stepped past the table where Hardcastle and Pierson sat and went into the passageway. She took a deep breath and headed back through the sleeper cars to the dome-observation car. The train was now heading across the Clio Trestle, the high railroad bridge with its panoramic view of the surrounding mountains, and Jill always enjoyed seeing the view from the Vista-Dome. As the train went through the forested slopes, approaching the little communities of Graeagle and Blairsden, she went downstairs and walked forward, to the buffet-lounge car. She wanted to talk with Mr. Griggs again, but first she checked the lounge. Pierson and Hardcastle had gone.

"Those two men you're looking for," Mr. Griggs said from behind the bar. "They went up to the Vista-Dome."

"How did you know I was looking for them?" Jill asked.

"Just a feeling I had." Mr. Griggs was washing coffee cups in the bar sink. "They sure were looking at you as you left."

Jill didn't like the sound of that. "The man with the mustache is Mr. Pierson. The other man is Mr. Hardcastle. We were both here in the lounge that day in May, when you showed me the picture of your daughter. They were having words with Mr. Randall, the man that died."

"Yes, I remember it well."

"Do you think they recognized us?"

He smiled. "Me? I'm just another black man to most passengers. But you? Yes, Miss McLeod. I think maybe they recognized you."

Mr. Griggs had a point. Many passengers couldn't see past the skin color of the waiters and porters who provided service aboard the train. The Zephyrette, as the only female crew member, was more visible. She had been counting on her uniform as camouflage, but perhaps that was naive, particularly since Saturday, when she'd been quite visible at the party. Visible, certainly to Hardcastle. The big man had worked with Kevin. He must have known about Kevin's weak heart. Surely it was he who had suggested the method of murder to Pierson, who had access to his father's Digoxin. The numbers on the sheets of paper that Kevin had mailed to Margaret must show the reason why. Kevin had gone to Portola at the behest of his employer, the Vennor Corporation, to audit the books of a business that the company had acquired, presumably Pierson's family business, based on what Jill had overheard earlier. Pierson must still have a hand in the business. And, according to the old woman, there was tension between Pierson and other family members regarding the business.

Jill was sure the gossipy Mrs. Bowman could tell her more about the Piersons.

The train was approaching Spring Garden. The 7,344-foot tunnel bored under the divide at Lee Summit, which separated the Feather River's middle fork drainage from the north fork drainage. Jill had heard that while the tunnel was being constructed, the workers found gold in an ancient river channel. She made her way to the Silver Ranch as the *CZ* went through the tunnel, plunging the car into darkness. When it emerged, she looked for Mrs. Bowman. She had seen the woman board this car, but when Jill checked the seats, she didn't see her. Mrs. Bowman might be in the ladies' room on the lower level, beneath the Vista-Dome. Or she might be up in the dome. If she could find the nosy old woman, perhaps Jill would strike gold of another sort.

Jill climbed the steps to the upper level and looked around. Mrs. Bowman sat by herself in one of the front seats. Jill moved up the aisle and sat down next to her. The train was moving slowly into the Williams Loop, where the track made a continuous one-mile loop in a one-percent grade. Depending on how many cars were on the consist, the train might cross over itself.

Jill pointed. "This is called the Williams Loop."

"I know what it is, young woman." Mrs. Bowman's voice was tart. "I live in Portola and I'm certainly familiar with all the sights along the Feather River route."

"I should have guessed," Jill said, smiling. "I saw you earlier in the lounge with Mr. Pierson. He's from Portola as well."

The older woman gave Jill a sharp look. "Indeed he is. And how do you know him?"

"He was on the train a couple of months ago. In May, right before Memorial Day, going from Portola to Oakland."

"Yes, he would be going to Oakland," Mrs. Bowman said. "He makes that trip frequently these days."

"Something to do with his business, isn't it? The family sold it, I believe."

It didn't take much to get an inveterate gossip going, and Mrs. Bowman was no exception. Her face held an avid look as she dished the dirt. "Yes, they certainly did. The Mohawk Valley Lumber Company. The Pierson family has been in the lumber business since the early days. They started that company in nineteen-ought-eight, the year before the Western Pacific completed the railroad down the canyon."

"That's over forty years," Jill said. "It must have been hard for Mr. Pierson to sell the company."

Mrs. Bowman sniffed. "That lumber company was not entirely his, you know. His two sisters had a say, too. Equal shares, the three of them. They sold the business last year, to some big company in Oakland. The younger sister, Mabel, didn't want to sell, but Harry and the older sister, Ruth, they outvoted her."

Why did they sell? Jill wondered. Money, I'll bet. It's always money.

Her suspicions were confirmed by Mrs. Bowman, who had stopped talking briefly to pull a sack of lemon drops from her large bag. She offered one to Jill, who took it, then continued with her tale about the Piersons.

"They were in financial trouble, at least that's what I heard. And I gather that they still are. Not that I'm surprised. Harry Pierson always did have a way of letting a dollar slip through his fingers."

"How so?" Jill popped the lemon drop into her mouth. She glanced out the curved Vista-Dome window in front of her and saw that the train was coming out of the Williams Loop.

Mrs. Bowman lowered her voice. "Not the best businessman in the world, if you get my meaning. Certainly not the businessman his father was. His sisters have more on the ball than Harry ever did. But that's not the only reason. If you ask me, Harry Pierson has a gambling problem. He spends a good deal of time in Reno. Why, Georgia Markley's husband has seen him in several of the casinos in that town. I rue the day they legalized gambling over in Nevada."

It had been more than twenty years since the Silver State had legalized gambling, in 1931, in the heart of the Depression. Portola was only about fifty miles from the Reno casinos, an easy trip to make if someone had a yen for gambling.

Jill had heard enough. "Thank you for the lemon drop." She stood and looked around the Vista-Dome. Uh-oh. Harry Pierson was sitting in an aisle seat near the back of the dome. She wondered if he'd seen her talking with Mrs. Bowman. The hard stare he gave her as she walked past him seemed to confirm that. As she took the steps down to the lower level, she had the unmistakable feeling that his eyes were boring a hole in her back.

When she reached the vestibule, Wade Hardcastle was there. He, too, gave her a lingering look as she stepped past him. Now Jill was sure he recognized her. She walked quickly back through the next car and entered the buffet-lounge car, heading through the coffee shop. As she passed the lounge, she waved to Mr. Griggs. Then she made a brief visit to her own compartment before going through the dining car. It was after nine and breakfast service was winding down.

She looked out the diner windows and glanced at her watch, guessing at the train's location. The *California Zephyr* had already passed Quincy Junction, and was heading toward the little settlement of Keddie, and the famous Keddie Wye. Now the train rumbled past the high three-legged trestle, descending further down the canyon, with the tracks crossing back and forth over the river, on several bridges. On either side, granite cliffs soared high. Here the train ran close to the river, with State Highway 70 high above on the side of the mountain. There were two places along this section of the route, at Pulga and Tobin Bridges, where the highway and railroad bridges intersected, crossing over one another.

Jill walked back through the sleeper cars, heading for the Silver Planet, the dome-observation car at the very end of the train. Her mind wasn't on the scenery, though. Now that she'd heard what Mrs. Bowman had to say about the state of the Pierson family business, Jill was connecting the dots. The Piersons were having financial difficulties before and after the sale to the Vennor Corporation. Selling the company to Vennor was supposed to solve the lumber business's money difficulties, but it hadn't. This had led to tension between Pierson and his siblings, according to the old woman. Now Jill wondered if the financial problems had something to do with Pierson and his way of letting dollars slip through his hands. Mrs. Bowman had said Pierson had a gambling habit.

Money. That was the key, and the motive.

Jill recalled the argument she'd overheard when she came upon Kevin and Hardcastle in the vestibule. "The figures don't add up," Kevin had said. He'd traveled to Portola to look at the Piersons' books. He'd found something amiss, Jill realized now. Hardcastle must have known what he'd find, and he was protecting Pierson, his accomplice. Or was it the other way around? What if Pierson was embezzling money from the lumber company, and using Hardcastle to cover his tracks? That scenario made sense. It was the Piersons' company, even though it was now owned by the Vennor Corporation, and Harry Pierson, who had been intimately involved with the business for years, would know how to siphon away the money.

Jill stopped in the Silver Poplar, the sixteen-section sleeper, answering a question from a passenger. "Yes, we're due into Oroville at eleven twenty-five. We'll make a stop in Marysville at noon, and be in Sacramento by twelve fifty-five."

She went through to the Silver Rapids. The Greenleafs, the passengers who had come all the way from New York City, were just stepping out of their bedroom, headed back to the Silver Planet. "I want to get a seat in the Vista-Dome," Mrs. Greenleaf said. Jill followed them to the car, passing the four sleeping accommodations at the front of the dome-observation car. The lounge in the middle of the car was full, and Mr. Garson, the porter, was busy behind the bar. The lounge area at the back of the Silver Planet was full of passengers, and when Jill took the stairs up to the Vista-Dome, she saw that the Greenleafs had gotten seats near the back, across the aisle from the Hagedorns. Jill stayed in the dome for a few minutes, chatting with passengers and answering questions as the train reached the Tobin Bridges. She went downstairs again, intending to head for her own quarters in the lounge car, a brief respite before the train arrived in Oroville.

As Jill entered the Silver Gorge, the porter's compartment was empty. Many of the passengers were no doubt in the Vista-Domes, looking at the scenery. But roomette one was occupied, judging from the loud, rattling snore she heard. She smiled at the sound. It appeared Colonel Lusco was taking a post-breakfast nap.

Harry Pierson rounded the corner in the middle of the car, walking toward her. She stopped outside roomette four and stepped inside to let him pass. Then she glanced back the way she had come and felt a frisson of alarm. Wade Hardcastle had just walked into the car, coming from the back of the train. All too late, she realized that he must have been following her.

Pierson grabbed Jill's left arm, twisting it behind her. She winced with pain as he shoved her back into the roomette. "You were eavesdropping on me and that old biddy. And later, in the Vista-Dome, I saw you talking to her. Why?"

Hardcastle crowded into the roomette. It was barely big enough to hold two people, let alone three. He shut the door. "I told you. She knows."

"How could she?" Pierson glared at him. He gave her arm another vicious twist and she gasped. He put his hand over her mouth. "Shut up."

Now Hardcastle leaned close to Jill, malice in his cold pale eyes. "You were the Zephyrette on that run, back in May, when I was in the vestibule with Randall. You heard something. Now you've been talking with his fiancée. Oh, yeah, I remember you from the party at Vennor's house. All that nonsense that brassy woman and the Vennor girl were talking about. You were watching me all the time." He shook her, so hard she was dizzy. "What did Randall do with those ledger sheets? You must know. You must have helped him hide them. Do you have them? Does the Vennor girl have them?"

"What nonsense?" Pierson asked, his voice urgent. "Who was talking at the party? About Randall?"

"Some twaddle about a ghost and a séance."

"A ghost?" Pierson's mouth thinned under his mustache. "What the hell kind of crap is that?"

Hardcastle smiled, but it didn't extend to his eyes. His voice dripped with contempt. "Randall's girlfriend, the Vennor girl. At the party she was going on and on, spouting a bunch of nonsense about how Randall was murdered and his ghost is haunting the train. And this brassy blonde was egging her on, saying they ought to have a séance, to get in touch with his spirit. I think they were doing it just to see how I'd react. So this one—" He squeezed Jill's arm hard. "This one knows too much."

"She sure as hell does. She was pumping that nosy old bitch for information."

Pierson's hand on Jill's mouth shifted. She bit him, on the fleshy part below the thumb, and tasted blood. He swore and pulled his hand away, but before Jill could scream, Hardcastle slapped her. She reeled back against the window. Hardcastle grabbed her, covering her mouth with his own large hand. She tried to bite him, but he pressed his hand too hard over her mouth. She couldn't gain purchase with her teeth.

"She's not going to tell us a damn thing," Pierson snarled. "We've got to get off this train. What are we going to do with her?"

"Don't lose your nerve," Hardcastle said. "We're getting off in Oroville, just like we planned. I have a car waiting. As for her, she stays in the roomette, all the way to the end of the line. By the time they find her, we'll be long gone. And so will she."

Jill's eyes widened and she looked from Hardcastle's hard blue eyes to Pierson's brown eyes, eyes that looked as though he didn't like the direction this was going.

"I don't think this is a good idea," Pierson said. "Can't we just lock her up someplace and get off the train?"

Hardcastle laughed, a harsh, unpleasant sound. "Don't tell me you're having second thoughts. A little late in the game, Harry. The time for second thoughts was before Randall figured out the money was missing and who took it. It was before we grabbed him and you forced those pills down his throat. Little Miss Zephyrette here has been asking too many questions, poking her nose in where she shouldn't. We've got to get rid of her. There's no other way."

Hardcastle moved his hand from Jill's mouth to her throat. He began to squeeze, hard and harder. Jill clawed at his hands, fighting, but she was struggling for air. He pushed her back toward the window. She hit her head. And she saw stars.

But was it really stars? Or a trick of the light?

It was no trick. The roomette had gotten colder, a bone-chilling cold that raised gooseflesh on Jill's skin. The light shimmered and moved.

Tap, tap, tap, tap. Four loud taps. Pierson jumped, looking around for the source of the noise. The taps sounded again, and the pressure of Hardcastle's hands on Jill's throat lessened. Now Jill heard buzzing, and it wasn't because she was lightheaded. These were the same sounds she'd heard last night, riding here in roomette four. The buzz and sibilance of spoken words, recognizable words, the argument between Kevin Randall and Wade Hardcastle.

"The figures don't add up, the figures don't add up, the figures don't add up."

The words kept repeating, over and over again, louder, more insistent.

Hardcastle's eyes filled with panic. He took his hands away from Jill's throat and put them over his ears, trying to shut out the words. But the words wouldn't stop.

"The figures don't add up, the figures don't add up, the figures don't add up."

Jill elbowed Hardcastle in the stomach and lunged toward the door. Pierson intercepted her, his hands on her arms, his legs wide apart. She saw her opportunity, swung her knee up, and struck him hard in the groin. He cried out and fell back. She shoved him out of the way and made her escape from the roomette, screaming as she hit the passageway.

The door to roomette one slammed open. Colonel Lusco stepped into the passageway, blocking Hardcastle, who was heading for the rear of the car. He looked at the angry red marks on Jill's throat, and then down at Pierson, who was curled on the floor of roomette four. The colonel's face darkened with anger and he tightened his grip on Hardcastle's arm.

The college student from roomette nine rushed into the passageway, nearly bumping into Lonnie Clark, who came running from the forward part of the car.

"Miss McLeod, are you all right?" The porter looked at Jill and his eyes widened as he saw her throat.

"I'm fine," she told him, though her heart was pounding and her hands shook. "Go find the conductor, please."

Chapter Twenty-Three

I F JILL MCLEOD SAYS those guys are killers, you can take it to the bank," Pat Haggerty declared. His face looked like a thundercloud as he glanced at Jill's throat. The red marks had given way to bruises.

Thank goodness Uncle Pat was here. Jill was relieved to see that he was the Western Pacific conductor boarding the *California Zephyr* in Oroville. Right now, she needed his familiar face and his support.

Jill stood on the platform at the train station, with Uncle Pat on one side and the departing conductor, Arthur Wylie, on the other. In front of her was Lucas Neal, the Butte County sheriff, a rangy man in his fifties, a tanned face beneath his wide-brimmed hat. Nearby were three deputies who had Hardcastle and Pierson in handcuffs.

"It's true." Jill's voice sounded rough, an aftermath of being choked. "Pierson and Hardcastle killed a man on the train last May. His name was Kevin Randall. When we arrived at the Oakland Mole that day, I found Mr. Randall dead." She pointed at the sleeper car. "It was roomette four of this car, the Silver Gorge. The autopsy showed that Randall died from an overdose of digitalis. He had a heart condition, so he took a prescription drug called Digoxin, which contains digitalis. So the murder was meant to look as though Randall died accidentally."

"How do you know about the autopsy?" Sheriff Neal asked, his bushy eyebrows going up.

"My father's a doctor. He has a friend at the Alameda County

Coroner's Office. Dad was able to look at the autopsy report. He told me what was in it."

The sheriff nodded. "I'll be interested to see a copy of that report. Go on."

"The day Mr. Randall died, I overheard Hardcastle arguing with him, in the sleeper car vestibule." She gestured at the two men who stood a few yards distant, both in handcuffs, between two deputies. Hardcastle glared at her, malevolence in his pale blue eyes. Pierson looked down at the ground, his tall frame looking as though it would fold in on itself. Jill continued her story. "Later that day, I saw Pierson pour a lot of pills into his hand, from what looked like an aspirin bottle. Today I found out that Pierson's father takes Digoxin. So Pierson would have access to the drug. What's more, when they had me in the roomette, Hardcastle said something about Pierson forcing pills down Randall's throat. The autopsy report also says that Randall had bitten his own tongue, and he had abrasions around his mouth."

She stopped. The picture her words evoked was dreadful. Hardcastle holding Randall, and Pierson forcing open Kevin Randall's mouth, pushing in a handful of pills, then closing and covering Kevin's mouth, so he would eventually be forced to swallow the fatal dose of Digoxin.

Beside her, Mr. Wylie scowled as he looked at Hardcastle and Pierson. "They attacked a railroad employee on the train. I want them prosecuted for that. I don't know if this happened when we were in Plumas County or Butte County, Sheriff, but we're in Butte County now. I'm turning these men over to you. Throw the book at them."

"Be happy to. We can sort out the jurisdiction later." Sheriff Neal signaled to the deputies. "Take those two down to the jail and put them behind bars."

Two of the deputies took Hardcastle and Pierson by their arms and hustled them to a pair of cars waiting near the station, in full view of the passengers standing on the platform and in the vestibules. Mrs. Bowman was among them, staring at Pierson with avid curiosity. Jill was sure the old woman would have plenty to tell her fellow townspeople when she returned home to Portola.

"I need a statement from you, Miss McLeod," the sheriff said. "And from the passengers and crew members, anyone who can shed some light on this incident."

"I want to cooperate, of course," Pat Haggerty said, watch in hand. "The train has a schedule to keep, though. We're already twenty minutes late leaving the station. The stationmaster sent a wire to WP headquarters in San Francisco, to explain the delay. We'll have to leave soon."

"I thought of that." The sheriff waved to the third deputy, a tall young man who had remained on the platform. "This is Deputy Coleridge. He'll board the train here and ride it to Sacramento. That gives him more than an hour to take statements."

With this course of action agreed upon, Pat stuck his watch in his pocket, straightened his billed cap with its shiny badge that read WESTERN PACIFIC CONDUCTOR, and called, "All aboard."

The passengers who'd been on the platform climbed aboard the train. So did Jill and Deputy Coleridge. As the *California Zephyr* pulled out of the Oroville station, Jill and the deputy set up shop in the Silver Club's lounge, where Coleridge took Jill's statement, probing with questions to get a clear and complete picture of what had happened during that morning's journey down the Feather River Canyon.

"Hardcastle had you by the throat, right?" Coleridge gestured at Jill with his pencil, as the train moved south, toward Marysville.

"He did." Jill touched the tender spots on the right side of her neck.

"How did you get away from him?"

This was not the time, she thought, to bring up what had really happened in roomette four. How could she explain it? The shimmering light, the penetrating cold, the insistent knocks, the voices that kept repeating that phrase, over and over, until Hardcastle had pulled his hands away from her throat and put them over his ears, in a vain attempt to shut the voices out.

"Hardcastle released his grip for a few seconds," Jill said. "I saw an opportunity to get away, and I took it."

When Coleridge finished interviewing Jill, it was Colonel Lusco's turn, and that of the college student who was heading to

Berkeley for school. Finally, the deputy spoke with Lonnie Clark and Alonzo Griggs. It was only after the deputy left the train in Sacramento that Jill had a chance to go to the dining car for lunch. Uncle Pat joined her at the table near the dining car steward's counter.

"Back in Oroville," Pat said, "I sent a wire to your father."

"You didn't have to do that. He'll be worried and so will Mom."

"As well he should. He'll meet the train, and I imagine some folks from Western Pacific headquarters will, too. When I think of those two trying to kill you—" He broke off as a waiter came to their table.

"Are you all right, Miss McLeod?" the waiter asked. "We could hardly believe it when we heard what happened."

"Thank you for your concern, Mr. Delmond. I'll be fine. I think I'll just have iced tea and a bowl of that split pea soup." Jill handed him her meal check. The creamy soup should soothe her throat.

"A ham sandwich for me," Pat said.

Mr. Delmond collected the meal checks and smiled. "I'm glad you're all right, Miss McLeod. We have chocolate cream pie today. I know it's one of your favorites. I'll bring you a piece. With extra whipped cream."

Jill chuckled. Chocolate cream pie would soothe her throat, too. "That would be lovely. I believe that chocolate in any form makes everything better."

———

The *California Zephyr* made up some time on the long flat stretches of the Central Valley, and was only a few minutes behind as the train climbed over Altamont Pass for the last leg of its westbound journey to the Bay Area. Jill did her best, performing her duties as Zephyrette, conscious of the looks from passengers and crew members alike. The attack had left her tired and shaken. As the train wound through Niles Canyon, she went to the lounge. Without asking, Alonzo Griggs poured her a cup of coffee and set it on the counter, along with the cream pitcher. After stirring cream into the coffee, she carried the cup to the corner table, where she pulled out her notebook and pencil and wrote an account of the incident for her trip report.

Dr. McLeod was waiting when the *CZ* pulled into the Oakland Mole. When Jill got off the train, he put his arms around her, then examined the bruises on her neck. "The bruises will go away soon," he told her. "I'm so glad you weren't more seriously hurt. Your mother is frantic."

"I knew she would be. I have a few things to do before we leave, Dad."

He took Jill's suitcase from her and waited patiently as she took her leave of the onboard crew, the waiters, cooks and porters, especially Mr. Clark and Mr. Griggs. She finished all her usual tasks, including her trip report. She talked with the Western Pacific representative who was there at the Mole.

Then the McLeods, father and daughter, went home. Her mother, upset and on the verge of tears, fussed over Jill, who found time to make a few phone calls before taking a hot bath. She went to bed early, cuddling her cat. There was something so comforting about the little ball of fur, purring on the pillow next to her.

———

Jill slept deeply and woke late Sunday morning. Mike was there for breakfast, invited by Lora McLeod. He swept Jill into his arms, kissed her, then held her close, not saying a word. He stayed for Sunday dinner. Drew had made himself scarce again, and Lucy and Ethan were out with friends.

Tidsy arrived at two o'clock that afternoon, followed a few minutes later by Margaret, her aunt and uncle. When they were seated in the living room, glasses of iced tea all around, Tidsy took charge of the conversation.

"I went over the pages from the ledger, and Kevin Randall's notes." She gestured at the pages she'd spread out on the coffee table. "There's enough information there to determine that Harry Pierson has been siphoning money from the family lumber company for quite some time. The embezzlement probably dates back years, before Dan Vennor even acquired the company. It looks like Hardcastle found out what was going on after Dan bought the company. He covered it up and he was taking money off the top as well."

"I can't believe it," Dan Vennor said, shaking his head. "I've known Wade for years. I trusted him."

"Your trust was misplaced," Tidsy said. "This scheme of theirs went on undetected for a while, since Hardcastle was the man in your financial department responsible for auditing the Pierson company books. Then you promoted Kevin Randall. Was it because he was planning to marry Margaret?"

"That was only part of it," Vennor said. "Kevin deserved that promotion. He was a good worker, honest. I could count on him."

"When you promoted him, the jobs in the financial department got shifted around," Tidsy said. "Kevin got the task of auditing the Pierson books. He found discrepancies. When he brought them to Hardcastle's attention, he got put off. At some point he must have told Hardcastle and Pierson he was going to tell you, Dan. If I were you, I'd do a top-to-bottom housecleaning. I'll bet this wasn't the only place Hardcastle was cheating you."

Helen Vennor had been sitting quietly, holding her glass with both hands. "So all this business about a ghost and a séance, what you said at the party, that was just to make Hardcastle nervous."

Jill and Margaret exchanged looks. When they had spoken the night before, Jill had told her everything about what happened in the roomette, the real reason she had been able to break away from the men who were trying to kill her. There was no need, they decided, to tell Aunt Helen about the séance at Tidsy's apartment.

"That's true," Margaret told her aunt. "We wanted to see what Hardcastle would do. Jill said he went white as a sheet. We made him nervous. And as Tidsy put it, nervous people make mistakes."

"You could have been killed," Mike said, squeezing Jill's hand. "But knowing you, I'm not surprised you did it."

Lora McLeod shuddered and got up from her chair. "I don't even like to think about it. Enough of this talk about ghosts and murder. Now, I've got a chocolate cake in the kitchen and I think we all need a piece."

Jill stood as well, heading for the kitchen to help her mother.

Before she left the living room, Tidsy intercepted her. "You did good. You could even be a government girl."

————

Margaret called Jill on Monday morning, providing a welcome interruption from the laundry and ironing that were Jill's tasks when she returned from a trip. "I talked with my friend who works for Western Pacific. The Silver Gorge is still in the rail yard."

"So it hasn't been put on a consist yet." Jill sat down on the hall chair and twisted the telephone cord around her fingers.

"I want to go visit the car. Before it leaves the yard. Just to say good-bye."

"I understand. At least I think I do. Can your friend get us into the yard?"

"He should be able to," Margaret said. "After all, he works for the freight department."

"And I know several brakemen," Jill said. "I'm sure one of them would do it. Tidsy will want to come with us, of course."

All it took was a couple of phone calls. On Monday evening, as the sun dropped below the San Francisco skyline and turned the bay copper and gold, Jill, Margaret and Tidsy got out of Tidsy's convertible and walked toward the siding where the Silver Gorge and several other sleeper cars waited for their next journey. They were in the rail yard south of the Oakland Mole. It was never really deserted here, as there were railroad employees in the yard. But it was different from the crowds of people that Jill would have seen at the Mole on a morning when the *California Zephyr* was about to depart. They were surrounded by rail cars and equipment.

"This won't take long, will it?" the brakeman asked. He'd let them in the gate and now he was lowering the steps that led to the vestibule. "I could get into trouble doing this."

"I know. And I really appreciate it. I won't tell anyone if you won't. And it won't take long."

Jill had worn dungarees, a shirt, and a pair of sturdy and comfortable shoes. Margaret and Tidsy were similarly dressed. Jill climbed into the vestibule first, then turned to help Margaret and Tidsy. They entered the deserted Pullman car. Jill led the way past the porter's compartment and stopped at the doorway to roomette four. Margaret went inside. She was carrying a deep red rose clipped from a bush in the Vennors' garden. She held it to her nose, breathed in the fragrance, and set it on the seat. Then she stood looking out the window at the utilitarian, industrial landscape, shadowed now as the day moved from dusk to darkness.

Tidsy had gone into roomette three, across the corridor. She, too, looked out the window, at a freight train moving slowly south on a set of tracks about fifty feet away. Jill leaned into the roomette. "I'm glad you came with us. I didn't think you believed in ghosts. I'm not sure I do either, not entirely, but after what happened, I'm hedging my bets."

Tidsy smiled. "I said good-bye to my husband, Rick, after I got that telegram from the war department. It's been eleven years since I saw him last. But every now and then, I think I see him, out of the corner of my eye."

"I don't see Steve. I think of him, though. Especially now, with the Armistice ending the war in Korea." It had been nearly three years since Steve died at "Frozen Chosin." If he was a ghost, he wasn't haunting her. Except with the occasional memory. It really was time to move on and she was doing that. "I said good-bye to Steve when I wrapped his engagement ring in a handkerchief and put it away in my jewelry box."

Margaret was saying good-bye to Kevin now, here in the roomette where he had died. She hoped her new friend would be able to move on as well.

It was getting dark and there was no electricity operating in the car. By now it was dim in the roomette, and even darker in the passageway. "We should go," Jill said.

Margaret turned from the window. With one last look at the rose she'd left on the seat, she stepped out of the roomette. Her face was composed and she smiled. "I'm ready." She went down the corridor to the vestibule. Tidsy followed.

Jill stood for a bit longer, taking one last look around roomette four. She could smell the strong scent of the rose on the seat. Then she shivered. Now that the sun was going down, it was chilly in here.

Or was it something else?

Jill saw the shimmering light at the same time the knocks began. Long and short. Morse code.

She had brought a pad and a pencil, for some reason, force of habit, perhaps. Or maybe because she thought this might happen. Now she pulled them from the pocket of her dungarees and wrote down dashes and dots. There was silence, then the sequence repeated, and she wrote it down again. The same sequence.

"I've got it now," she said, her voice sounding strange and quiet in roomette four.

She would translate the Morse code when she got home but she had a feeling she already knew what it said.

   – .... .– –. –.– ...

Thanks.

AFTERWORD

ALL THREE OF THE California Zephyr mysteries are the result of much research. I took train trips, I interviewed people, I read books, and I climbed around on old railroad cars. I even drove a locomotive.

When writing about a historical period or a particular subject, I strive to be accurate in conveying information. I worked hard to make this book as accurate as possible, though I may have tweaked facts from time to time for the sake of plot, characters, and a good story. Any errors are my own.

My heartfelt thanks go to two of the Zephyrettes who worked aboard the historical streamliner known as the *California Zephyr*. Cathy Moran Von Ibsch was a Zephyrette in the late 1960s and rode the Silver Lady on her last run. The late Rodna Walls Taylor rode the rails as a Zephyrette in the early 1950s, the time period of the book. I greatly appreciate their generosity in answering my many questions. I couldn't have written this book without them.

In 2010 I was a passenger on a special train to and from Portola, California via the famous Feather River Route, which gave me the opportunity to see what the passengers of the original *CZ* saw on their journey through the Sierra Nevada. This route has been primarily traversed by freight traffic since the old *CZ* ceased operations, so traveling the canyon on a passenger car was a treat. My accommodations for that trip were aboard the Pacific Sands, a 1950 Budd 10/6 Pullman sleeper built for the Union Pacific, a car very much like those that traveled on the *CZ*. The car is owned by Doug Spinn of LA Rail. I met several people on this trip and we called ourselves the Pullman Pals, taking a subsequent trip on the Pacific Sands from Los Angeles to San Diego. It was on this trip that Doug Spinn mentioned the ghost. He reported that, at various times, passengers aboard the car would report hearing voices during the night. At other times, the porter call button in a particular roomette would ring, but no one was there. A haunted roomette? That's music to a writer's ear. From such stories, novels arise. Thanks for the story, Doug.

Many thanks to two of my Pullman Pals, Roger Morris and Glenn Stocki, both railfans and both generous with answers to my many train-related questions. A special thanks to Roger, who has created the cover art for all three of the California Zephyr mysteries.

Here's a link to LA Rail, with information on its trips and articles about them, including one by Roger Morris:

http://www.larail.com

Here's a link to Plumas County's Seven Wonders of the Railroad World, which describes some of the sights on the Feather River Route:

http://www.plumascounty.org/documents/Spec%20Tour %207.pdf

On another note, my brother plays bass guitar and he loves the blues. He plays a song I like, "Mercury Blues," that I've used in this novel. I researched the date the song was written, to be sure Jill's brother, Drew, would know the song in 1953. "Mercury Blues," originally "Mercury Boogie," was written by bluesman K.C. Douglas and Robert Geddins, musician and record producer. Both men came to Oakland, California during World War II, Douglas from Mississippi and Geddins from Texas. Douglas first recorded the song in 1948 and in the past 60-plus years it has been covered by many musicians. Geddins had a recording studio on Seventh Street in Oakland, which used to be called the Harlem of the West. The thoroughfare, and its side streets, were lined with nightclubs, including the famous Slim Jenkins' Supper Club. The clubs were patronized by customers of all races, as described in the novel, who came to listen to what was called race music, the term for blues and rhythm & blues.

Do a search on "Mercury Blues" and you'll find all sorts of YouTube videos of musicians performing the song. Here's a link to K.C. Douglas's 1952 recording of the song:

https://www.youtube.com/watch?v=QsTfCITzISM

For more information on Seventh Street in Oakland:

https://localwiki.org/oakland/Harlem_of_the_West
http://7thstreet.org/category/sources/other
http://www.blackpast.org/aaw/jenkins-harold-slim-1890-1967

In writing about the 1950s I find myself doing research on a variety of things, such as appliances (yes, dishwashers were used), movies and television programs, books, music, cars, hairstyles, and clothes. Especially clothes. It's important for me, and my readers, to know what clothes Jill McLeod and the other characters in the California Zephyr books are wearing. A book titled *Everyday Fashions of the Fifties as Pictured in Sears Catalogs*, edited by JoAnne Olian, proved invaluable. The book is published by Dover Publications, which also publishes books for other decades, a terrific resource for anyone writing historical novels.

The Key System was a privately owned transit company that was vital to transportation in the East Bay, with streetcars that were replaced by buses in the late 1940s. As described in the book, employees did go on strike on July 24, 1953. The strike lasted a record 76 days, dealing a crippling blow to public transit in the East Bay. At one point, California Governor Earl Warren (who eventually headed the US Supreme Court) called a special session of the legislature to discuss the possibility of a government seizure of the system. The strike was a factor in the eventual demise of the system, which was replaced by AC Transit in 1960.

The internment of Japanese American citizens and their families is a sad chapter in the history of the United States. People lost their livelihoods and properties. In some cases, as discussed in the novel, their neighbors stepped in to run farms for families who were interned. As also mentioned in the book, Italian residents of California who were not citizens were also scrutinized and restricted by the US government.

We are fortunate to have railroad museums to preserve the remaining artifacts of this country's rail era, particularly the streamliners like the *California Zephyr*. Both the California State Railroad Museum in Sacramento and the Colorado Railroad Museum in Golden have excellent research libraries as well as rail cars and locomotives. The Western Pacific Railroad Museum in Portola, California, is a treasure house of rolling stock.

I recommend the *California Zephyr* Virtual Museum, at: http://calzephyr.railfan.net. Here I found old timetables, menus, and brochures, as well as information on the Zephyrettes.

The Amtrak version of the *California Zephyr* is not the same as the sleek Silver Lady of days gone by. But it's great to ride a train through most of the same route, getting an up-close look at this marvelous country. The journey may take longer, but the scenery is spectacular and the relaxation factor is 110 percent.

The *California Zephyr* story, and that of railroading in America, is told in books and films. Some of them are listed below, along with other sources I used in writing the California Zephyr series. Many of these books are full of photographs and firsthand accounts of working on and aboard the trains.

PUBLICATIONS ABOUT THE CALIFORNIA ZEPHYR,
RAILS, AND RAIL TRAVEL IN THE UNITED STATES

Portrait of a Silver Lady: The Train They Called the California Zephyr, Bruce A. McGregor and Ted Benson, Pruett Publishing Company, Boulder, CO, 1977. Full of beautiful photographs, lots of history and technical information, and firsthand accounts of what it was like to work on this train.

CZ: The Story of the California Zephyr, Karl R. Zimmerman, Quadrant Press, Inc., 1972. Excellent overview of the train's history, with lots of old photographs.

Zephyr: Tracking a Dream Across America, Henry Kisor, Adams Media Corporation, 1994. An account of Kisor's journey westward on the Amtrak *California Zephyr*.

Waiting on a Train: The Embattled Future of Passenger Rail Service, James McCommons, Chelsea Green Publishing Company, 2009. A thought-provoking account of the author's travels on various Amtrak routes and his interviews with passengers, employees, rail advocates, and people in the railroad business, with discussions about the future of passenger rail in the United States.

A Guidebook to Amtrak's California Zephyr, Eva J. Hoffman, Flashing Yellow Guidebooks, Evergreen, CO, 2003, 2008. There are three volumes: Chicago to Denver, Denver to Salt Lake City, Salt Lake City to San Francisco. I discovered these courtesy of a railfan while riding the Amtrak *CZ*. A detailed milepost-by-milepost guide to what's outside the train window, with history and anecdotes thrown in. A useful resource for finding out how far it is from one place to another and how long it takes to get there.

Rising from the Rails, Pullman Porters and the Making of the Black Middle Class, Larry Tye, Henry Holt & Company, 2004. There is also a PBS video. The book discusses the history of the Pullman Company, African Americans working on the railroad, and their legacy.

The Pullman Porters and West Oakland, Thomas and Wilma Tramble, Arcadia Publishing, 2007. A look at the lives of porters in Oakland, CA. Full of wonderful photographs.

FILMS

The California Zephyr: The Story of America's Most Talked About Train, Copper Media, 1999

The California Zephyr: Silver Thread Through The West, TravelVideoStore, 2007.

The California Zephyr: The Ultimate Fan Trip, Emery Gulash, Green Frog Productions, Ltd., 2007.

American Experience: Streamliners: America's Lost Trains, PBS Video, 2006

Promotional films from the *CZ* and other trains are viewable on YouTube.

The original *California Zephyr* appeared on film in the 1954 movie *Cinerama Holiday*, as well as the 1952 noir *Sudden Fear*, starring Joan Crawford and Jack Palance. During the train portion of that movie, a Zephyrette comes to Joan Crawford's bedroom to tell her it's time for her dinner reservation. That Zephyrette is Rodna Walls, whom I interviewed.

I hope you enjoy *The Ghost in Roomette Four*. Now go ride a train!

ABOUT THE AUTHOR

Janet Dawson has written twelve books about Oakland private eye Jeri Howard, including *Kindred Crimes*, winner of the St. Martin's Press/PWA contest for Best Private Eye Novel, and a nominee for several Best First awards. Her most recent Jeri Howard book is *Water Signs*. *The Ghost in Roomette Four* is the latest in her California Zephyr series of historical mysteries. In addition, Dawson has authored a suspense novel, *What You Wish For* and several award-nominated and -winning short stories. A past president of Northern California Mystery Writers of America, Dawson lives in the East Bay region. She welcomes visitors and email at www.janetdawson.com and on Facebook.

More Traditional Mysteries from Perseverance Press
For the New Golden Age

K.K. Beck
Tipping the Valet
ISBN 978-1-56474-563-7

Albert A. Bell, Jr.
PLINY THE YOUNGER SERIES
Death in the Ashes
ISBN 978-1-56474-532-3

The Eyes of Aurora
ISBN 978-1-56474-549-1

Fortune's Fool
ISBN 978-1-56474-587-3

The Gods Help Those (forthcoming)
ISBN 978-1-56474-600-9

Taffy Cannon
ROXANNE PRESCOTT SERIES
Guns and Roses
Agatha and Macavity awards nominee, Best Novel
ISBN 978-1-880284-34-6

Blood Matters
ISBN 978-1-880284-86-5

Open Season on Lawyers
ISBN 978-1-880284-51-3

Paradise Lost
ISBN 978-1-880284-80-3

Laura Crum
GAIL MCCARTHY SERIES
Moonblind
ISBN 978-1-880284-90-2

Chasing Cans
ISBN 978-1-880284-94-0

Going, Gone
ISBN 978-1-880284-98-8

Barnstorming
ISBN 978-1-56474-508-8

Jeanne M. Dams
HILDA JOHANSSON SERIES
Crimson Snow
ISBN 978-1-880284-79-7

Indigo Christmas
ISBN 978-1-880284-95-7

Murder in Burnt Orange
ISBN 978-1-56474-503-3

Janet Dawson
JERI HOWARD SERIES
Bit Player
Golden Nugget Award nominee
ISBN 978-1-56474-494-4

Cold Trail
ISBN 978-1-56474-555-2

Water Signs
ISBN 978-1-56474-586-6

What You Wish For
ISBN 978-1-56474-518-7

TRAIN SERIES
Death Rides the Zephyr
ISBN 978-1-56474-530-9

Death Deals a Hand
ISBN 978-1-56474-569-9

The Ghost in Roomette Four
ISBN 978-1-56474-598-9

Kathy Lynn Emerson
LADY APPLETON SERIES
Face Down Below the Banqueting House
ISBN 978-1-880284-71-1

Face Down Beside St. Anne's Well
ISBN 978-1-880284-82-7

Face Down O'er the Border
ISBN 978-1-880284-91-9

Sara Hoskinson Frommer
JOAN SPENCER SERIES
Her Brother's Keeper
ISBN 978-1-56474-525-5

Margaret Grace
MINIATURE SERIES
Mix-up in Miniature
ISBN 978-1-56474-510-1

Madness in Miniature
ISBN 978-1-56474-543-9

Manhattan in Miniature
ISBN 978-1-56474-562-0

Matrimony in Miniature
ISBN 978-1-56474-575-0

Tony Hays
Shakespeare No More
ISBN 978-1-56474-566-8